# Strangers In The Land

## Georgette Sable

Previously-published titles authored
by Georgette Sable:

**Murder on M99**
**The Avengers**

# Preface

**D**etective Constable Elisabeth Andresen was pretty sure that she knew what was going to happen when she got a call from her immediate superior, Detective Inspector Lydia Mussett to come see her in her office. A few minutes previously, the room in which she sat had been emptied as, one by one, her colleagues had left. One of them, a particular favourite, DC Nathan Green, had said, "see you in a bit, Liz," as he passed her desk on his way out of the room.

A short time later, Liz knocked on Lydia's office door and entered. Her 'boss' greeted her by saying, "morning, Liz. I've no doubt that you've already guessed what's going on, but the AC has asked me to bring you along to the briefing room, so I'm only obeying orders! Let's go."

As she entered the briefing room, Liz was surprised by receiving a round of applause from her assembled colleagues. As the clapping halted, the man in charge of her division of New Scotland Yard, Assistant Commander Barlow, stood up and began speaking. He started by saying, "I take pleasure in announcing that, with immediate effect, Elisabeth is being promoted to detective sergeant." Then, in a rather long-winded speech, he chronicled her history with the Metropolitan Police, ending by saying, "now, Liz, your outstanding qualities are being recognised."

After the speech by the AC, the next in command, Detective Chief Superintendent Rignell, added his appreciation of Liz's merits, mentioning that she had achieved one of the highest scores recorded when she took the sergeant's exam.

When he said that, Liz recalled the surprise that she had had when she had taken the exam a few months earlier: the questions had placed heavy emphasis on the candidate's knowledge of the law. There were precious few questions relating to the actual tasks that police officers are called upon to carry out.

Finally, it was Lydia's turn to speak. She smiled at Liz when she said, "I remember when I first met Liz; we sang together in a London choir; I thought that she was a very bright young lady then, and I've seen no reason to change my mind since. Let's give Liz another hand for a job well done!" Despite the fact that there were a few cries of "speech!" from her colleagues, Liz, blushing profusely, could only stammer her thanks to everyone for being so kind to her.

# Chapter One

**A** young girl lay on her back on the bed of her room apparently sleeping peacefully. It was a warm night, and she lay uncovered wearing only a flimsy night dress. Moments later a noise was heard: that of a key unlocking the door of the girl's room. The door opened quietly, and a dark form entered, closing the door. The form, a man, went to the bedside and bent over the apparently-sleeping girl. Then he proceeded to remove his clothing. A short time later, the man lay down on top of the girl, apparently causing her to awaken, startled. When she felt the weight of the body holding her down on the bed she shouted, "no, no!" The man covered her mouth with his hand, ignoring her muted sounds of protest and her attempts to push him away from her. Eventually, he positioned himself so to have sexual intercourse with her. As his frenzied efforts were rewarded her cries changed to moans of pleasure. Moments later, he was nearing climax when he placed both of his hands around her neck, his thumbs pressed hard against her throat. Now she was truly alarmed; she was unable to breathe or to make a sound. She struggled frantically, managing to scratch him on his face with her long fingernails. That action on her part caused him to tighten his grip on her throat as he cursed her. Finally, the hammering of her feet against the mattress of the bed ceased. As the man climaxed, he again tightened the grip that he had on the neck of the now inert form that lay beneath him.

When the man had finished he raised himself onto his elbows, trying to see into the face of the young woman. He got onto his feet and looked closely at his victim, moving her head back and forth. She made no response. Panicking, he dressed himself quickly and left the room. His only thought was to escape from the building. In the dimly-lit hallway outside of the room, he looked both ways and walked hurriedly in a direction indicated by a well-lighted sign that showed the route that had to be taken in order to evacuate the building during a fire. However, when he got to the fire-escape door, he found that it was locked. He knew that he would have to leave the building by the same route that he had taken to get to Karina's room. He would have to encounter the persons to whom he spoke when he first entered the brothel; he thought that one of them, a rather muscular black man, very likely was a guard. He would have to talk his way out of the building.

A short time later, he came to a reception area in which sat a man and a woman who were talking to each other. He gave the key to Karina's room to the woman. Despite his attempt to turn his face away from the woman, she noticed the scratches on his face; she made a joke of them by suggesting that Karina had got carried away. He laughed and said, "yeah, it was something like that." To the woman's question: did he wish to book another appointment; he said that he wasn't sure of his movements during the immediate future, so that he would get in touch. He then left the building.

After he had gone, the woman spoke to her companion, telling him that she thought that the man who just had left was a "strange one. I've never liked the look of him, but Stan says that we can't go turning away customers just because we don't like the look of them. Nonetheless, I'd hate to meet him in a dark alley way."

Over the next several minutes, more men arrived at reception, identified themselves, and paid some money. After that, they seated themselves on a comfortable settee until young women arrived and went to the reception desk. A short time later each man would be escorted out of the reception area by a young woman. After each client left, the only sounds heard in the reception area came from a television set sitting in the corner. The man and the woman stationed there seemed intent only upon watching one of the more mindless quiz programmes that was on offer on the 'telly'.

Several minutes after Karina's client had left the brothel, the woman in reception looked at her watch and spoke to her male companion: "I wonder what's keeping Karina? We should have got a signal from her by now; she's got another client coming in a few minutes. Derek, why don't you go have a look and see what's keeping her. If she's got herself high again, I'll kill her; I don't know where she gets the stuff, but I suspect she performs 'little extras' for her clients if they bring her some junk."

Derek went to one of the rooms of the building where he found the inert form lying on the bed. He shook Karina, shouting her name; the young girl did not respond even when he slapped her face. Then he walked hurriedly to the reception area, telling the woman, "something's happened to Karina, I can't get her to wake up. Can we get hold of Hazel? She looks to me like she's dead, but Hazel will know." The receptionist telephoned a number, but there was no reply. "Nah, she's not there. Let's lock the front door and go have a look. I'm sure the little bitch has just knocked herself out on some of that junk she's been taking."

After slapping Karina's face and shouting at her to wake up, the woman looked up at the man and said, "there ain't nothing more I can do. Does her skin feel cool to you? It does to me. Either she's taken an overdose of something or that bastard who was with her last got carried away and killed her. I told Stan that we should at least keep an eye on him. I remember once before he almost killed another girl we had here. What in hell are we going to do? It looks like we've got another dead girl on our hands and you know as well as I do that we'll get the blame from Stan and Hazel."

Derek said that he couldn't be expected to know which of their clients would do such a thing. "That's just a chance we've got to take, I thought that he looked like he had a screw loose when he came in, but then most of them look that way." The woman said, "well, it's too late now to do anything about it. I'm pretty sure she's dead. Let's get hold of Stan and see what he thinks we ought to do. We can't leave her here, that's for sure."

\* \* \*

In a 999 telephone call to the emergency services, a Mrs Barbara Taylor reported sighting what she was fairly sure was a human body floating in the Grand Union Canal just up from where it crossed under one of the bridges opposite the London Zoo. She had been walking her dog, which drew her attention to the body; the animal wouldn't stop barking at something that it saw in the water. The Camden Town police were alerted, and a police constable was sent to meet with Mrs Taylor who agreed to remain at the scene. The constable ascertained that what Mrs Taylor had seen was, indeed, a dead body: that of a woman in her late teens or early twenties.

4

A forensic team was sent to the spot to perform their various examinations. It was thought likely that the dead woman had been killed elsewhere, and her body transported to the Grand Union Canal and dumped. She was dressed only in a skimpy night dress.

Ten days later, it had been established that the cause of death had been strangulation; the killer had gripped the young woman's throat so hard that the cartilages of the voice box were completely collapsed. The toxicology report on the body indicated that the deceased was a heroin user. This was borne out also by sites of injection at various places on the body. Still-active sperm had been found in her vagina and the lower part of her uterus, indicating that she had had sex not long before her death.

The fact that she had been strangled was presumptive evidence that her death had occurred during a rape. This presumption was supported by forensic evidence. The DNA profile of the sperm found in her reproductive tract indicated that its source was an unknown male who was wanted by the police because he had committed rape twice previously.

Efforts were made by the Camden Town police to discover if any member of the public had seen anything suspicious. However, no witness had come forward who could give any information that was helpful in apprehending the rapist. The file containing details of the crime that were known to the police was kept open and photographs of the dead woman were circulated to the usual UK and international police destinations.

# Chapter Two

**D**etective Sergeant Elisabeth (Liz) Andresen was seated at her desk at New Scotland Yard; she'd arrived at work late because of utter confusion on the London Underground that morning, caused, as usual, by a breakdown of equipment somewhere on the network: either in the signalling system or of one or more trains. That morning, the stoppage had affected all westbound trains on the District Line east of Mile End station; that had made her late. In the detectives' room she read hurriedly over the latest reports of investigations being made by the group of police officers of which she was part. She had arrived at the 'Yard' that morning too late for the usual 'briefing' session.

The principal efforts of her team currently were being concentrated on the identification and detention of illegal immigrants. The Scotland Yard team was but one of four such groups of police officers from several of the forces that comprised the Metropolitan Police. Her immediate superior, Detective Inspector Lydia Mussett, was in charge of the group of which Liz was a part. In addition, Lydia had the added responsibility of co-ordinating the actions of all four of the 'illegal-immigrant' teams.

Acting on information received from various sources, including the immigration service and the public, the teams were attempting to counter what was perceived as a growing menace: not only illegal immigration, but also the exploitation of such immigrants. Lydia's team had had some success in locating and detaining illegals, but up to that point, at least, the police had not seen even a single prosecution amongst those who had exploited the unfortunate persons.

The official attitude toward the immigrants was rather harsh: they should be hunted down and expelled from the country. Liz did not share that attitude. Many members of the public and, regrettably, quite a large number of politicians held the view that the immigrants came to the UK to take advantage of generous welfare provision, or that they were taking jobs from the UK residents. That had not been Liz's perception. Most of those whom she had encountered were hard working, usually doing jobs that UK residents had no interest in doing. The main difference between legal and illegal workers, as far as Liz had seen, was the poor wages and working conditions of the latter. It was for that reason that Liz was particularly keen that the efforts of the team of which she was part should be directed at exploiters of the illegals rather than the illegals themselves.

Much to Liz's regret, so far, all of the exploiters that her team had investigated had covered themselves so well that it had been impossible to charge them with criminal acts. In two cases, companies had been shut down because of infractions of various provisions of the Health and Safety regulations; such things as badly heated and ventilated premises or inadequate provision of safety devices on machinery. However, the employers were able to evade the main charge against them by pleading that they were ignorant of the illegal status of some of their workers. Unfortunately, employment law worked in favour of employers of illegal immigrants. All such an employer had to do was treat his workers as casual labourers; that procedure obviated the necessity of entering them into the national insurance system.

Liz had discovered very quickly during the investigations that the attitude even of most of her fellow police officers was unsympathetic to the view that it was the employers of illegals who were at fault. Liz could understand the view taken by politicians; most of them had no idea of the conditions under which many, if not most illegal immigrants lived. However, her fellow police officers saw those conditions virtually on a daily basis; their lack of sympathy was difficult for her to understand.

Early in her investigations, Liz had complained to Lydia about the apparent lack of interest shown by the Crown Prosecution Service in evidence that she had gathered against an employer of illegal immigrants. Lydia had explained the attitude of the police as clearly as she could saying, "our task is hard enough without getting a bunch of employers on our backs. If I were you, unless you can get irrefutable evidence of an employer's wrong doing, I would forget about it. By 'irrefutable' I don't mean statements by illegal immigrants. Any good lawyer will make mince meat of them should they be asked to testify in court." Nevertheless, Liz made up her mind that she would persist in her efforts to get evidence of an employer's wrongdoing that would hold up in court.

* * *

An opportunity to go after exploiters of illegal immigrants arose when a telephone call was put through to Lydia from a Detective Inspector Leighton at the Paddington Green station of the Metropolitan Police. He said that a young woman named Julia Gomes had showed up at his station making accusations against some men who, she said, had held her in captivity and had raped her. Inspector

Leighton said also, "she came right out and admitted that she had entered the country illegally from Mozambique. At first, we thought that she had been beaten badly, but it turned out that her injuries were incurred during her escape from captivity. Anyway, she's in hospital now, but she's about ready to be discharged. I thought I'd better give you a tinkle to see what you want done with the girl. My super thinks that it might be more appropriate for one of the police teams currently investigating 'illegals' to involve itself with her claims." Lydia agreed, asking that the young woman be transferred to Scotland Yard. Lydia then asked Liz to interview the young woman and determine whether or not it was worth enquiring further into her allegations.

Liz made preparations for her interview of Julia Gomes. Lydia had been told by her informant at Paddington Green that the young woman's command of English was poor, so Liz had attempted to find a translator. She rang the Portuguese embassy, asking their advice. A spokesman there said that there were significant differences in the Portuguese spoken in his country and that spoken in Mozambique; he suggested that she contact the Mozambique consular office. That she did and was able to engage the services of a person they had recommended: a young woman of Mozambican nationality who was in the UK legally and earned spare money by providing a translation service.

On the day that Julia Gomes was transferred to the 'Yard' from Paddington Green, Liz entered the interview room in which the illegal immigrant had been placed. Liz was chatting with the interpreter, who had arrived at Scotland Yard earlier and had come to the detectives' room where Liz had her desk.

When they entered the interview room they saw Julia Gomes who was seated at a table on which was the equipment that would be used to record the interview. Miss Gomes was speaking to a woman police constable who, presumably, had accompanied her from Paddington Green. Liz was quite taken by her first sight of Julia Gomes. She was very pretty. Her prettiness was emphasised by her pale-brown skin, much lighter than that of the Mozambican woman who was to act as an interpreter. Liz could see that Julia's right hand and lower arm were encased in a plaster caste and her left hand was bandaged. Liz introduced herself and the interpreter, and the two women seated themselves opposite Miss Gomes and the WPC.

In her statement, Julia Gomes said that she had come to Britain from Mozambique. Her parents were amongst an unknown number of Mozambicans who had been swindled by a man who called himself "Henry." He was a white man who spoke the Portuguese that was used in Portugal; however, he said that he was British.

Anxious to get their daughter away from what they perceived as the turmoil of the East African country in which they lived, Julia's parents had paid Henry the equivalent of £2000 to get her to Britain. Henry had told Julia's parents that the money he charged would be used primarily to "smooth the way" with British officialdom so that Julia would be given the appropriate documents to enable her to enter and stay in Britain. Julia's parents did not question the man when he said that most of the money they gave him would be used to pay off corrupt British officials. They understood the ways of 'baksheesh', a well-established means of "way smoothing" in their part of the world. They had assumed that a similar system operated in Britain.

Julia had finished secondary school; it was there that she had learned English. She had hoped that when she got to England she could go to university.

Julia, along with four other young Mozambicans whose parents also had parted with £2000, entered Britain at Heathrow Airport in London to which they had flown from Portugal. The young women had begun their journey when they had been placed on a cargo ship that called at a port in Mozambique. They were smuggled ashore when the ship reached its destination: Lisbon. The girls had been kept in a house in Lisbon where they were provided with Portuguese passports and given instructions that they were to follow when they got to London.

At Heathrow Airport they passed through the immigration controls without difficulty because they held passports indicating that they were citizens of another country of the European Union. Immigration officers took the passports and made only cursory glances at the young women before indicating that they were free to pass through the barrier. As each of the five young women cleared the immigration barrier, she was detained by a man who spoke to her in Portuguese telling her to wait until all of the girls were together.

Julia continued the narrative, speaking for a time in rapid Portuguese and then pausing briefly for the interpreter to speak. "Once we were all together, the man told us to give him our passports. He said that he would keep them safe for us because it would be necessary to show them when we tried to get a job. Like fools, we all handed over our passports. Then the man told us not to wait in the baggage hall for our luggage because that would be delivered to us. He told us to go through the green line at customs and then out the door where a man would be waiting with a sign reading, 'Maputo'." When Liz asked what Maputo meant, Julia smiled for the first time during the interview and said, in English, "why, ma'am, that's the capitol of Mozambique." She then continued in Portuguese, "we waited by the man with the sign until everyone showed up. Then the man who had spoken to us in Portuguese came through the door to join the man with the sign. They then told us to follow them. They seemed to be in a hurry. We went into a building where a lot of cars were parked and got into a van. I don't know where they took us, but it took quite a long time to get there."

Liz waited for Julia to continue her narrative, but the young woman seemed disinclined to say anything more. The interpreter said something to the young woman in Portuguese and received an answer, none of which meant anything to Liz.

Finally, Liz looked at the young woman and said, "you told the other police officers that you had been raped. Can you tell me about that?" Before the interpreter could speak, Julia nodded her head, saying, in English, "it was strange thing; we were, you know, the little sheeps who went to the slaughter house."

Then she continued in Portuguese: "here we were thinking that the two men who were taking us into London were doing us a favour. I was the only one of the group that knew any English. I took it at school, and I read some books in English. I guess the two men didn't realise that I could understand some of what they were saying, although they spoke with an accent I had never heard before."

"When I heard them talking about the 'good prices' that they were going to get for us, I became worried. I had heard about young Africans who had been kidnapped and sold into slavery; however, I didn't think that that would happen in England. Finally, the van stopped, and we were taken into a large house where there were two other men. The two new men put us in a room that had small beds in it and then left us. We were sitting there wondering what was going to happen, when the two men who picked us up at the airport came into the room and closed the door. The one who spoke Portuguese told us that contrary to what we had been told, we now were illegal immigrants to Britain. Unless we did everything that we were told to do, we would be turned over to the police, and we would go to prison, where horrible things would happen to us before we got sent back to where we came from. Then those two men left the room, and we never saw them again."

"A short time later, the two new men came into the room and began gesturing to us. They made us take off our shoes. One of the girls attempted to make the men understand that we were worried about what had happened to our luggage; that the only clothes we had were what we were wearing. Several times, I was tempted to say something to the men, explaining what we wanted. However, I had decided by then that I would keep the fact that I understood a little English a secret. I presume she finally made herself understood because one of them did say, in English, 'don't worry; you won't be needing it'. Then the men left the room again."

"We were sitting around in the room, talking; all of us were bewildered by what had happened to us so far, and we were wondering what was going to happen in the future. Then, one of the men came in and pointed at one of the girls, motioning to her to come with him. I almost said something then, but I thought that I had better not. Not long after that the door of the room opened again and the girl was pushed in. She was undressed and she carried her clothing in her arms. She told us that both men had raped her. That led to a great deal of excitement, with all of the girls looking frightened."

"For the next few days the girls were taken out one by one and raped. Three of us, myself included, had never been with a man before and there was blood, but they wouldn't let us wash ourselves. Also, they didn't feed us very much. They brought in some bread and butter, but that was about it. They told us, in English, that if we wanted to eat proper food, we would have to earn it. Once they had left the room, I told my three companions what they had said about earning our food; I also told them what I thought that we would have to do in order to earn our food. One of the girls, the youngest of us; she was only fifteen, said that she was so hungry that she would do what they asked. It was disgusting. When she discovered what it was that they wanted her to do, she refused. However, they hit her, indicating that the beating would continue until she did what they wanted. She was forced to suck one of them whilst the other put his thing up her backside. That poor girl hadn't recovered from that by the time I left. She just lay on her bed all of the time."

Liz asked Julia to tell her how she had escaped. "Well, after we had been there for what I think was two or three days, two of the girls were taken from the room and they didn't return. Those of us remaining were very worried. We thought it likely that the girls had been killed. Then another of us was taken from the room and didn't return. Except when that girl went they left the door to our room open and I could hear them speaking. They were talking about getting the girl looking presentable because she was going to be picked up in a short time. Then, a day or so later my turn came; they took me out of the room with the beds and let me bathe myself. Then they gave me clean underpants and a new dress to put on. The dress was too small for me, but one of them joked in English that the client wouldn't mind that I was showing off my 'tits'. I didn't understand what they meant by the word, 'client'. I know what the word means, but I didn't know how it applied to me. Not long after that they grabbed me; one of them held me whilst the other put plastic bands around my wrists and ankles. Then they tied a piece of cloth around my head that covered my mouth. After that they put a cloth bag over my head. Then, both of them grabbed me and carried me to one side of the room, laying me down on a couch."

"I lay on the couch for what seemed like a very long time. Then I heard several voices speaking in English, and the hood was taken off of my head. The two men who were my captors had been joined by two other men, one of whom was black. I thought that he would take pity on me because we were of the same race, but, if anything he was worse than the white man. He said, 'oh, she's just perfect; I want to have first crack at her,' or something like that. He then reached down and unbuttoned my top. I closed my eyes, then; I didn't want to see what he was going to do. However, the other man said, 'c'mon, Derek, let's get goin'. You can take care of her when we get back to Paddington'."

Liz interrupted Julia to ask: "you're sure that he said Paddington, Julia?" Julia said that she was sure. "They put the hood back over my head and then one of them lifted me and carried me into the outside. I was wearing only a thin dress, and I was very cold. I heard a car door open, and I was laid down on a seat. It was very uncomfortable. I lay there for a time, and I could hear the two men arguing. The black man, Derek, wanted to ride in the back with me, but the other who the black man called 'Stan', said that there was no way he was going to allow that. It seemed that Stan was the boss because the two men got into the front of the vehicle and they drove off."

"Whoever was driving the car was going very fast; I was worried that I would fall off of the seat. Finally, I heard Stan's voice tell his companion to slow down; that all they needed was to be stopped by the cops with what they had in the back of the car. After that, the car went slower."

"Finally, the car stopped and I was carried up some stairs and into a building. I was shaking, both because I was very frightened and because I was cold. I was pretty sure of what Derek was going to do to me when we got to where they were taking me. The two men took me into a room where they laid me down on a bed. I closed my eyes, thinking that now Derek was going to do what he had said he wanted to do. However, nothing happened; the next thing I knew I was alone."

Julia then went on to say that some time later she heard the door of the room open and two women came in talking to each other. She felt a tug at her ankles and then relief as the ankles were freed; her wrists were freed also allowing her to rub one wrist that had been worn by its binding. Moments later, the hood was taken off of her head so that she could see, and the gag was removed from her mouth. She was lying on a high bed. Standing on either side of the bed was a woman, one of whom was wearing a white dress that looked like the uniform usually worn by nurses. The 'nurse' said, "there; that should make you a little more comfortable."

The other woman told her companion not to waste her words; that Julia did not understand English.

Julia continued her narrative in Portuguese: "as the two women talked, I looked around me. I was in a small room that looked like it was set up for medical examinations. It had two tall beds in it. The other bed was occupied by another young woman who appeared to be sleeping. The women made no effort to disguise what they were saying. The one in the nurse's uniform gestured to me that I should remove my dress and underpants, and lie back down on the bed on which the two men had placed me. Then she examined me all over, even pushing something into my bottom so she could examine me by the light of a torch. As she was looking at my bottom she told her companion that it didn't look like I was pregnant, but she'd ask the lab to check that when they did the test for AIDS. Then she put a needle in my arm and removed some blood. After that the nurse gave me my underpants and pulled back the bed clothing, gesturing to me that I should get into the bed. The two women left the room, turning out the light and locking the door. I lay there for a time, trying to gather my thoughts. Everything that had happened to me since arriving in England seemed so strange. I had no idea why I was where I was. I felt very lonely, missing my parents and my home, so I began to weep. Then I heard a voice asking me, 'do you speak English'?"

Julia went on to relate the conversation that she had had with the young woman whom she had seen lying in the other bed in the room. The girl; she was no more than that, said that she was one of three girls who had been brought to Britain from Albania several months earlier by a man who had told the girls that he would help them to get jobs and places to live. He had done that alright; he had turned her over to Stan and Derek and she had been working for them ever since.

Julia asked the girl, who said that her name was Karina, what it was that she did. The girl's answer so shocked Julia that she remembered it clearly. Karina had said, her job was to "fock." Then she corrected herself to say that she didn't even do that; she just lay there while she was focked. She said that she was supposed to pretend that she enjoyed it, which she did because if she didn't Stan would not give her her injections. Julia said that Karina had said that most of the time when she "focked" it was OK, but some of the men that did it to her were crazy. Unless she pretended that she was being raped and tried to stop them, they didn't like it, and would get angry with her.

Liz interrupted Julia to ask about the injections, but Julia said that she had not understood about them. "When I questioned Karina about it she said only, 'you will find out soon enough. That is the way they make you stay here and make you let men fock you. You'll see, it will be the only pleasure that you will have'."

Liz knew that many prostitutes were addicted to drugs, usually heroin or crack cocaine and that prostitution was a way to finance their habit. However, from what Julia was telling her of the conversation she had had with Karina, it appeared likely that the girl had been forced into addiction and her addiction had been used to control her.

Liz asked Julia to continue her statement. "Karina told me, 'once they are sure that you don't have any diseases they will put you in a room. If you have not done much focking before they will charge a higher price for you at first. However, after you have been here for awhile the price will come down.' Then Julia said that she had asked Karina why she was in the bed in the room. 'They took a dead baby from my body; it was only a tiny thing, so it died. You are not supposed to get babies; they make you take pills so you won't, but something happened that mine didn't work. They made me stay in here until I am healed enough to go back to work. They told me today that that will be tomorrow'."

Julia said that at that point there was a noise indicating that the door to the room was being unlocked and Karina left quickly to go to her bed. The lights of the room came on and the 'nurse' and her companion came in. Julia said that she could see that Karina had closed her eyes and was pretending to be asleep. The nurse's companion had returned Julia's dress to her, and, by gestures, indicated that she was to put it on. Then Julia had been taken from the nursing room, the door of which again had been locked. She had been taken along a hallway to another room which, she was told, would be her's. At that point, the two women had left Julia alone; the young woman had heard it as the door to her room had been locked.

* * *

The room in which Julia had found herself had a double bed, a settee, a low table that was placed before the settee and two overstuffed chairs. At one side of the room was a door which, the 'nurse' had pointed out to her with gestures, led into a small bathroom with a shower, a washbasin and a toilet. Julia said that the 'nurse' had indicated by further gestures what was required of her. She was to shower and put on a gown that was lying on the bed. Julia said, "she even made it clear to me that I was to wash my bottom with a little bulb thing that she took from a drawer of a small table that was at one end of the bathroom. The clothing I was given to wear consisted only of a loose-fitting dress with a tie at the waist. The woman was having quite a lot of difficulty getting across to me by gestures what it was that I was supposed to do, so now and again she would say something out loud. From what she was saying, it was obvious that I was expected to allow men to have sexual intercourse with me and I was to thoroughly douche myself after each client."

"When I indicated that I would never do what she said that I was to do, the woman went to the door and called out, asking Derek to come into the room. She told him that I wasn't being co-operative, so he came over to me and grabbed me, placing me on the bed and holding me by the arms. I tried to struggle but he was just too strong. He slapped me across the face and told me, in English, to calm down. As he was dealing with me the woman left the room. A short time later, the woman in the nurse's uniform came into the room, and whilst Derek held me, she injected me in the arm. Then I just lay there gasping for breath; finally, I closed my eyes. Whatever they injected into my arm seemed to make me sleepy. At that point, they left the room turning out the light and locking the door. As they left I heard the 'nurse' say, 'I don't think we'll have any trouble from her from now on'."

"After Derek and the woman left, I opened my eyes once more. I was feeling very strange, but I knew that I had to get away if it was possible. I got out of bed, almost falling over, I was so dizzy. I looked around the room to see if there was any way that I could get out of it. There was what looked like a window on one wall, but there was no glass in it, only a painted panel. I went over to the window and knocked on it, but it seemed to be made of wood or metal."

"Then I remembered that I had seen a window above the toilet in the bathroom when I had showered, but that was very small and quite high up. Nonetheless, I went into the bathroom and looked at it. It had a fan in the upper part, but it looked like the lower part might be just large enough for me to get through. It was hard to tell, because I found it very difficult to focus my eyes, and I had to support myself with the frame of the bathroom door. Also, I thought that maybe I could get through the window, but I didn't know how I could get up to it. I climbed up onto the seat of the toilet, but still it was above my head. I almost fell when I got down from the toilet seat."

"I went back into the bedroom and dragged one of the overstuffed chairs into the bathroom, just managing to lift it up and rest it on the toilet seat. That allowed me to climb up high enough so that my head was almost level with the window, but it was very wobbly. I took one of the pillows off of the bed and held it against the glass whilst I banged on the pillow with my fist. However I could not break it. I wrapped my fist in the pillow case and hit at the window. At first, it was very painful. Finally, a large crack appeared in the glass. I again put the pillow against the window and hit it. Then the glass began to break, making what seemed to me to be very loud noises. Obviously the sounds were not heard by anyone in the house because no one came. I removed the pieces of glass that remained in the window frame and looked out of the window. I couldn't see how far it was to the ground or whatever was below the window. I was feeling very unsteady on my feet, but I was fighting the feeling that I wanted to lie down and sleep. I knew that I would die rather than have happen to me what had happened to Karina."

"I could see that there was a pipe going down the wall that was just outside of the window. My first thought was to try to use it to get to the ground, but I couldn't see any places along its length that would give me a good grip. Instead, I took the bed sheets off the bed and tied one end of one of them to the drainpipe under the washbasin. I tied its other end to the second sheet, which I then shoved out of the window. Fortunately, when I was a little girl my mother taught me to weave, so I was very practised in tying knots that would not come loose."

"As I made my way out of the window I tried to keep myself right side up by holding on to the pipe, but the opening was only just large enough to allow my chest to squeeze through and I ended up hanging onto the sheet with my head down. Once my feet cleared the window, I tumbled over backward. I didn't loosen my grip on the sheet, but I slipped down it getting severe burns on the palms of my hands. I didn't feel those until much later. I slipped to the end of the sheet and then fell to the ground below, which wasn't very far. I sat for a time with my back leaning against a surface. My inclination was to close my eyes and go to sleep, but I knew that I had to get away from that place. Derek and the 'nurse' would be looking for me."

"Finally, I felt able to get to my feet. It was so dark, I could see nothing. Once on my feet I had to support myself by leaning against what I could feel was a structure that had a very rough texture. I thought that it might be the wall of the building from which I'd just fallen. I could not feel my feet, which were completely numb. I felt my way along the structure, a short time later seeing a lighted area ahead of me. I was having less difficulty staying on my feet, so the effects of whatever had been injected into me must have begun to wear off. I continued to feel my way, until I came out from between the outside walls of two adjacent houses. There was a well-lit street just in front of me. I didn't hesitate. I climbed over a low wall and onto the sidewalk and began to run."

"At first I nearly fell over because my feet wouldn't do what I wanted them to do. However, eventually I found myself running very fast. I don't recall even breathing as I ran. I know that when I finally did stop, it took me a long time to get my breath back."

"I saw the lights of a car approaching, so I ran out onto the road waving my arms. It was a woman who stopped. She stared at me through the window of her door, but she didn't say anything. I shouted at her to help me; finally she opened the window a tiny amount and asked what had happened to me. When I told her about being held captive and having escaped, she started to close her window. I shouted at her again, asking her to help me. She stopped closing the window and said something like, 'alright, get in'. She said that she hoped that she would not be sorry for helping me. Once I was in her car I told her what had happened to me. She was very kind and took me to a police station where she told them what I had told her. I was so relieved to have been rescued I didn't even stop to worry if what the men had said about us being illegal immigrants was true. I didn't care."

"It wasn't until I was seated in the police station talking to a lady police officer that I noticed that the fingers of my right hand were all swollen and bleeding, and the palms of both of my hands were all red. My hands hurt horribly, as did my left arm. Also, I had holes in my stockings, and, in places, my feet were very sore and bleeding. The police woman who spoke to me was very kind to me. She insisted that I be taken to emergency room of a hospital before anything else was done. She went with me and stayed."

# Chapter Three

**D**uring her conversations with Julia Gomes, Liz had grown to admire the resilience of the young woman. She was being kept in a holding cell at Scotland Yard. Although Liz thought that the conditions in which the young woman was being kept were far from adequate, Julia seemed quite happy with them. Before Liz had been able to ask her, the young woman had told her that she would like very much to help the police to find the men who had done such terrible things to her and her fellow Mozambicans. She said that she was sure that the others who had come with her to Britain now were being treated horribly. She would do anything that she could to put a stop to that.

Each morning, after arriving at the 'Yard', Liz would go to the area of the holding cells and have a friendly chat with Julia. After such visits she came away with feelings of guilt that the young woman was being so friendly and co-operative and yet the police were treating her no better than they would a criminal. Liz had spoken to Lydia about the possibility of moving the young woman to more comfortable surroundings; perhaps renting a room for her in a nearby hotel. However, her superior had said that she thought it unlikely that "the powers that be" would approve of such a procedure, which would be expensive both in terms of money and manpower. The young woman would have to be supervised twenty-four hours of the day. Then, with a twinkle in her eye, Lydia had said, "of course if someone would volunteer to put her up, and if that someone were, herself, a police officer; that would be a different story."

That evening, an elated Julia Gomes accompanied Liz to her flat in Plaistow, East London, where the young woman would be accommodated during the time she would be co-operating with the police.

Liz thought that the logical first step in locating the places where Julia had been incarcerated was to begin in the area from which the young woman had escaped. She began by questioning the woman driver who had picked up Julia Gomes shortly after her escape. Fortunately, the identity of Julia's rescuer was known.

The rescuer could recall only approximately where she had picked up Julia. She retraced her movements on a map of West London that showed the various roads and land-marks in great detail. She said that she had been on her way home after dropping off her daughter at Paddington train station. She thought that the place must have been close to the Harrow Road because she remembered crossing that going under the Marylebone flyover not too long before the girl had run into the road in front of her. She remembered that after picking up the girl, she had had to turn around to go to the Paddington Green police station.

Liz questioned Julia closely, attempting to get her to re-call every detail about her surroundings on the night that she had escaped from the house in Paddington. From the young woman's answers to Liz's questions, it became clear that the house occupied by Julia's captors was on a road where most of the houses on either side had had their front gardens sur-faced so to provide parking spaces for cars. However, Julia had had to climb over a low wall to get to the pavement in front of the house in which she had been held.

Lydia decided that there was nothing for it; the only way to find the captors' house was on foot. She assigned three detective members of her team as well as some uniformed officers to a duty in which they walked along roads in a part of West London. The area chosen was that indicated by Julia Gomes' rescuer as one in which there were good possibilities for finding the place where she had picked up the young woman. It was hoped that the presence of a low wall would not be a common feature of houses in that area, but that proved not to be the case; the houses along many of the roads in the likely area of West London had their front gardens separated from the 'sidewalk' by a low wall.

Whilst three of the detective constables on her team were walking along roads, noting those with appropriately-located low walls, Liz undertook the task of ringing the premises of glaziers in the area. She had looked them up in the Yellow Pages, being surprised at just how many there were in such a limited area. She knew that the odds were against her, but it was just possible that the bathroom window that Julia had broken had been repaired by someone who was paid specifically for that job. Usually, building owners relied on 'handymen' who would effect any general repairs required. One of the shops that she had rung told her that there seemed to have been a "run" on broken bathroom windows of late. "I've re-glazed two in the past fortnight!" Liz got the addresses of the buildings where the man had worked, both of which were private houses. One address was well outside the area indicated by Julia's rescuer, but Liz included that address when she drove Julia to see the houses. Neither house had a low wall in front, and Julia said that she could not recognise either of them.

Liz, discouraged, returned with Julia to the 'Yard', telling her that perhaps a nice cup of tea would brighten their spirits. When the two women entered the detectives' room, one of the PCs assigned to her team, John Yardley, was standing talking to one of the detectives. He said, "ah, Sergeant Andresen; I think that I may have seen one of the men that Miss Gomes described; the man called Derek. This morning, I was walking down one of the roads that has houses with low walls in front, when this black man came out of one of the buildings and got into a car that was parked in front of it. The front garden of the house that the black man came out of was used as a car park. However, the house next door had a wall around its front garden, and there appeared to be a passageway that went from that front garden between the two houses. Anyway, I made a note of the address. Also, I've spotted a couple of places on the road where we can park a surveillance van in case we want to keep a watch on the house." Liz was quite impressed with John Yardley's show of initiative and said so. She asked the PC to describe 'Derek' as best he could to Julia to see if she could recognise him as the man who had assaulted her. Constable Yardley described the man he'd seen as relatively tall, probably over six feet. Also, he had what looked like a muscular build. He had a full head of hair which was short. Julia said that nothing that John Yardley said contradicted her memory of 'Derek', but that she was sure that she would recognise the man if she saw him again. Liz concluded that she would have to speak to Lydia and make arrangements for the suspect house to be kept under surveillance. That would be the next move, anyway, if the man did turn out to be 'Derek'.

A week later it, had been established that the black man seen first by PC Yardley was the same as the man who had assaulted Julia. A small van that had been converted especially for surveillance operations had been parked in the road not far from the house from which Derek had exited a few days earlier. From the surveillance van, close-up videos were taken of everyone entering or leaving the house. At the end of each period of surveillance, the videotape made of that period's recordings was shown to Julia. After two days of surveillance, it was established that Derek and Stan, as well as the woman who locked Julia in her room, were permanent inhabitants of the house. The second woman that Julia had described, the 'nurse', was not seen. As PC Yardley put it not so delicately to Liz, it was obvious that the house was being used as a "knocking shop;" that is, a house of prostitution. Each day, during the late afternoon and evening, the house was visited by several men who usually arrived by taxi. However, no young woman ever was seen to enter or leave the house. That observation, Liz thought, confirmed Julia's observation that the young women who worked there very likely were being held captive.

From Julia's description of the treatment of her and her companions after their arrival at Heathrow, Liz thought it likely that the place where she had been taken first must serve as some kind of distribution centre for illegal immigrants. Liz hoped that surveillance of the house in Paddington might be helpful in locating that place. One of the members of her team was placed in an unmarked police car that was parked a short distance away from the surveillance van. Whenever Derek and/or Stan came out of the house and got into a car, the officer in the surveillance van would alert the officer in the unmarked car, who then would follow the suspects' car. Liz didn't wish to continue surveillance of the house in Paddington for too long a period because she thought it likely that imprisoned in the house under surveillance were some very distressed young women.

Liz's first inclination upon finding the house had been to arrest Derek and Stan and the two women and free any of the young women who were imprisoned there. However, she knew that it would be far more useful to cut off one of the sources of prostitutes. That could be done only if the house where Julia had spent her first few days in Britain could be found and kept under surveillance.

\* \* \*

Finally, the break for which Liz was waiting, occurred. Stan, accompanied by Derek, drove to Hampstead to a house that was located on a tree-lined street just off the Finchley Road. The police constable following the two men kept up a running commentary of his progress on the radio in his car. He said that the car he was following finally had come to a halt in the driveway of a large house. The two occupants of the car then had got out and entered the building. He gave the street address, indicating that he was in some difficulty because parking was not permitted on the road in front of the house. He was told to go ahead and park as inconspicuously as possible; Traffic Division would be alerted in case his car was detected by a member of that group.

A short time later, the PC again contacted the radio room and said that he had observed two men to carry a bundle out of the house and put it into the back seat of their car. He was in the process of following them.

As it turned out, Stan and Derek had gone to the house in Hampstead to pick up a new inmate for the brothel in Paddington.

Liz was of the opinion that the house in Paddington should be raided and all of its occupants should be taken into custody, if for no other reason than to rescue an unknown number of young women from depraved conditions. However, she had discussed with Lydia the hope that Stan, Derek and the two women could be arrested on more serious charges than those involved with prostitution. Also, she had hoped that some of the clients of the brothel could be made subject to charges more serious than consorting with prostitutes.

During the surveillance operation, Liz's team had collected close-up photographs of thirty-two men, who had entered the house, stayed for varying periods of time and then left. If what Karina had told Julia was true, and the police had no reason to believe it wasn't, at least some of the men who frequented the house as clients were committing offences much more serious than that of consorting with prostitutes. Nevertheless, with the exception, perhaps, of a minority of cases, it was unlikely that charges of rape against the men could be sustained.

Lydia overrode Liz's opinion that the Paddington brothel should be raided, telling her younger colleague that very likely it was only one of several such locations that were supplied with illegal immigrants by the house in Hampstead. "To raid it at this time might alert the whole of the network to police activity, causing them to shift their operations elsewhere. Then we would have to start all over. No, Liz, I think that we will have to allow the operation of the brothel for the time being. However, it shouldn't take us too long to determine the extent of the prostitution ring, if, indeed, that is what it is. Then we can close down the whole operation all at once."

# Chapter Four

The activities of Liz's team now were shifted to the building in the Hampstead area of London. Because of Julia Gomes' testimony, it was thought likely that that house was the first place in the UK to which some of the illegal immigrants were taken. Surveillance of the building quite possibly would offer the police the opportunity of apprehending not only persons acting as 'middlemen' in the illegal immigrant 'trade', but also the procurers.

Because of the difficulty of locating a surveillance vehicle near the house, Liz had to expend effort to find the owner of a building along the same road who would allow the police to make use of his or her premises.

Liz's first place of asking was a small hotel, the Heath, that was on the opposite side of the road and about 50 meters further along. Liz hoped that the manager of the Heath Hotel would co-operate by allowing the police to occupy one of the rooms at the front of the building that overlooked the road. Much to her delight, the manager was happy to oblige. He said that with the exception of the summer and of festive seasons, the rooms at the front of the hotel usually stood empty: people generally preferred the rooms at the rear of the hotel; they were less likely to be disturbed by traffic noise.

Liz realised that much of the activity of her team would depend upon the co-operation of Julia Gomes. Although, officially, Julia was facing deportation still, Liz was hopeful that such an event would not occur. She was sure that the

Home Office would take into account Julia's help to the police when her case came up for review.

In the meantime, Liz was finding Julia to be a very companionable flatmate. In their spare moments, and at Julia's request, Liz was helping the young woman to perfect her spoken English. Fairly often, Liz would find herself giggling at one of Julia's errors either of pronunciation or the use of an inappropriate word. Like most native speakers of romance languages, she had found the irregular pronunciation of vowels in English to be particularly difficult.

Lydia had managed to get the young woman some money out of police funds which gave her enough to live on. Also, the money was sufficient to provide Julia with several new items of clothing. There was an added bonus for Liz in having Julia living with her because the young woman was an excellent cook; she introduced Liz to a number of dishes that were part of the diet in Mozambique.

Liz had hoped to be able to give Julia some official status so that the young woman could take part in the police operation. During the surveillance of the Paddington house, Julia had helped by each day reviewing videotapes recorded the previous day. By that means she had been able to identify Stan and Derek, as well as two female occupants of the house. The procedure proved to be awkward and didn't permit of a rapid response when one was needed, such as the time when the car containing Stan and Derek had been driven to the building in Hampstead. However, Liz's request for official status for Julia had not been approved, so she decided to 'use her own initiative': a course of action she had been encouraged to utilise by several of her superiors up to that point in her police career. She asked Julia to make herself available for as much time as possible during an eight-hour period between two or three in the afternoon and ten or eleven at night. Julia said that she would be pleased to do so.

Police experts in covert surveillance had set up a room in the Heath Hotel from which the suspect house could be kept under observation constantly. The most useful of the surveillance equipment was a video camera that was fitted with night-vision optics. The image it took could be both recorded on tape and displayed on two television monitors. One of the monitors was located within the room from which surveillance was being maintained; the other was located in an adjacent room that was occupied by Julia Gomes. Because, technically, Julia could not be in the surveillance room, Liz took the responsibility upon herself to hire the hotel room into which the young woman was to remain whilst she was 'on duty' at the hotel. Prior to taking this action, Liz had mentioned her plan to Lydia. Lydia had responded in a manner typical of her: neither approving nor disapproving but saying only, "well, I've always found that what bureaucrats don't know about they don't grieve over!"

The police officer who was in charge of the surveillance camera was in radio communication not only with Julia, but with two members of Liz's team who sat in an unmarked police vehicle located in the small car park of the hotel. Liz hoped that the method of surveillance that she was using would allow the team to cover two contingencies: the investigation of activity at the suspect house as well as permitting any vehicle arriving at the suspect house to be followed once it left.

\* \* \*

Liz was getting rather bored with the surveillance operation of the house in Hampstead. Consequently, she occupied some of her time, whilst not actively making observations, attempting to discover the ownership of the observed house. She knew that that detail would be required when it came time to make charges against those involved in the prostitution ring.

Through offices of the borough council responsible for Hampstead, she discovered the name of the entity that paid the rates on the house. It was a property company. Enquiries with that company indicated that the house was under lease to a named individual. That was all that they could tell Liz about the premises. Liz managed to persuade the manager of the property company to help the police with their enquiry. He agreed to send a representative to inspect the house, an act permitted by the tenancy agreement between his company and the current tenant.

Initially, the representative of the property company had been refused access. However, the manager of the company contacted the firm of solicitors who acted on behalf of the tenant and access was granted. By this rather round-about procedure it was established that only the two men seen to come and go by the surveillance team were actually living in the house. Julia had confirmed that they were the same two men who had kept her and her four companions from Mozambique prisoner.

Late one evening Julia shouted something in Portuguese into the microphone that was attached to the collar of her blouse; she was sitting before the television monitor in her room. Moments later she said, "sorry, I get so excited I forget myself. I am sure that van that just stop at house bring me from heatrow. Yes, I am almost sure." Liz was seated in the police surveillance room when she heard Julia's excla-mation so she went to the television monitor, asking DC Green to focus the camera as close up as possible. Two men got out of the van and went to the side door of the vehicle, opening it; moments later four women exited.

Accompanied by the two men, the women went into the suspect house. Liz asked DC Green to see if he could get close enough so that they could see the registration number of the van. That proved to be possible, so Liz alerted the two PCs seated in the car in the hotel car park, telling them to stand by, ready to follow the vehicle when it left.

Once the van left the suspect house, Liz had a very emo-tional discussion with Julia. The young woman had urged Liz to send the police team to the house in order to arrest the two men who lived there and rescue the young girls who had just arrived. Julia said that the two men who lived in the house were animals and would very soon start to rape the girls if the police did not act. Liz was sure that what her young friend said was true, but she knew that an immediate raid on the house was not part of the police plan of operation.

Rather than reveal the police plan to Julia, Liz tried to deflect the argument with one that was equally emotional. That is, the continuance of the surveillance of the suspect house would make it possible for the police to wind up what very likely was a large and widespread ring of prostitution. If the procedures of the whole ring were like those that had been in operation at the house in Paddington, then the suffering of a large number of young women, not just four, would be ended.

Liz's argument did not calm Julia, who seemed more concerned about what went on in the suspect house imme-diately after the arrival of the young women in the country than what would be their ultimate fate. Finally, in order to calm Julia, Liz said that she would discuss the matter with her superior.

After a rather brief discussion, Lydia made it clear that from that time on Julia Gomes would have to be treated as an illegal immigrant. In other words, she would have to be sent to a detention centre where she could be looked after properly until it was decided what to do with her. "Her usefulness to the surveillance operation is over. We may have to use her if and when we start bringing people to trial, but until then she will be treated like every other illegal immigrant. I'm sorry, Liz. That probably seems harsh considering how helpful Julia has been. However, you can blame me if you like. I will send a car to collect the young woman, but don't say anything to her about going into a detention centre. She might try to do a bunk."

Liz explained to Julia that her superior had affirmed that surveillance of the suspect house would be maintained. Julia seemed to accept that that was the way things had to be. Not long after the two women had talked together, a car arrived from Scotland Yard and a WPC asked Julia to accompany her. As Julia was about to leave, she went to Liz; gave her a hug and then thanked her for being so kind.

Liz was to remember Julia's parting actions and words for some time. She resolved that she would make some enquiries to discover if there was anything that could be done to help the young woman. At the very least, Liz was determined that she would find out where Julia was detained, and she would visit her there as often as she could.

On the evening that Julia left police custody, Liz was not required for surveillance duties, so she managed to get home to her flat at a reasonable hour. There were three things that she had to do, and she was determined that on her first free evening for over a week, she would do them. She had to telephone both her mum and her best friend, Patricia Moffatt, just to let them know that she had not forgotten them. Also, she thought that she should explain that she'd neglected them because she had been very busy. The third thing she needed to do was to have a talk with Pat's husband, Roger. He was a solicitor and Liz was hopeful that he could offer good advice about what legal steps, if any, could be taken to help Julia Gomes. She thought it unlikely that Roger would be knowledgeable about immigration law, but he might know someone who could help. Liz had decided for herself that the Metropolitan Police had treated Julia rather shabbily and she was going to do what she could do to put things right.

\* \* \*

When Liz rang her mother's number there was no response; it was obvious that Audrey, as usual, was spending the evening at the pub. After putting down the receiver, Liz found herself returning to a worry that she had had for well over a year. Her mother was drinking far too much. The worry was fortified by the knowledge that there seemed to be nothing that Liz could do to help.

To keep her mind off of her mum, Liz then dialled Pat's number, saying, "c'mon, Pat, be in, be in!" Fortunately, the woman, herself, answered, not the answering machine. The obvious pleasure in Pat's voice was very cheering and soon the two of them were chatting along happily. By the time Liz put the 'phone down, she had promised faithfully that she would visit Pat in Cambridge on her next free weekend. Also, she had spoken briefly to Roger, who gave her the name and address of a London solicitor who specialised in pleading the causes of persons who had fallen foul of UK immigration laws. He said that the solicitor, a Miss Parmeeta Khan, could be a "right pain in the arse," but she had been very successful in arguing on the behalf of people treated badly by Home Office bureaucrats.

When she had a spare moment the next day, Liz telephoned the number she had for Parmeeta Khan. To her surprise, the lady, rather than a secretary, answered the telephone. Liz identified herself and then quickly outlined her view of the difficulty in which Julia Gomes found herself, asking, finally, if Miss Khan would give an opinion as to whether or not there was anything that could be done. Miss Khan said that it didn't sound as if there was any basis in law for an appeal against wrongful detention. "I would think that the only thing that might be done is to make an appeal to the Home Secretary. Even though Miss Gomes is illegally in the country, it could be argued that she had been unaware that her entry was unlawful, and she would not have entered had she known. Also, if what you say about her help to the police can be substantiated formally, that should help the appeal. Unfortunately, I have rather a lot on at the moment, so I won't be able to give Miss Gomes' case my undivided attention; however, I'll do what I can to help."

Miss Khan continued, "it would be helpful if you could find out where Miss Gomes is being detained. As soon as you let me know that, I'll try to get to see her; I know that drill pretty well. I'll have a chat with the young woman to be certain I have the full story of her entry into the country. Then I'll ask a few of my colleagues their opinion of the best course to pursue in this particular case. Probably I shall have to have a statement from someone in authority in the police that describes the rôle played by Miss Gomes in police enquiries. I appreciate that the latter could be difficult. Since both the police and the immigration service come under the jurisdiction of the Home Office, there is usually a tendency for them to back each other up rather than oppose each other. However, we'll worry about that at the appropriate time."

Before ringing off, Liz asked Miss Khan about the cost of her enquiries. She said, "well, I usually charge £100 an hour, if I can get it. However, I assume that Miss Gomes has no money, and as a sergeant in the police you aren't exactly rolling in it. Sometimes I can get the money from public funds; let's worry about that later." Liz added that she did have some savings, so she would be able to help out. Miss Kahn repeated, "let's worry about that later, sergeant. Oh, I hope you won't mind me saying so, but you've gone quite a little way in restoring my faith in the police. As I'm sure you're aware, coppers aren't overly popular with the Asian and black communities. However, the fact that you appear to be worrying about Julia Gomes makes me think that there are still some human beings to be found amongst our police brethren."

# Chapter Five

After delivering four young women to a house in Hampstead, Northwest London, a van drove to an address in North Hillingdon, near Heathrow Airport. Unknown to the van's occupants, their vehicle had been followed by an unmarked police car. The two men in the van then were observed to enter a house. Officers in the police car kept the house under observation until it was obvious that the occupants had retired for the night.

Liz checked with the Driver and Vehicle Licensing Centre in Swansea, finding that the van driven by the two men was registered to a person who gave his address as that at which the van was parked. A check with the local borough council indicated that the rates on the property were paid by a property company. The manager of the property company told Liz that he was not allowed to reveal the name of the man to whom his company had leased the property. Liz knew that she could get a court order to force the manager to reveal the name, but she thought that she would try a simpler means first. She told the manager that she would mention a name. If the lessee of the house was not that person would he tell her? He said that he saw no reason not to do that. She mentioned the name of the registered owner of the van and the manager responded by saying that he saw no need for Liz to get a court order.

Liz rang Lydia, asking to have a word with her as soon as possible. Lydia suggested that they go to afternoon tea together. At tea, the main subject of conversation was the pattern that seemed to be emerging as the result of investigations made by their team. Liz said that everything official was in the reports, but she wished to appraise Lydia of some speculations and to get her superior's thoughts about them. "As you know; so far, we have located three properties being used by what, obviously, is a prostitution ring. The house in Hampstead, which seems to serve as a reception centre and distribution point for young women brought into the UK to serve as prostitutes. Also, there is a house not far from Heathrow Airport that is occupied by two men that supervise the import of the women into the country. However, we've located only one place of ultimate destination of the young women: the house in Paddington that is being used as a brothel. Nevertheless, I am sure that we are dealing with an organisation that is larger than that indicated by what we've found so far."

"Because the whole operation appears to be so well organised, I am fairly certain that only one person is behind it. All of the properties that I have mentioned are leased to different individuals by what appear to be legitimate property-management companies. Those companies act on behalf of owners through the mediation of firms of solicitors. So far, I have been unable to discover who is the true owner or owners of the properties we know about. However, I must admit that I have given the identification of the property owners a low priority. Also, it is far from clear how the young women who show up in this country as prostitutes are recruited. The fact that they have come from several different countries suggests that there are several different recruiters. Are the recruiters somehow connected to the prostitution ring?"

Lydia said that she agreed with Liz that the likelihood was great that her team was dealing with a well-organised prostitution ring. She thought that the first priority of the team should be to locate as many as possible of the places where prostitutes were operating. "I suspect that the only way you can do that is to maintain surveillance of the house in Hampstead. Also, I think that for the time being at least you should back off from looking too closely at the owner-ship of the various properties. Of course, find out from lo-cal councils who pays the rates on the properties; that won't arouse any suspicions. However, let's wait until we're ready to shut down the whole operation before we resort to legal means to discover the identities of the true owners of the properties." Lydia closed the discussion by saying, "there seem to be quite a lot of unanswered questions. I think that we've got a long way to go yet before we begin to crack this case, Liz. Here, let me get you another cup of tea; would you like a biscuit to go with it?"

Lydia and Liz were just rising from their seats in the can-teen preparing to go back to their respective offices when the radio transceiver carried by Liz in her handbag indicated that she was being called. It was one of the PCs involved with surveillance in Hampstead. He said that he had been having no luck trying to contact Inspector Mussett; he asked Liz if she would contact the inspector and pass on a mes-sage. Liz said, "ah, she's just here, constable;" she handed the transceiver to Lydia, telling her, "it's for you."

The constable said that about ten minutes earlier a car had arrived at the suspect house and he had alerted the two PCs waiting in the hotel car park. He wanted to know whether or not Lydia would wish to send a backup car just in case another one might be needed. Lydia thanked the PC for thinking so far ahead; she would see to it that a backup car arrived at the hotel as soon as possible. Both women went off to their respective offices.

Some time later, Liz contacted the team at the Heath Hotel, wishing to know how things were going. The PC who had radioed earlier told her, "it got really exciting here a short time ago. Our blokes had no sooner taken off to follow the car from the suspect house when another car shows up at the place. I thought briefly about radioing you again, but I figured it would be too late anyway. Fortunately, a few minutes later I got a call from the backup car the DI sent telling me that they were in position in the hotel car park. I don't know if you've been following the conversations, Liz, but the first car that came to the suspect house today now seems to be on its way to Kensington. I'll keep you informed of their progress, if you want me to." Liz asked him to do that, telling him that she would be seeing him fairly soon because she would be arriving for the evening watch.

* * *

A fortnight later, Lydia's team still was maintaining surveillance of the house in Hampstead, but there had been no activity there for several days. The four young women who had arrived just over three weeks earlier all had been removed, one each, to four houses in West and Southwest London. Although the team had received extra help from the uniformed branch of the Metropolitan Police, there had not been sufficient manpower to mount surveillance on the four houses.

During the lull in activity, Liz had made the usual enquiries about the ownership of the four premises the police had located as a result of their most recent surveillance. Like the previous three houses associated with illegal immigrants, the four were under the control of property-management companies. Again, like the previous three, the property-management companies had been engaged by firms of solicitors.

Based on what was known by the police about the fate of the young women removed from the house in Hampstead, Liz was exasperated by the slow pace of the investigation. She wished that there was something that the police could do to speed the end to the suffering of the young women. However, she was aware also that the secrecy surrounding the ownership of the houses meant that one or more premises might be overlooked if the police moved too quickly.

It was always a mistake to make plans more that a day in advance if you're a member of the police, but Liz made that mistake almost habitually. She had planned to go to Cambridge over a weekend to stay with her mum and have a meal with Pat and Roger Moffatt. However, on the Thursday before her planned departure, she had been told that it was very likely that a new consignment of illegals would be arriving in Hampstead that evening. Since its discovery by Lydia's team, the house in North Hillingdon had been kept under twenty-four-hour surveillance by the police of the nearby town of Uxbridge. Movements of the two men who lived there and drove the van that delivered illegal immigrants were monitored constantly.

On Thursday morning the van from North Hillingdon had been followed to the channel port of Dover and was seen to pick up five young women in the car park of a pub not far from the passenger terminal for the cross-channel ferries. Liz was present in the surveillance room of the Heath Hotel when the van arrived and discharged its passengers. She knew that this meant a wait of an indeterminate length until the young women were dispersed. She tried not to think too much about what would happen to the victims both during the next few days and when they reached their ultimate destinations.

Over the next week, the five young women all were taken from the suspect house. Four went to premises that were known to the police and the fifth went to a new place: this one a house in West Hampstead which was only a short distance from the Heath Hotel. Liz had hoped that Lydia would conclude from the most recent results of surveillance that it was time to raid the known premises and arrest their occupants. However, her superior said that in her opinion they should wait just a little longer.

Lydia expressed her frustration at not having the manpower to keep watch on the various premises whose locations were known. "We're only assuming that the premises are being used as brothels, but if that is the case, what happens to the young women that causes them to have to be replaced?"

As Liz left Lydia's office she was distracted completely by a thought planted in her mind by one of Lydia's remarks: "what happens to the young women that causes them to be replaced?" Liz was pretty sure that she would find that the answer would turn out to be: "the young women are dying, probably from drug overdoses."

During a lull in the surveillance operation, Liz searched through police records recording the incidences of deaths of women by suspected or actual drug overdose. She found that there was a record of thirty two such deaths in the previous year in the London area. Twenty four of the deaths were of women whose identity had remained unknown, suggesting that they could be illegal immigrants. The ages of those twenty-four dead women had been estimated to be twenty five years or less. Liz scanned the files kept on the dead women by the police national database. She was looking specifically at the reports of autopsies carried out on the bodies. Usually, a pathologist performing an autopsy will make some comment on the sexual history of a dead woman, remarking upon anything unusual about her genitalia or breasts. However, the autopsy reports revealed nothing except that in all cases the pathologist had commented that the woman had been sexually experienced.

# Chapter Six

**E**ach time she sat down at her desk in the detectives' room, Liz saw the note that she had written and sticky taped to her OUT basket. The note reminded her to get in touch with Parmeeta Khan to see how things were getting on with respect to Julia Gomes. She had tried to telephone the solicitor a couple of times, but there had been no answer. It was obvious that she did not have a telephone answering machine.

This morning, she had just got seated and once again had resolved to ring Miss Khan, when her extension 'phone sounded; it was Lydia. Liz could tell that Lydia was displeased about something the minute she heard her superior's voice. Dispensing with the usual niceties like "good morning," Lydia had asked Liz to come to her office as soon as it was possible. Liz said that she would be there right away.

Lydia opened the conversation by saying that she had just got off the 'blower' from speaking to a permanent secretary at the Home Office. "He said that his minister had made enquiries with the Metropolitan Police and had been told to ring Superintendent Rignell; typically, Rignell has passed the buck to me, so I've had to spend half an hour talking to the permanent secretary. Anyway, he told me that he had been in receipt of a letter from a solicitor saying that the Home Office was treating an illegal immigrant, a young woman named Julia Gomes, very shabbily."

Liz smiled when she heard the name. It was obvious that Parmeeta Kahn had got started in her efforts to help Julia.

Lydia continued, "the permanent secretary went on at me about someone he described as 'that wretched woman, Parmeeta Khan. He said that once she gets hold of something she never lets go. Anyway, he said that Parmeeta Khan had told a story that this Julia Gomes had been unaware that her entry to the UK was illegal. However, once she had become aware of her illegal status she had turned herself in to the police. He said also that Miss Khan had told him that Miss Gomes had been of considerable help to the police, and she felt that it was unforgivable for Her Majesty's government to show their gratitude by threatening to throw the young woman out of the country." Lydia continued, "I hope I have done Julia some good, Liz. I told the permanent secretary that because of Julia's help we are well on the way to closing down a major network which is involved with bringing young women into the country illegally and exploiting them."

"The permanent secretary asked me to put in writing what I had told him; he said that it was likely that the Home Secretary would grant an exception in the case of Miss Gomes and allow her to become a resident." Lydia ended by saying, "the only thing I'm miffed at you about is going behind my back to this Parmeeta Khan. You might at least have told me."

Liz was so pleased that it was likely that Julia would be allowed out of detention and permitted to stay legally in the UK that she merely thanked Lydia for saying what she had to the permanent secretary. She tried to apologise to her superior for not consulting her, but Lydia told her not to worry about it. Obviously the woman had calmed down between the time Liz received her summons, and Lydia had explained what it was all about.

Once back at her desk she rang Parmeeta Khan's number, but there was no answer. She spent the next fifteen minutes typing a letter to the solicitor, thanking her for all that she had done and insisting that she would be willing to compensate her financially for her time.

Liz had just put her letter to Parmeeta Khan in the out-going post and returned to her desk when she received a telephone call from a person whose voice caused her to close her eyes and think, "oh, no!" It was Reginald Marshall, a very dear friend who, of late, she had been neglecting badly. She knew that she had a good excuse: her occupation with the investigation of the prostitute ring. However, she did not wish to make excuses; she had been horribly neglectful and she would have to make amends, no matter what. She began her side of the conversation by saying, "oh, Reg; how wonderful to hear from you. How are you?" Then she said, "I'm ever so sorry; I have been intending to call you, but I been up to here in work. Can you ever forgive me?" Reg said that he quite understood, but his voice betrayed the fact that very likely he didn't entirely believe. However, he said, Liz thought rather formally, "I know that you're a very busy young woman, Liz. However, are you so busy that you couldn't go out with me Thursday week? I can get two tick-ets to the London Choirs Concert at the Albert Hall. I re-membered that you used to sing in a choir, so I thought that you might enjoy the concert. We could have an early dinner at my flat and then go to the concert afterwards. You can stay overnight with me so you won't have to go all the way out to Plaistow late at night."

Liz could think of nothing that would stop her accepting Reg's invitation, but, of course, she never could be certain that her work wouldn't interfere. She thanked Reg for the invitation and told him that she would love to go to the concert, even if it would make her feel guilty. "A couple of weeks ago, I got a notice about the performance from the choir to which I belong. However, all it did was to re-mind me how badly I have been neglecting my singing since I moved to Scotland Yard. I keep intending to take it up again, but I never seem to get around to it." Reg said that he was sorry to remind her, but maybe it was a good thing. Maybe she should develop a few more outside interests, "like a cer-tain lonely old man who sits alone in his flat!" Liz told him that now he really was making her feel bad, and that she was going to do better in the future. "Anyway, Reg, I'll try to get to your flat by about four thirty or five on Thursday."

After speaking to Reg, Liz found herself day dreaming about her relationship with him. She supposed that that relationship would be thought odd by many people. He was an old man who was approaching seventy, and she, a woman in her mid twenties. However, she got on famously with Reg. He was a retired professor of English, whose special interests were Shakespeare and the literature and history of Elizabethan England. Those also were her favourite literature and history topics. Reg wasn't just knowledgeable and intel-ligent; he was full of common sense. She would never tell anyone, but occasionally, just occasionally, she caught herself fantasising about making love with him. She expected that he would be shocked by the idea, but then she was pretty sure that none of the fantasies with which she occasionally entertained herself ever would turn into reality. Liz would really look forward to her date with Reg. She hoped that nothing would come up that would force her to cancel it.

\* \* \*

The surveillance operation on the house in Hampstead very obviously was beginning to bore all of the police officers involved. One or both of the two male occupants of the house would leave it on occasion, taking the car that otherwise was garaged on the site. That would necessitate pursuit by the police car that was parked in the Heath Hotel car park. So far, at least, the excursions made by the house occupants in the car had proved to be entirely innocent: trips to the market or, occasionally, a social night out at a nearby pub. One of the detectives on the surveillance team had struck up a conversation with the two men during one of the pub evenings. He said that they seemed to be "two ordinary blokes." He had tried to get them talking about prostitution, but they'd shown a distinct lack of interest in the topic.

Liz was intrigued still by the idea that the young women who arrived at the house in Hampstead were replacements for prostitutes who had died because they had taken or had been given a drug overdose. Consequently, each morning when she arrived at her desk she read over the report of activities involving the police that had occurred in the London metropolitan area during the previous day. She was looking specifically for reports of the finding of bodies of young females where the cause of death was either suspected or confirmed to be from a drug overdose. She knew that it was a long shot, but she thought that it was just possible that the numbers of illegal immigrants that arrived at the house in Hampstead could be correlated with the deaths that she was reviewing. In order for her idea to have any credence, she would have to be able to predict the time of arrival of illegally-immigrated women.

About two months after beginning her analyses of the deaths of young women, the number of new deaths that were related to drugs numbered five. Liz thought it likely that in the very near future the van that delivered illegal immigrants to the house in Hampstead would be making another trip. She alerted the detective inspector of the Uxbridge police who was in charge of the surveillance of the house in North Hillingdon. She was relieved when he didn't enquire as to the source of her intelligence. He said that he had given the surveillance low priority, of late, because nothing seemed to be happening. However, he would put a couple of extra men on it right away.

Two days later Liz was greatly relieved when she heard a message sent over the radio to the officer in the surveillance room of the Heath Hotel. The message was describing observations being made at a motorway service area on the M 20 near Folkestone. Some young women were being transferred from a lorry into the van that had been followed there from North Hillingdon. Because of the location of the service area, it was thought likely that the young women had been smuggled into the country on the Calais to Dover ferry route. The women were being moved singly from the lorry to the van with long intervals between each transfer, presumably to minimise the chances of arousing curiosity.

The police officer describing the transfer said that the lorry must have had a special compartment just behind the driver's cab that housed the illegal immigrants. The women had got out of the lorry by stepping down from the driver's cab. So far, three women had been transferred, but the police officer describing the scene was sure that there would be more to come.

Late that evening, the van that had made the pick-up near Folkestone discharged its cargo: four young women, at the house in Hampstead. Over the next week, the same women were transferred to three addresses in West London, all of which were known to the police surveillance team.

Liz was pleased when Lydia told her that she thought it likely that the police had located all of the premises that were involved in the prostitution ring, and that now it was time to act. That pleasure turned to disappointment when Lydia added, "however, I think that we should delay things for a few days until we have had a good look at the people who occupy the five premises that appear to be used for prostitution. I'd like you to take charge of another surveillance operation; you'll need some help from uniform, but I've already arranged for that with Assistant Commissioner Barlow. I've called a meeting for tomorrow morning in the briefing room, so all of the new uniforms should be there. I'll leave you to manage things from now on."

As she returned to her desk in the detectives' room, Liz knew that she would have to ring Reg and tell him that she would be unable to make it for their date to go to the Albert Hall. She knew from experience that the surveillance operation under her direction would occupy most of her time for its duration. She hoped that she would be able to get home on occasion to cook herself a meal, but very likely that would be the extent of her 'freedom'. Liz didn't often have feelings of regret about choosing police work as a career, but such a feeling had crept into her consciousness by the time she reached the detectives' room.

# Chapter Seven

During the next week, the group of which Liz was part gathered the information necessary to identify persons permanently associated with the buildings used by the prostitution ring. All of the premises that had been watched were in locations where street parking was allowed, although few spaces were available except early in the day. Use was made of small vans that had been fitted out with video cameras of the same type used for the surveillance of the house in Hampstead. The vans were driven to the sites early in the morning and parked in a place where an unobstructed view of the entrance to each of the premises could be had. As usual, everyone entering or leaving the building was photographed using both video and still cameras.

Once the surveillance operation was concluded, Lydia organised the follow up. In what could be described only as a massive operation, involving one hundred and five police officers, all seven buildings involved in the suspected prostitution ring were raided simultaneously, and their occupants were taken into custody. Also confiscated in the raids was a surprising amount of heroin. Hidden away in the buildings in which the prostitutes worked were heroin stores ranging from 2.5 kg to 6 kg. The persons detained during the raids numbered sixty three. These were dispersed to several local police stations, no single one of which being able to keep such a large number of persons.

All of the detainees were held overnight without charge. The next day, twenty four of the twenty seven persons detained who had been 'temporary visitors' at the houses of prostitution, were released. No charges had been brought against the twenty seven, but all of them had been asked to 'volunteer' a blood sample for DNA analysis. Three of the 'temporary visitors' had refused to do so, and they had been detained on a charge of consorting with a known prostitute. Lydia knew that that charge was easily challenged, but she hoped that the men could be detained long enough to discover if a much more serious charge could be brought against at least one of them: that of murder.

\* \* \*

Lydia had formed the opinion that the young woman whose body had been found in the Grand Union Canal in Regent's Park some weeks earlier very likely was one of the prostitutes who were held captive in the various brothels that were raided; quite possibly the one in Paddington, which was relatively close to Regent's Park. The young woman's identity still was unknown, despite widespread circulation of her photograph and description, so it was possible that she was an illegal immigrant. Also, she was a drug user. In fact, all of the young women who had been arrested in the police raids were drug users.

Lydia had no doubt that police questioning would establish that it was a deliberate policy of those in charge of the prostitution ring to make drug addicts of the young women as a means of controlling them. If Lydia's assumption was correct: that the murdered woman was a prostitute, then very likely her murderer would be found amongst the clients of the prostitution ring. Surveillance of the various premises indicated that women who were later identified as prostitutes never left the buildings in which they were working.

Therefore, it seemed logical that the murderer would have visited the prostitute, rather than vice versa. It was probable that someone in the prostitution ring could give the police valuable information about the death of the young woman whose body had been found in the Grand Union Canal.

Immediately after the raids on premises in West London, the police had detained and dealt with three groups of people. These were men and women who were members of the prostitution ring, men who were clients of the prostitutes, and, finally, the prostitutes themselves.

The police attempted to retain in custody the men and women who were known to be associated with the prostitution ring. The spokesman for the Met had argued that the release of the ring members would put in jeopardy the entire police investigation. Bail was granted nevertheless.

All but three of the client group were released after they had presented proof of their identity and an address at which they could be contacted. The three men who refused to give a blood sample for DNA analysis were released later when solicitors they had retained presented the police with 'show cause' documents.

\* \* \*

The group that proved to be the most difficult with which to deal was that that contained the prostitutes: none of them had documents indicating that they were in the UK legally; therefore they had to be detained. Because all of the young women were addicted to heroin, they were placed in detention centres that contained or were close to drug rehabilitation units.

The command of spoken English by most of the prostitutes was very limited except when it came to words associated with their job, such as cunt, cock, blow job, tits, come, etc. Of those English slang words, they were very knowledgeable. The words had been taught to them presumably because they were part of the everyday language that passed between a prostitute and her client.

\* \* \*

Lydia and Liz both were very happy to see the end of the interviews of the twenty seven young women who had acted as prostitutes. The stories that they told depicted almost unbelievable depravity on the part of most of the people under whose control they had found themselves. The stories had caused great distress amongst the translators, mostly female, who had had to be present during the police interviews.

The degradation of the young women began as soon as they arrived in the country. The place where they were taken first was run by two men who had raped them. Ten of the young women had been virgins prior to that. Each of the young women told a similar story of how they had been introduced into prostitution. After arriving at the place where they were to work they had been placed in a room where their bodies had been examined by a nurse who also had taken blood samples from them.

Then they were put in other rooms; the places where they were to live and work. Nothing happened to them for a few days. They were locked in their rooms and fed at intervals. However, after a couple of days, the nurse visited them again and injected them with something which, at first, made them feel very peculiar. After the injections were continued for awhile, the feeling afterward became quite pleasant, and the young women began to look forward to receiving the injections.

After the first few injections, a man came into the room with the nurse. After she had injected them, the man demonstrated what it was they were to do. Whilst he had sexual intercourse with them the nurse made noises that she made clear to them that they were to imitate. The young women were unanimous in saying that it was the nurse and her male companion who had undertaken to train them as prostitutes. The young women were asked to identify the nurse and her male companion from photographs taken of all of the members of the prostitution ring who lived in the brothels. The prostitutes identified the same woman as the nurse, but there were five different men who served as companions to the nurse.

Some of the prostitutes: those who had a reasonable command of spoken English prior to arriving in Britain revealed a variant on the training programme. They were told that some men liked to imagine that they were raping women. With those men, the young women were told to pretend at first that they were resisting. Then, when the man had begun to penetrate them, they were to act as if they were enjoying it. The women were told that the clients who liked a bit of what was called 'hard sex' would be identified to them, and that they were to be treated differently. Instead of the woman going to reception to fetch the client they were to wait in their rooms with the light out until the client came to them. When the client entered the room she was to pretend to be asleep. Then, when the client got into her bed, she was to pretend that she was resisting and let the client take it from there.

Taking evidence from the prostitutes had proved to be a complicated task. Only a few of them were sufficiently fluent in English that the police could be certain that they fully understood the questions that they were being asked. Consequently, persons who could interpret between English and the native language of the prostitute had to be present in the interview.

The twenty-seven young women between them spoke eight different languages; most of the languages were those of Eastern Europe and the Baltic states. The primary purpose of the interviews was the identification of the persons who had been in control of them, and detailed statements of the actions those in control had taken against the captive women. Those statements made it possible for the police to bring a whole series of charges against the nine men and seven women who had been detained after the raids.

One of the women, Hazel Cook, was a state registered nurse and had served in that capacity at all of the properties used as brothels. Even though she had played a rôle in training the young women to be prostitutes, there seemed to be no charge that covered such activity. Had she used films or printed matter, she could have been charged with dealing in media that tended to deprave and corrupt. For her rôle in injecting the young women with heroin sufficiently often to get them addicted to the substance, she could be charged only with inflicting grievous bodily harm.

The men removed from the raided premises were charged with one count of rape for each of the prostitutes under their control. The two men who occupied the house in Hampstead were identified by all twenty seven of the prostitutes as the men who had raped them. The men who drove the van that delivered illegal immigrants from their port of entry to the house in Hampstead were charged with offences under various parts of the Immigration Control Act. If convicted of those offences they faced little more than fines.

* * *

Liz sat in on all of the interviews of the prostitutes because she was certain that they would be able to help her with an enquiry in which she was involved that paralleled the much larger investigation of the prostitute ring. She showed photographs of the young women whose bodies had been found in various parts of the West End of London. The bodies of all of the women showed evidence of drug taking. Since it was known at the time that all of the prostitutes had been forced into drug addiction, Liz thought it likely that the unknown women had been prostitutes and, very likely, had been involved with the ring that just had been broken up. Five of the six women were recognised by one or more of the prostitutes interviewed, but they had been known only by their first names.

The results of Liz's interviews had made it clear, if nothing else had, that the prostitute ring had worked with deadly efficiency. When a prostitute died, her body was dumped someplace, and then she was replaced by some other hapless illegal. Liz knew that she was being naïve, but she still could not get used to such acts of callousness by her fellow humans. Nutters? OK. She could believe that a nutter could do anything. However, the nine persons in control of the premises of the prostitution ring couldn't really be described as mad.

Liz also had shown the prostitutes a photograph of the young woman whose body had been found in the Grand

Union Canal. Three of the young women said that they thought that she looked familiar, but they didn't know her name. Liz noticed that the three women all had worked at the building in Paddington. She noticed that they spoke very guardedly when they talked about the dead woman. Liz concluded after the interviews that she would have to speak to the three prostitutes again when the confusion was less great. There had been three police officers and an interpreter in the room during their interrogation. Perhaps under quieter circumstances the three women might be encouraged to reveal more.

Lydia and her team were applauded by their colleagues for the success that they had had in breaking up an operation that not only imported illegal immigrants but exploited them. However, whilst talking with Liz, Lydia expressed herself dissatisfied with two aspects of the investigation: firstly, the failure to uncover the identity of the person or persons behind the organisation of the prostitution ring. Secondly, the failure to find the man who had been responsible for the death of the young woman whose body was found in the Grand Union Canal. "I'm pretty sure, Liz, that the dead woman was one of the prostitutes. I would like you to follow that up, if you will. Meanwhile, I shall spend my time digging beneath the surface of the various property management companies and firms of solicitors. Somewhere there must be a common thread that will tell us who ran the whole operation."

# Chapter Eight

Liz had discussed with Lydia the approach she thought that she should make in attempting to solve the murder of the young woman whose body had been found in the Grand Union Canal. Liz had taken to calling her "Miss X." Since three of the prostitutes interviewed a few days earlier said that they thought they recognised Miss X, it was possible that those young women would prove to be helpful. The women had worked in the brothel in Paddington which was less than a mile away from the place where the body had been found.

All of the prostitutes detained during police raids on the brothels in West London had been sent to a Home Office detention centre near Heathrow Airport. That centre had hospital facilities incorporated, thereby permitting medical supervision of the drug-addicted women during the initial period of their rehabilitation.

The three women with whom Liz was concerned were from Eastern Europe: two Bulgarians and a Romanian. At the time of their interrogation by the police after their arrest, use had been made of interpreters supplied by the consular offices of the two countries concerned. Liz rang the Bulgarian and Romanian consuls, asking if, once again, they could make interpreters available. In both cases a consular spokesman had been quite obliging in agreeing to supply the interpreters required.

Liz and a colleague, DC Blackthorne, along with two interpreters, were spending the better part of a full morning at the detention centre near Heathrow. It was proving to be much more difficult speaking to the detainees than Liz had imagined it would be. She had begun by attempting to speak to each of them individually, the usual police procedure, but they had refused to co-operate. Each wanted her two friends to be present.

It became clear both from their appearance and from what they told the interpreters that they were going through hell and feeling very sorry for themselves. By the time that they had been transferred to the detention centre from the various police stations at which they had been held, they had spent several days during which they had been given neither heroin, nor a substitute. All of them had been very ill. Once they got to the centre they were told that they could be given nothing until they had been cleared by a doctor.

When they had spoken to the doctor, he had acted completely callously, telling them that it was their own fault that they felt the way they did. Liz noticed that none of the young women had a good command of spoken English, so, through the interpreters, she asked if perhaps the doctor had failed to understand them. The replies were spoken simultaneously in rapid Romanian and Bulgarian: "two of the other inmates translated what we said into English, so he had understood us alright." Liz tried to move on but the young women were far too upset. She realised that it was very likely that the journey was going to be wasted; the women were showing no interest whatsoever in talking about anything that was related to their recent experiences as prostitutes.

Liz asked her colleague to take over; she thought that she would try to have a word with the doctor who had spoken so callously to the young women. She was sure that if he knew the circumstances under which the women had become addicted to heroin he would be much more sympathetic.

After several enquiries, Liz was shown by one of the nurses where she could find the doctor concerned, a Dr Davis. He was a man who looked to her to be no older than she; it was obvious that he could not have been practising his profession for very long. His first response, when Liz was introduced to him by the nurse, was one of wariness. Liz explained that the police had been involved with several young women who now were under his care at the detention centre; presumably the young women were being treated for drug addiction.

Doctor Davis said that perhaps 'treatment' wasn't entirely accurate. "What we are attempting to do is keep them under observation whilst they get over the worst effects of their habit. I know that some of them have been complaining, but, with respect, officer, no one forced them to become addicted to hard drugs. I have tried to make it clear to them that addiction to heroin poses a serious health risk, and the sooner they kick the habit, the better. Unfortunately, not many of the ladies speak good English, and it's hard to get the message across."

Liz said that she was sure that most heroin addicts would agree with him. To get back onto the subject about which she wished to speak, Liz asked Dr Davis if anyone had told him about the previous history of the young women who had arrived recently at the detention centre. He said, "as I understand it, all of them were picked up in raids on brothels in London. All of them are prostitutes. I'm afraid I really can't have much sympathy for women that sell their bodies like that. I don't wonder that they are all heroin addicts."

Liz continued, "have you not been informed that all of those young women were forced into heroin addiction, and when that had been accomplished, their addiction was used to force them into a life of prostitution."

Liz saw that now she had Dr Davis' full attention. Although he said, "I can't believe such a thing would be possible," it was obvious that there wasn't much conviction in his voice. Liz went on to tell the doctor of the backgrounds of virtually all of the prostitutes. They had been recruited in their homelands, most of which were in turmoil. They or their relatives had paid sums of money to men who said that they could get them into the UK where they could have a new life. "We know now of what that so-called new life consisted."

Doctor Davis was silent for a time saying finally, "I had no idea; no one told me. I shall see what I can do to help them. I think that most of them have got over the worst of the withdrawal symptoms, but I'll keep a close watch on them anyway. Of course, it would have been helpful to have been told what you just told me when the women first came. I can assure you that I would have been much more sympathetic." Liz thanked Dr Davis and returned to the place where she had been interviewing the three young women.

Liz explained through the interpreters that the doctor who was looking after them had not known about their background, and that from then on he would be much more helpful. One of the Bulgarians said that she could only speak for herself, but she was over the worst of it now, so that made her happy, "I know that I never would have been able just to stop taking heroin, unless I had been forced to." Both of her companions nodded in agreement. Liz hoped that the time had come when she could introduce the topic about which she had come to the detention centre to enquire: the identification of the young woman whose body had been found in the Grand Union Canal.

From her handbag Liz removed a colour photograph of the deceased. The photo showed the woman's head and shoulders, as she lay on an autopsy table. The bruising high up on her neck was very obvious. Liz asked the interpreters to ask the three young women if they could tell her anything about the person shown in the photograph.

The two Bulgarians started to speak to each other in tones that obviously were questioning. The two women mentioned a name that sounded like Karina. Then one of them looked at the Romanian girl, tapped the photograph and said, "Karina?" The Romanian girl looked at the interpreter and said something which was translated immediately as, "yes, I think that the girl's name is Karina."

As the young women continued to discuss the dead girl, Liz was thinking quickly of the statement that Julia Gomes had made shortly after her detention by the police. Julia had said that she had met a prostitute whose name was Karina whilst she was being held captive in West London. Liz was hopeful that Julia would be able to positively identify the dead woman as Karina. That would greatly help the investigation into the death.

Liz's thoughts were interrupted by the Bulgarian interpreter, who said, "my two women think that the girl's name definitely is Karina. They say that she was in the same place where they were but she went away a long time ago. They are worried about the girl in the photograph because she looks like she is dead." Liz said, "sad to say, she has died; that is why I am asking questions about her."

Both interpreters repeated Liz's statement to the young women, one of whom spoke rapidly to an interpreter, who repeated, "probably she was given too much drug; that happened often, especially to the new girls."

Another of the women said something which was interpreted as, "maybe she was killed by one of the crazy men!" Liz asked what the women meant by "crazy men;" who were they? The young woman looked at her two companions and said, "some of the men who came to us were rapers. Some of the girls were told to pretend that they were being raped. Those men must have been crazy." Then followed a long discussion carried out between the young women, the interpreters, and Liz, during which the views on prostitution of the former were well aired.

During the return journey to Scotland Yard, Liz and her colleague had to agree with the two lady interpreters that the story revealed by the three young women to whom they'd just spoken was almost unbelievable. One of the interpreters, the one from Romania, said at one point, "I pray nightly that the economies of Eastern Europe and other parts of the world will improve soon. Then our young women won't have to be sold into slavery." By the time the police car stopped at the relevant consular offices to drop off the interpreters, the mood within had grown reflective. That mood continued as Liz and DC Blackthorne returned to Scotland Yard.

After visiting the detention centre, Liz was satisfied that she had got as much information as it was possible to get from the young women to whom she'd spoken. It was obvious that Miss X's name was Karina, and that she had worked at the brothel in Paddington. She had disappeared one day, and no one had seen her again. Aside from learning the first name of Miss X, Liz had learned something of potential importance to the success of her attempts to find Miss X's killer. One of the young women said that she thought that Karina had been forced to take part in a game that Mrs Bond, the receptionist at the brothel, let some of the clients play. The young woman had said, "a girl would pretend that she was being raped. If she did it well, Mrs Bond would give her little extras like a heroin injection well before she had come down from the previous one." Liz had remembered the feeling of sadness that she had felt when the girl had said that. To think that the high point in the daily lives of those young women was the receipt of a heroin injection.

Liz was looking forward to the interview she was going to have with Mrs Bond. She would have to find some way to put that woman behind bars. Liz wasn't a religious person, but the only word of which she could think to describe Mrs Bond and her cohorts of the prostitution ring was 'evil'.

\* \* \*

After discussing the results of her visit to the detention centre with Lydia, Liz decided to re-interview all of the persons who worked in the brothel in Paddington. There were two men, Stanley Impcress and Derek Cassell and two women, the nurse, Hazel Cook, and, most particularly, the receptionist/manageress, Myra Bond. Liz wanted to focus particularly on the interview with Mrs Bond because she was sure that the woman would know something about Karina's murder.

Liz looked up the addresses given by the four individuals at the time of their bail applications. She thought that she would begin the interview process with Myra Bond.

However, two PCs sent to Mrs Bond's address returned to Scotland Yard without her. The address had been that of her sister-in-law, who had explained that Myra was on holiday in France. The PC who spoke to the sister-in-law had said that it had been stipulated when bail was granted to Mrs Bond that she was not to leave London without notifying the police. The woman had said that she knew nothing about that, and that she had no idea where in France Myra had gone.

Liz next sent a car to fetch Derek Cassell who actually was living at the address that he had given in his bail application. Liz had asked the PC who had gone to fetch the man to let her know as soon as he had returned to Scotland Yard and then to hold the interviewee at reception for ten minutes or so. That would give Liz time to prepare an interview room the way she wanted it.

When Derek Cassell was shown into the interview room, Liz was seated at the table and she already had turned on the recording equipment. Before her on the table she had spread all of the photographs of Karina that had been taken at the dead girl's autopsy, excepting, of course, those showing anatomical details revealed by the pathologist's dissection. Liz wanted to record Derek's reaction when he saw the photographs; she was sure that, unless he was a hard case, he would react to them if her face was familiar.

She had been right; Derek did react, particularly to the photograph that showed the dead girl's face and neck with the obvious discolouration where her killer had placed his hands. Liz allowed Derek to look at the photos for a brief time and then asked him, "what do these pictures mean to you, Mr Cassell?" He shrugged, saying, "what are they supposed to mean? I ain't never seen the girl in my life."

Liz said, "well, if that is true, let me tell you about her. Her name is Karina and her body was pulled from the Grand Union Canal just north of where you used to work. We think that she had been raped and strangled. I should have thought that if nothing else you would have read about it in the papers. Are you sure you have never seen her before?" Derek replied, "oh, yeah, I think I might have seen something about it in the papers."

Liz said, "that's curious, just a few days ago I was speaking to some young ladies who said that you and Karina were well acquainted. Don't you remember that at all? I guess I will have to get in the three young women to whom I've been speaking, and then you can tell them that you don't know Karina. I am sure that you should remember the three young women to whom I've been speaking. They were arrested at the same time as you when the police raided the place in Paddington where you were working. However, instead of being released on bail like you, they are being held in a detention centre for illegal immigrants. I suppose that in one sense they are lucky. All that is going to happen to them is that they will be deported. You're going to be tried for rape. The young women told me that not only did you rape them, but that you raped Karina."

Derek protested, saying, "nobody's proved that I raped nobody, and, anyway, nobody's gonna believe a bunch of illegals." Liz said, "well, that may well be true, Mr Cassell, but you should see the young ladies. Now that they have kicked the heroin habit that you and your colleagues gave them, I think you will find that all kinds of people will believe them, especially the sorts who make up juries in criminal trials. I hope that you are enjoying your freedom now, Mr Cassell, because I have a feeling it's not going to last."

"Anyway, that's not what I got you in here to talk about. I'm really trying to find out if you can tell me anything about Karina's death. I am pretty sure that you had nothing to do with it, but it's just possible that you have some idea who was responsible. I can tell you right now, Mr Cassell, if you can help us with the investigation of Karina's murder, it's just possible the police won't push too hard to get you convicted of rape. After all, few would argue with the fact that rape is a much less serious crime than murder."

At that point, Liz got out photographs of the three men who had refused to give blood samples so that a profile of their DNA could be constructed. It had been established already that the DNA of none of the 'clients' who had volunteered tissue samples immediately after the police raids had matched that of the sperm found in Karina's body. "Is there anything that you can tell me about any of these three men; could any of them have been involved in her murder?" Derek said, "nah, it wasn't none of them. I don't know what his name was but it wasn't none of them."

Liz caught her breath; had she been mistaken or had Derek implied that he knew who the murderer was? Liz just nodded at him saying, "go on, Derek." "Well, there was a couple of men who used to come to our place now and then. They was real creeps; they only wanted to go with girls who knew how to pretend that they was raping them. I never understood it. They must 'ave known that they wasn't really raping them, but they kept comin' back. Ol' Myra encouraged 'em because she could charge them double for the girl. Karina was good at it, and this one man always asked for her. As you can see, she looked like a little kid."

"Well, one night he must 'ave lost it. He came in as usual, did his thing; paid up and then left, except he didn't try to book another appointment. Me and Myra sat around for a time, waiting for Karina to let us know that she was ready for her next appointment. When we didn't hear from her, I went to her room. I almost shit myself when I saw her; poor, bloody kid. She was just lying there, limp. We called Hazel, and she came 'round, but she said that Karina had been dead for some time. Me and Stan just put her in the car, and drove her into Regent's park near the zoo, and dumped her in the canal."

Liz asked Derek if there was any way that the identity of Karina's killer could be established. During their raids on the brothels the police had found no records identifying clients. Derek said that he thought that Myra Bond might be able to answer that question, but he couldn't.

Liz was not too sure how to proceed. What Derek had told her was potentially extremely helpful in the solution of Karina's rape and murder. However, he had implicated himself in at least one further act which was illegal. She decided to use her initiative by thanking him for his help and releasing him. After all, if her decision was wrong, the police knew where to find him.

# Chapter Nine

The glass of wine was most welcome, as was the wonderful view from Reg's flat which was situated well above the Thames where it flowed through East London. Liz could see Tower Bridge and the Tower of London in the foreground, and, of course, the lights of boats on the river. The view from the picture window in Reg's sitting room was her favourite. She hoped that her friendship with her retired university professor would go on for a long, long time.

Liz's musing was interrupted by Reg coming into the room, saying, "dinner will be ready in a little bit, but let's have a chat about a scheme that I have in mind for our next big adventure. First, however, you've got to tell me if you think that you'll be able to get away for a few days within the next month or so."

Liz thought quickly of work and everything that was going on there in which she was involved. She was certain that the police now were aware of the full extent of the prostitution ring, but there still were several unknowns. The most important, as far as both she and Lydia were concerned, was the discovery of the organisation behind the ring; the person or persons who owned all of the properties used by the ring and the person or persons who procured the young women used as prostitutes. Fortunately, Lydia was involving herself with that aspect of the investigation. However, Liz was actively involved in finding the killer of Karina: the young woman whom she continued to call Miss X. Probably that investigation would be tedious, but it wouldn't involve her in a lot of overtime.

Her thoughts had been rapid enough so that Reg had not felt it necessary, as he did fairly often, to repeat his enquiry, thinking that Liz, once again, was daydreaming, which she preferred to call "musing." Liz said that for a short time, at least, she thought that it was unlikely that she could get away for very long, but maybe three or four days, if that would be suitable for "your grand scheme, Reg."

"Ah, well, then, Liz; I have had a thought that we might take ourselves off to York. We can go there and back by train and then spend a couple of days wandering around the city. The buildings and sites that are of historical interest are in a fairly confined area, within the walls of the old city, so we won't have to walk our legs off."

"I went to a conference at York University once, not too long after it was established. The university was one of the new ones opened in the sixties, and it was built from the ground up as a campus. In those days that was unusual. More typically, universities started out as a scattered collection of a few old buildings to which more were added as the institutions grew. However, I thought that the university campus was quite attractive; several of the buildings were built around a pleasant artificial lake. However, we won't spend much time there on the university campus. Mainly, I thought that we would just walk around the old city, stopping occasionally for a glass of wine and to do whatever takes our fancy."

After staying overnight with Reg, Liz went straight into work from his flat. She and Reg had agreed that he should go ahead and book their hotel accommodation in York, as well as their seats on the train. Every time she made such definite plans, she then would proceed to worry that something would come up to interfere with them. That worry ended only when she was seated on some form of transport that was taking her to wherever it was that she had planned to go.

For the next several days, seated at her desk in the detectives' room, Liz was apprehensive every time her extension 'phone sounded: she was sure that the call would be from someone preparing to ruin her plans to go with Reg to York.

Not until she was making her way to King's Cross train station to meet Reg and to catch the train to York, did Liz relax. It was a sign that Reg was getting to know her well that once the two of them were seated in their carriage, and the train had begun its journey, he reached up to the overhead baggage rack and took down a small pack that he had brought onto the train. From the pack he removed a cold bottle of white wine and two plastic cups. Liz demanded to see how he had kept the wine chilled. He said that he had emptied his fridge of ice cubes and put them in a couple of plastic bags along with the pre-chilled wine. He hadn't been certain that the wine would stay cold, but, fortunately, it had. Liz felt much more relaxed after her first cup of wine. She felt too relaxed after she and Reg had finished the bottle. After they had arrived in York, Liz was unable to recall very much of the journey; she had slept for most of the time.

Upon returning to the hotel with Reg after their second day of walking around the old city, the receptionist got the key to their room from its hook, saying, "there's a message for you Miss Andresen. You are to call the Accident and Emergency Department of Addenbrooke's Hospital in Cambridge, as soon as you can. The number is on the sheet of

paper I wrote the message on; it sounded rather urgent."
Liz's spirits fell. That message could mean only one thing;
something had happened to her mum. She and Reg went
to their room, where Liz at once picked up the 'phone, asking to be put through to the number listed on the sheet of
paper given to her by the hotel receptionist.

In due course, Liz was put through to a woman who was
one of the administrators in the admissions department of
Addenbrooke's Hospital. The woman apologised for ringing
her whilst she was on holiday. "Missus Audrey Andresen
has been admitted to hospital. She told us that you worked
in Scotland Yard, so I telephoned them, and they told me
where you were. Anyway, Mrs Andresen was brought into
the A&E Department of the hospital from the place where
she works because she collapsed. When questioned, your
mother would say no more than she had passed out; there
wasn't anything wrong with her other than a feeling of light-
headedness. They had a good look at her in A&E but they
couldn't find anything wrong. They were just on the point of
sending her home, when she said that she was ill and asked
to go to the toilet. Instead, the duty nurse handed her a
basin, telling her that it would be better for her to be sick in
that; it was far more hygienic. Your mother then became ill
and her stomach contents were composed almost entirely
of blood. Your mother finally admitted that that had happened to her at work, and it was the sight of the blood that
made her pass out. Anyway, Miss Andresen, your mother has
been admitted to the hospital with a suspected gastric ulcer.
Her condition isn't life threatening, but we thought that you
should know."

Reg, of course, was listening to Liz's side of the telephone conversation, and when she put the 'phone down he

said, "well, it was a nice, short holiday whilst it lasted; how soon do you think that you will have to get to Cambridge?" Liz said that she didn't think that things were that urgent, but that probably she had better get off the train when it stopped in Cambridge on their homeward journey. "Also, I'd better ring Lydia and tell her what has happened; I hope there's nothing urgent awaiting me in London."

\* \* \*

When Liz got to her mum's bed in the hospital ward, she was hoping to be greeted by something other than, "oh, Elisabeth, why are you never here when I need you? They keep insisting that I have to stay here when all I want to do is go home. There's really nothing wrong with me." Liz knew from long experience with her mother that it would be useless to attempt to do anything other than agree with the woman's complaints. Liz said, "well, let me have a word with them, mum, and see what it is they think you ought to do."

Liz looked away to see if she could see anyone to whom she could speak, but her mother continued: "it would all be alright if you could just look after me, Elisabeth. Why do you have to be so far away? I'm sure you could find a good job in Cambridge." Liz could only say what she always said: "ah, mum, you know I'd be closer to you if I could, but unfortunately, my job is in London. Maybe someday I will find something suitable in Cambridge." Liz realised, too late, that she had left her mum the perfect opportunity to voice an opinion she voiced often when the two of them spoke together about the future: "I'll probably be dead by then." Liz patted her mother's hand and then said, "let me just go see if I can speak to someone about when you can go home, mum; I won't be a moment."

As she was walking toward the front of the hospital ward an older man in a white lab coat entered and came over to her. "Is that Miss Andresen? I'm Mr Muir; I've been looking after your mother. Well, Miss Andresen, I can't find too much wrong with her, except she seems a bit undernourished. I think the blood in her stomach contents must have been due to some massive insult the stomach had received immediately before she became ill. Your mother won't tell me anything, but I think it likely that she could have eaten or drunk something that set up a breakdown of the inner lining of the stomach. Does your mother drink much, do you know?" Liz said that she was aware that her mother often drank to excess, but whether or not she had done so just prior to coming into hospital, she couldn't say. "Well, let's take that as an explanation for now. If the problem is what I think it is, it should clear up after a few days on a careful diet. I suppose all that I can really tell you is to try to get her to eat more frequently, and, above all, not to drink heavily, especially on an empty stomach. I'll go now and arrange for your mother's discharge. By the way, is there anyone at home to look after her? I don't think that she will need too much looking after, but it would be helpful if there were someone there to help her out a bit."

Liz had planned to be firm with Audrey during the taxi ride home. She was going to tell her mum that she would have to take better care of herself. She knew that saying that would risk provoking a bout of self pity, but somehow it had to be said. As usual, Liz had underestimated her mother's ability to monopolise conversations that she had with her daughter. She cast ridicule on what she called Liz's lies about how much her mother drank. A pint of beer or so in the pub of an evening was not drinking to excess. Also, she would eat more, but she had no appetite. She said that the meals in the canteen where she worked weren't fit for pigs, and it just seemed so much of an effort to get in food at home. When the two of them got home, Liz discovered that there was no food to be found. She seated her mum on the settee before the 'telly' and took the shopping cart, going to the local shops.

During the first evening her mother was home from the hospital, Liz had to endure constant comments from the woman about how lovely it was to have her daughter cooking a meal; wouldn't it be wonderful if it happened all of the time, and so on. At least for that one evening, her mum didn't insist that the two of them go to the pub. Liz sat with her mother watching Audrey's favourite evening programmes. Liz didn't watch much 'telly' when she was in London; she found that reading was a very much more enjoyable occupation.

During the visit with her mum, Liz became convinced that Audrey needed some kind of supervision. Despite being a relatively young woman: she was only in her mid forties; Audrey seemed to have given up on life.

After Audrey had gone off to bed, Liz telephoned Pat, both to say hello and to get her friend's opinion as to what she should do about her mum. Pat thought that Audrey needed a companion. Liz had protested that her mother showed no interest in men. "Not that long ago there were a couple of men who came around from time to time, but mum never was interested." Pat said, "no, I don't mean another man; I wonder if she shouldn't have some one like an au pair or someone like that. You say that she doesn't eat properly; maybe if there was someone there to help her with meals and that sort of thing, she might like that."

Liz thought that Pat's idea of a companion might be a good one; certainly it was well worth looking into. Her mother's work was of a rather menial variety, and the pay was low. Liz was sure that Audrey wouldn't be able to afford an au pair. However, if the cost wasn't too great, Liz might be able to pay for it. Her police pay was more than adequate for her needs; maybe it could supply some of her mum's needs also.

Unfortunately, Audrey would not hear of having another woman, except Liz, of course, living in her house with her. Liz had begun an attempt to persuade her mum, but the woman was obstinate. Several times during their lives together Liz had encountered her mum's form of bloody mindedness. Consequently, she knew it would be futile to attempt to convince the woman that she could use some help around the house.

Liz had hoped that she would arrive back at work refreshed by her brief holiday. Unfortunately, the two days with her mum had obviated any chance of that happening.

# Chapter Ten

**W**hen Liz returned to work after visiting with her mum, there was a letter in her IN box containing a long note from Parmeeta Khan in which she had written, "thus far the results of my entreaties on behalf of Julia Gomes are encouraging. The response of the Home Office to my arguments has hardly been positive, but then I never expect that when I deal with civil servants on the subject of illegal immigration. They always seem too worried about what their political masters will say." Miss Khan then went on to ask if Liz could tell her whether or not the Home Office had been in contact with the police; she continued by writing, "if the Home Office has contacted the police, it would be a good sign; it would show that they had accepted that it was worth investigating the argument that I made, that Julia Gomes had been helpful to them."

After twice reading over Parmeeta Khan's note, Liz tried to telephone the woman, hoping that she might be lucky and catch her in her office. Having no luck with that effort, she wrote to Miss Khan, answering the solicitor's questions as well as she was able.

Having written off to Parmeeta Khan, Liz turned her attention back to the murder of Miss X, now known to be an illegal immigrant whose first name was Karina. She reviewed the contents of the file that she had set up and labelled, "Miss X." It contained very little except copies of the reports of forensic examinations of the body, and, of course, photographs of the deceased taken during the autopsy. Liz read over the transcript of the interview with Derek Cassell. From his statement it seemed reasonably certain that the man who probably had killed Karina was not one of the faceless clients of the brothel in which both Derek Cassell and Myra Bond had worked. His appearance and actions were sufficiently unusual that both people had noticed him. It seemed clear that if anyone could tell Liz details that might help identify the man suspected of killing Karina, it would be Myra Bond. She handled the finances of the brothel and had accepted payments from the clients.

Although no documents of any kind were found when the brothels had been raided by the police, it seemed likely that records of client payments had been kept. Myra Bond appeared to be a relatively minor player in the prostitution ring. It seemed unlikely that she would have been trusted to give an honest accounting of the earnings of the brothel in which she worked. More likely, that accounting would have to have been backed up with some kind of permanent record. Derek had said that most of the clients paid by credit card. Possibly there was a depository of credit-card receipts tucked away that the police search had not revealed.

Liz, accompanied by a uniformed constable, Dave Hendricks, who drove, visited the address that Myra Bond had given on her application for bail. Once again the only adult present at the address was Mrs Bond's sister-in-law, Mrs Cooke. Missus Cooke said, "I told Myra when she got back from France that the police wanted to speak to her; I'm surprised that she hasn't got in touch. Anyway, she's out looking for work at the moment. I believe she went down to the local employment exchange this morning, but she should be back before too long." Liz said that the two police officers would wait in the car for her return, but

Mrs Cooke invited them to be seated in her lounge where, she was sure, it would be much more comfortable.

Liz tried not to discuss the prostitution ring with Mrs Cooke but the woman was very talkative, asking questions about what was going to happen to her sister-in-law. She said that she had every confidence that Myra must have been misled by someone because she was really a very nice and kindly person. She continued, "I can't believe that she would be involved, knowingly, in anything as sordid as prostitution." Fortunately, Mrs Cooke's two pre-school-age children were present, so Liz and PC Hendricks were able to deflect the conversation by getting the woman to talk about them.

Although she had never seen the woman, Liz had formed the opinion, despite Mrs Cooke's belief, that Myra Bond would prove to be quite a "hard case," to quote the police vernacular for someone who was callous.

When Mrs Bond arrived back from the employment exchange and saw that the police were waiting to interview her, she made it clear immediately that she had nothing to say to them. She said that she had made a statement at the time they arrested her, and she could think of nothing to add to that. From then on, if the police wished to speak to her, they could do so in the presence of her solicitor.

Liz's first impulse was simply to arrest the woman on a charge of violating a term of her bail and take her into Scotland Yard. However, whatever satisfaction that would give Liz, would be countered by the possibility that it would make Mrs Bond totally unco-operative. Liz opted for the 'softly, softly' approach.

First she spoke to Mrs Cooke, asking if there were some place that she and PC Hendricks could speak to her sister-in-law alone. Missus Cooke volunteered to absent herself and her children from the lounge so "you and Myra can carry on in private." Liz thanked the woman for her courtesy and said that she hoped that they would not be too long.

Once Mrs Cooke had left the room, Liz said to Myra Bond:"we believe that you can help us with another enquiry: that of the murder of a young prostitute named Karina who was under your supervision at the time of her death. Let me make it clear that you are not under suspicion for committing any crime connected with the death. However, it is our understanding that you may be able to help us locate and identify Karina's killer. I am sure that you are aware that you have been arrested on some serious charges. I can tell you that the evidence against you is extensive; it is likely that you will be convicted of most of the crimes with which you have been charged. However, if you volunteer to help us with the murder enquiry, I can assure you that the fact that you were cooperative can only help in your defence. It's up to you, Mrs Bond."

Myra Bond said that she really didn't know how she could help with the murder of a young woman whom she didn't even recall. She said, "it must have happened before my time. I only worked at that place in Paddington for a little over six months before you lot shut it down." Liz told Mrs Bond what Derek Cassell had told the police about an event that had occurred during the time that she was working there. Missus Bond said that Derek had to be confusing her with someone else.

It was obvious to Liz that Myra Bond had no intention of volunteering her help. She concluded that it would be better to continue the interview at Scotland Yard where she would have access to the file on the murder of Miss X, so that she could quote times and dates to the woman. She said, "OK, Mrs Bond, that's it. I suggest that you ring your solicitor and ask him to meet you at New Scotland Yard, because we are going to take you there for questioning."

When Myra Bond said, rather belligerently, "you have no right to arrest me; I don't have to answer your questions," Liz replied in her most formal voice: "you are quite correct, Mrs Bond, in stating that you do not have to answer my questions. However, you are quite wrong in stating that I have no right to arrest you. You may not recall it, but one of the conditions stipulated when you were granted bail was that you were not to leave London without notifying the police. As I am sure that you are aware, your recent violation of that bail condition gives me every right not only to detain you but to keep you in custody."

Liz turned to speak to PC Hendricks, ignoring what Mrs Bond was saying. "Probably it would be well, constable, to restrain Mrs Bond whilst she being taken to the Yard." PC Hendricks reached into his back pocket bringing out a pair of handcuffs. As Liz had hoped would happen, Mrs Bond said, "just a minute; there's no need to take me to Scotland Yard. I'll tell you all that I know about the girl's death."

Liz nodded at PC Hendricks, and everyone seated themselves again. At Liz's prompting, Mrs Bond told a story that was identical to that told by Derek Cassell in all of its essential details. Liz asked Mrs Bond to describe exactly the procedure through which a client would go when wishing to engage a prostitute. She replied, "well, generally, the first time they came to the place they'd tell us that someone had recommended us to them. Then I would ask them for a name by which they would be known to us, and how they wanted to pay. I told them that the name didn't have to be their real name; it was more like a password. That would be recorded in a separate page in our log book so that every time the client rang in we could record his appointment time and the girl he wished to see, if he had a preference. I am pretty sure that the man that you're looking for called himself Mr Welwyn. I remember that a man who called himself that had a preference for Karina. I think that the fact that she looked to be very young and was a good little actress was what had attracted him. Her only problem was wanting to be stoned all of the time. Unfortunately, some of her clients brought her drugs as a tip for her performing acts we didn't allow our girls to perform if we knew about it."

Liz asked what had happened to the log book that she had used; no such document had been found when the premises in Paddington had been raided and searched. Missus Bond said, "the log book was only a loose-leaf binder. Except during the hours when men were visiting the premises, it was kept in a compartment made in the bottom of one of the drawers of my desk. Also, I was told that if the police made a raid, I was to do nothing else until the log book went into its compartment. I put it there when you lot raided us, and as far as I know it's still there."

Liz said, "we know that your clients usually paid by credit card; how did they do that without using their real names?" Missus Bond said, "of course they would have to use their real names then, because they had to sign the receipts, but I didn't pay any attention to that. I really wasn't interested in who the men were and what they did; that was their business. I was interested merely in how much they were willing to pay. To answer your question about the man who might have killed Karina, I don't know his real name, but I am pretty sure that his password name was what I said: Mr Welwyn. He was really quite a creepy-looking man; I suppose it was that that made me remember his password."

Liz asked Myra Bond if she knew whether or not a log book similar to the one that she had kept had been utilised in all of the brothels owned by the prostitution ring. She said that she didn't know for sure, but she thought it likely that it was a standard procedure.

Liz ended the interview with Myra Bond, telling her that it was likely that the police would wish to question her further, so that she should remember that she must still adhere to the conditions of her bail.

On the way back to the station, Liz discussed with PC Hendricks the possibility that records kept by credit card companies could be scrutinised in a search for Mr Welwyn. Liz did not use a credit card, so she was unfamiliar with the details of their operation. The PC said that he thought it unlikely, since millions of them were in use. "However, it's probably worth a try."

Liz was interested to know PC Hendricks' impression of Myra Bond and the story that she had told. He had come to the same conclusion as had Liz: the woman had told the truth after she had been given an incentive to do so. Liz knew that women who served as receptionist/managers of the five brothels had been interrogated at length immediately after the police raids. However, she had read nothing in the statements made by the women that agreed with what Myra Bond had told her about the keeping of a log book.

The statements of the other receptionists had confirmed what Myra Bond had said: that each day's receipts were put in the post late in the evening. On the day of the raid, the police had recovered envelopes that were ready for posting at three of the five premises raided. These had contained money and credit-card receipts. The envelopes had been addressed to a company called Landreach Associates c/o a P. O. Box in a main post office located in the King's Cross area of London. A watch had been kept within the post office for a few days after the raids, but no one called to retrieve envelopes from the P. O. Box involved.

Back at Scotland Yard, Liz consulted with Lydia, asking to get authority to enter the five houses that had served as brothels to see if she could find log books like that described by Myra Bond.

A day later, Liz, accompanied by DC Blackthorne, went to the house in Paddington. It was that log book which held the most interest for her. She hoped that it would provide evidence allowing her to identify Mr Welwyn. The front entrance to the house was barred by the usual blue and white plastic tape, and there was a PC on guard with whom Liz stopped to chat. He said that he had seen several men drive up in taxis, get out, and then come to a dead stop when they saw him. "For some reason, sergeant, they didn't want to stop and talk!"

Liz left DC Blackthorne talking with the PC, whom he knew. After ducking under the plastic tape, she entered the reception area of the brothel. It was a large single room that had been converted from two rooms and a hallway. At one side of the room was the desk described by Myra Bond. Liz opened the top drawer of the desk, but it lacked a false compartment. However, the topmost of the set of three drawers on the right of the desk had a false compartment in which Liz found the log book. She quickly looked under the name, Mr Welwyn, at the side of which was written the name of a prominent provider of credit cards and, in brackets, the fact that the card was part of the VISA network. Below the name was a column containing dates and opposite each of the dates was written a girl's name. The name entered most often was 'Karina'. The date of the last entry must have been the day that Karina had been killed; it was two days prior to the day her body had been discovered. Liz left the building, telling DC Blackthorne that they had better make a move because they had four more brothels to visit.

Liz found very quickly that she had wasted her time retrieving the log books. When she telephoned the offices of the company that supplied Mr Welwyn with his credit card, she learned that they could give her no help. The man to whom she spoke told her, in a voice that sounded as if he thought that she should have her head examined: if she thought that he could supply the details she required about an owner of a credit card without knowledge of either its number or the owner's name, she would have to think again. Persisting, Liz told him that she could supply him with a list of six dates on which the card had been used. Also, the owner of the card may have lived in the County of Hertfordshire. In a calmer voice, the man said that his company did not keep records that could be accessed by date alone, or by home address alone, although they were working on a method of access to the database by post code. He ended his part of the conversation by saying, "all of the relevant information is in our database, but even if it could be accessed, it would take a very long time and lots of manpower!" Liz thanked the man and rang off.

Liz feared that her attempts to identify Karina's killer were doomed to failure until she remembered that the police had other data that might prove useful. She had checked the log books of the four brothels raided on the same day as the one in Paddington. She had not found a listing of the name, Mr Welwyn. However, it was possible that the same man had visited other brothels using a different pseudonym.

During the surveillance operation, everyone entering or leaving the brothels had been photographed in close up and, of course, the date and time had been recorded simultaneously. It was possible that Derek Cassell and/or Myra Bond would be able to recognise Mr Welwyn from his photograph. That still wouldn't tell the police who he was, but the photo could be circularised in the hope that someone would be able to recognise him.

Both Derek Cassell and Myra Bond agreed to review the police photographs of the brothel clients taken during the surveillance operation. Both of them identified the same man as Mr Welwyn. Also, the photo identification session turned up a result for which Liz was hoping: the man who called himself Mr Welwyn at the West-London brothel also visited the brothel in West Hampstead. No man of that name was listed in the log book of that brothel, but there was a client listed there known by the name, Mr Hatfield. Liz thought that it was unlikely that the choice of the two names was coincidental: Welwyn Garden City, often shortened to Welwyn, and Hatfield being two adjacent towns in the County of Hertfordshire, just north of London.

The photograph of Mr Welwyn/Hatfield was published in the London papers with an accompanying article asking anyone who recognised the man to contact New Scotland Yard. Liz thought it prudent, also, to publish the photograph in papers local to Hertfordshire towns. Although most households in that area very likely read one or more London papers, it was better to cover all contingencies.

The day after the photo was published in the London papers, Liz had two telephone calls from persons who said that they recognised Welwyn/Hatfield; his last name was Berkowitz. They said that he lived in a flat in an apartment building in Streatham, Southwest London. They gave Liz the street address of the apartment building. Police officers who called at the address in Southwest London found that the 'flat' was, in fact, one-room in a large house that had been subdivided into eight separate places, usually termed "bed-sitters." Berkowitz's bed-sitter was unoccupied, but two of his neighbours were at home. They told the police that they had not seen Mr Berkowitz for several days. They said that some of the bed-sits in the house were rented out to companies for the use of their employees whilst they were in London on company business. The neighbours said that because of the infrequency with which Berkowitz used it, they had assumed that his accommodation was a company rental.

Liz had begun to despair that her attempts to find Berkowitz were going to be unsuccessful, when she received a telephone call from a woman who said that she hadn't known the suspect's name, until she saw his picture in her local paper. She gave Liz the street address of Berkowitz's home in Welwyn Garden City, Hertfordshire.

A car from the Hertfordshire police, which called at the address in Welwyn Garden City, found a most distraught Mrs Berkowitz. According to her statement, her husband had left home the previous evening after he had seen his picture and the accompanying article in one of the London newspapers. He had told her that it had to be a case of mistaken identity, but he didn't think that anyone would believe him, so he was going to go away for a time until it was all sorted out. She said that he hadn't told her where he was going; only that he would "be in touch."

Missus Berkowitz stated further that the article had said that her husband was wanted in connection with the rape and murder of a young girl. She broke down in tears as she said, "that's impossible. He has two teenage daughters of his own and he has never laid a finger on them. He's just not like that."

The Hertfordshire police kept a watch on the Berkowitz family home, and Scotland Yard co-operated with the national newspapers so to give maximum publicity to the fact that Nathan Berkowitz was wanted for rape and murder. Questioning of employees of the company for which Berkowitz worked provided no information that would suggest where the man might have gone. At first, it was thought to be unlikely that he could have gone far because his wife had said that he hadn't much money on him. She had said, "he got out £100 in cash from the bank on the day after he saw his photograph in the paper, and he gave me half of it before he went away."

Questioning of the accounts manager of the company for which he worked revealed that Berkowitz used a company credit card. It was the issuers of that card whose name had been written on the pages for Mr Welwyn/Hatfield in the log books kept by the London brothels that he had frequented. The credit card company was alerted to invalidate the credit card; only then was it discovered that Berkowitz had used the card to make £300 in cash withdrawals since he had fled his home. He and his wife also had a credit card account. Although there had been no charges against it since before the disappearance of Berkowitz, the cards issued on the account were invalidated and a new card issued to Mrs Berkowitz.

# Chapter Eleven

A month after Nathan Berkowitz fled from his home, there had been no new leads that would allow the police to proceed with the investigation of the murder of 'Miss X'. Consequently, police efforts were redirected to other investigations, although the file was left open.

Liz was working late on a new assignment that Lydia had given her. This one involved illegal immigrants again, but this time the immigrants were being used in an unusual way. They were all young men whose command of English was very limited. They were being sent 'round to houses in the more affluent areas of London where they were asking for donations for charities that had been found to be bogus. The police had been alerted because of suspicions raised by some of the people asked to donate.

Investigation of the first few collectors to be detained revealed that their identification papers had been falsified; they were in the country illegally. The police operation was concerned more with apprehending the organisers of the collections, rather than hauling in a bunch of illegal immigrants. Liz was staying late at her desk because she had to read through a stack of statements that her team had taken from people who had made donations to the bogus charities. That was necessary to determine if the illegal immigrants had violated laws other than the obvious one.

Liz had about decided that she had had enough of the boring job for one day and was going to depart for home, when her extension 'phone sounded. The voice of the police operator informed her that a Mrs Berkowitz was on the line and would speak only to Sergeant Andresen. "Sergeant Andresen? Please excuse me for bothering you; I got your name from the police in Hatfield; they said that you were handling the investigation of my husband. I wanted to speak directly to you about him."

Liz expected that Mrs Berkowitz would launch into an explanation of why her husband was innocent, and why were the police being so closed minded. However, the lady surprised Liz by saying that she had heard from her husband, and that he had decided to give himself up. "He asked me to talk to the police, and to ask them what he should do. He said that it had all been a dreadful accident, so he wanted to go to the police voluntarily. He told me that he was afraid that he would be killed. He said that last night a man had set upon him and had almost killed him. He's frightened for his life, sergeant."

Liz asked Mrs Berkowitz if her husband had indicated how he could be contacted. She replied that he said that he would ring her again in the morning. Liz told Mrs Berkowitz that should her husband call again, she should urge him to go to the nearest police station and give himself up. Before she rang off, Liz asked the lady for her telephone number, saying that it might be necessary to ring her back at some point.

The moment Liz got off the "phone, she was on to the technical department of Scotland Yard, asking them if a telephone tap could be set up on a private number in Welwyn Garden City within the next twelve hours. The sergeant to whom she spoke said that it would depend upon several things, but if Liz would give him the number he would make some enquiries and get back to her.

After she had stopped talking to the sergeant in the technical department, Liz looked at her watch. Probably she would be lucky to get home in time to have anything to eat. She went over to an adjacent desk where DC Blackthorne also was working late. Liz admired Blackthorne, thinking that he would go far; he was very conscientious. To her question of what he was doing, he replied that he was typing up a report. Then he said, "I'll probably be at this for a time, so I thought that I would take a break and get a sandwich or something; can I get you anything while I'm at it?" Liz told him that he was a genius; she would like nothing better than a sandwich and a fizzy drink.

Two hours later, DC Blackthorne had left for his 'digs' and Liz still was waiting by her 'phone. She had about made up her mind to again ring the sergeant in the technical department, when he rang her. He told her, "the wire tap on that number isn't too involved, so we should be able to set it up in a couple of hours. I got on to the Hertfordshire police who've authorised us to go ahead, largely because they're not set up to do it on such short notice. Therefore, with any luck, we should have things set up in no more than four more hours. Where do we go from there?" Liz gave him the details of the call that Mrs Berkowitz should be receiving: telling him, "it will be a man and she will call him by his first name: Nathan. We want to know where he is when he makes the call. Let me know on this number as soon as you have any useful information."

Liz was happy that DC Blackthorne had got her something to eat; she knew that she would not be getting any sleep that night, but at least she wouldn't be sitting there with her stomach making loud noises.

Liz was awakened by a loud ringing coming from a place that was close to her ear. She lifted her head, only then remembering that she was still at her desk in the detectives' room, and the ringing was her extension 'phone. She lifted the receiver at once to hear: "Sergeant Andresen, this is Sergeant Norton in technical; you know, we were putting a wire tap on the Berkowitz residence in Welwyn Garden City. Our man has just listened to a call from a hospital in Hatfield telling Mrs Berkowitz that her husband is there. According to the caller, Berkowitz had been brought by ambulance, unconscious, to accident and emergency of the hospital shortly after midnight. Then he was transferred to intensive care where he is at present. The caller would not tell Mrs Berkowitz what was wrong with her husband."

Liz asked if the Hertfordshire police had been made aware of the incident. Sergeant Norton said he had no idea about that; he was just passing on the information got by the men who had set up the wire tap. Liz said that she would get in touch with her contact at the police station in Hatfield. Sergeant Norton closed by saying, "I presume that we can stop listening to the lady's telephone conversations." Liz apologised for not mentioning that the operation could be halted. "I think probably we've got all of the information we're going to get from that source. Thank you very much, Sergeant Norton, you have been most helpful." Sergeant Norton rang off after saying, "well, that's what we're here for."

Liz rang her contact at the Hatfield police station, Police Superintendent Macleod, asking if it would be possible to quickly arrange for a police guard to be placed on a man who had been admitted to the Hatfield Hospital, and who now was in their intensive care unit. He said that that would be arranged at once. Liz gave Superintendent Macleod those details known to her: Berkowitz's full name and the approximate time he had been taken to the hospital, asking if he knew whether or not there had been any police involvement. He said that he would check and ring her back if he found anything useful.

The superintendent rang Liz a few minutes later, saying, "yes, we did, in fact, hear of the incident, but until you told me just now, we didn't know the name of the victim. The station got a call from the ambulance service at 12:10 am. A spokesman for the service said that they had responded to a 999 call from a man who reported seeing a body lying on the pavement outside of a pub. An ambulance was sent which reported back that the man on the pavement had been the victim of a physical assault. Consequently, the police were notified. The spokesman for the ambulance service said that the victim was unconscious and that he had been taken to A&E at Hatfield hospital. We intended to send a man to the hospital to speak to the victim when he recovered consciousness; the hospital already had agreed to notify us when that occurred. However, now that we know that the man is Berkowitz, I shall arrange to put a twenty-four-hour guard on him. I'll let you know as soon as he regains consciousness."

Liz spent the next four days hard at the rather boring investigation of the involvement of illegal immigrants in making collections for bogus charities. The investigation appeared to be going nowhere because the men behind the scheme appeared to have covered their tracks very efficiently. Therefore, she was pleased to get a telephone call from Superintendent Macleod telling her that Nathan Berkowitz had regained consciousness and had been transferred from intensive care into a general ward at Hatfield hospital. Berkowitz had been cautioned and arrested and told that someone from New Scotland Yard was intending to take a statement from him. Liz arranged to go to Hatfield at once, asking DC Blackthorne to accompany her. The arrest warrant they took with them listed only the rape and murder of Karina; the possibility of further charges awaited checks of his DNA profile.

On the way to Hatfield, Liz and DC Blackthorne discussed the Berkowitz case. She was of the view that it seemed inexplicable that a man who had what appeared to be a lovely wife and family would have to resort to prostitutes, let alone murder one of them. Constable Blackthorne said that he had read psychology at university, which, he thought, had given him some insight into what motivated human beings. "It's possible that as far as Berkowitz was concerned consorting with prostitutes was just his way of living out his fantasies. It's just that his fantasies may have been more eccentric than those of most people." Liz thought over what her companion had said, finding herself unable to agree. However, she said nothing. She was aware of the opinion that men who raped women really were expressing their hatred of them and their desire to dominate them. She was inclined more to believe the latter idea, than that expressed by DC Blackthorne.

When they arrived at the hospital in Hatfield, Liz and her companion where asked to wait a few moments in reception because the consultant who had dealt with Mr Berkowitz wished to speak to them. Not long after, a man in white coat introduced himself, saying that he was Mr Asheed, a consultant in internal medicine. "I have now concluded my examination of Mr Berkowitz. He has been beaten very badly, indeed. The injuries to his head will be quite apparent to you when you visit him. The swelling of his face is extensive, but that should go away in due course. Also, he was kicked in the head at least twice; both times causing wounds that required stitching to close. How he escaped having his skull fractured, I'll never know. However, the most serious wounds are internal and, very likely, caused because he was kicked repeatedly. Both of his kidneys have become detached from the body wall. That will require correction. Finally, and most serious, he was kicked repeatedly in the groin. As a consequence of that, both of his testicles have herniated and may have to be removed surgically. In short, officers, Mr Berkowitz is a very sick man, and I would appreciate it if you would bear that in mind if you feel that you must speak to him at this time."

Of course, Liz could not say so, but she felt no pity for Nathan Berkowitz, and as far as she was concerned the more the man hurt, the better; she hoped that he was in constant pain. She was so intent on that thought, that she almost forgot to ask the consultant an important question: "Mr Asheed, I wonder, if before we go, it would be possible to obtain a blood sample from Mr Berkowitz. Whilst we are waiting for him to get well we can get on with working up a DNA profile on him; we shall need that in any event." As Liz was speaking, she took a plastic bag out of her handbag in which was all of the paraphernalia needed for collecting and keeping a sample of blood. The consultant asked Liz how much blood was required, and when Liz told him just a few cc's he turned to a nurse and gave her instructions.

Nathan Berkowitz was, indeed, a sorry sight. One of his eyes remained closed and the skin of his face had blackened blotches of haematomas underlying the skin. Liz had come prepared to question him about two of the three crimes with which it was thought that he had been involved. Most of the details of his involvement with the prostitute, Karina, were known, but, aside from DNA evidence, there was nothing known of his possible involvement in the rape of two young women several months prior to the killing of Karina.

In order to get Berkowitz talking, Liz asked him to describe what had happened to him prior to being found unconscious. He said that he had been set upon by two men just as he left a pub, where he'd been for a short time. He said that he had no idea why the men had attacked him; "I never laid eyes on them before they jumped on me!" Liz was pretty sure that she knew why Berkowitz had been attacked. His picture had been seen all over the southeast of England, and it was likely that his assailants were just 'upright' citizens bestowing 'society's justice'.

After speaking to Berkowitz for several minutes and getting nowhere, Liz suggested to her colleague that perhaps they should leave. Liz was not totally unaware of a stern-faced nurse who kept coming into the ward and looking at them. She had been the one to tell the two police officers when they entered the hospital ward that they shouldn't stay long; "Mr Berkowitz needs as much rest and freedom from disturbance as possible." Liz wondered if the nurse would have the same opinion, if she knew who Berkowitz was.

\* \* \*

Until Nathan Berkowitz was well enough to be discharged from hospital, Liz had to content herself with gathering background details which would help in preparing the case against the man. She had had a long and at times distressing interview with Mrs Berkowitz in the presence of the two Berkowitz girls; they were aged thirteen and seventeen. Missus Berkowitz expressed herself completely at a loss to explain her husband's actions.

When Mrs Berkowitz had been questioned shortly after the discovery that Berkowitz had a family, she had denied that her husband could have made use of prostitutes. She claimed that she would have known if he were sleeping with other women. However, once the number of the credit card used by Berkowitz to pay for his visits to brothels was known, Mrs Berkowitz had to accept that her husband was a frequenter of such places.

Liz had ended the interview with the Berkowitz family both because she was obtaining no new information, and it was obvious that Mrs Berkowitz was becoming quite distressed. She thanked the family for their co-operation, and made to leave. The eldest daughter, Natalie, said that she would show Liz to the door. When they got outside the house, Natalie asked Liz if she had a card with her telephone number on it. Liz removed one of her business cards from her handbag. Natalie said, "I may call you in the next day or so and tell you a few things about my dad. But if I do, I want you to promise that you never will let my mother know about them. She wouldn't be able to cope." Liz said that she could not make such a promise. "If what you tell me involves criminal acts, I wouldn't be able to ignore them." Natalie told Liz not to worry, she was pretty sure that what she had to say didn't involve anything criminal.

The 'few things' that Natalie wished to tell Liz turned out to be the necessity of Berkowitz's two daughters to fight off his sexual advances ever since both of them had reached puberty. According to Natalie's account, when she and her sister were little girls they had loved their dad.

He did all of the things a good father did. Rather coolly, she said, "however, once we started to wear bras he became a different person. Mind you, he never actually succeeded in doing anything, but he always seemed to be trying. We didn't dare take a bath without locking the bathroom door, and we made excuses rather than be in the house with him alone during the evening."

"One year my mother took an evening course at the local church hall. It was hell. Even when we threatened that we would tell mum he laughed at us, saying that she never would believe us. I think the thing that worried us the most was the fact that he was right. I think the only way that mum would have believed what our dad was up to would have been if she'd come home one night and found him raping one of us. We could never have any friends over to stay with us because he would behave the same way toward them, if you gave him half a chance."

"However, now that mum knows about him and knows that it is her husband who raped and murdered that young girl, she is ready to believe that he is capable of doing anything. My sister and I talked it over, and we decided that I should tell you about our dad. I know that what I've said can't be used against him; at least I presume that it can't. However, both my sister and me think that our dad should be sent away for a good long time, and we want you to do anything you can that will make sure that that happens. I was worried when you talked to mum yesterday; you seemed to be so sorry for her. Don't be. She is much better off without our dad, who is sick. That's all there is to it; the man is sick."

At that point the young woman broke down, weeping and saying occasionally, "sorry." Liz thanked Natalie for her statement, telling her that it would strengthen her resolve to see that her father got all that he deserved. Liz added that she saw no reason why the knowledge that the girl had imparted about her father should be shared by anyone other than herself, Natalie and her sister. After Liz rang off she sat staring at the wall of the detectives' room for a considerable time. After that call she was going to dig hard to see if two rapes and a murder were the only things with which Nathan Berkowitz could be charged.

\* \* \*

When Berkowitz's DNA profile became available, it was placed on the police national database as usual. Also, Liz sent communications to police forces throughout south-east England asking them to review any cases of rape for which they had obtained DNA profiles of the rapist, but had been unable to find the culprit. The police forces were asked to make a comparison between such DNA profiles and that of Nathan Berkowitz. That appeal resulted in one further case of rape with which Berkowitz could be charged.

Not far from where Berkowitz lived in Welwyn Garden City, a girl of thirteen had been attacked. In her statement to the police, the girl had said that she was returning home alone from an after-school piano lesson, and, as usual, she walked through a small park. Just after she entered the park, a man had stopped her to ask directions to a nearby supermarket. When she started to show him the way, he grabbed her, put his hand over her mouth, and dragged her into some bushes. Once there, he tied a scarf around her head covering her mouth, which stopped her from screaming; then he raped her.

Liz was notified of this rape by a telephone call from an officer of the police force concerned. The rape of the young girl had occurred over a year prior to Karina's death. When Liz asked why the DNA profile of the rapist had not been posted on the police national database, the officer said, "to be frank, sergeant; someone made a monumental cock up. However, we've rectified the situation now, so maybe the kiddie will get some justice at long last."

The day came, finally, when Nathan Berkowitz was able to be delivered to Scotland Yard to be questioned. A few days earlier Liz had gone to Hatfield to see the prisoner and to revise the charges against him to four counts of rape and one of murder. As he had done when charged initially, he said nothing, so the process had been a short one. On the way out of the hospital, she encountered Mr Asheed who made the mistake of telling her that she should go easy on Mr Berkowitz. "He has suffered terribly at the hands of some thugs. Fortunately, we were able to save one of his testicles, but we had to remove one of his kidneys. The other kidney was badly damaged also, so we're not to sure how long it is going to last him."

With barely-controlled anger Liz said, "Mr Asheed; that man has raped four young women, murdering one of them. You think we should go easy on him?" A clearly embarrassed consultant apologised saying that he had not been aware of the seriousness of the charges faced by his patient: "of course, I wouldn't dream of suggesting that what has happened to Mr Berkowitz is in any way comparable to what he has done to those women." He looked distinctly relieved when his 'beeper' began to sound. He said, "excuse me, someone wants me urgently," as he rushed off.

Nathan Berkowitz was interviewed by Liz with DC Blackthorne in the presence of Berkowitz's solicitor. After the formalities of the interview were over, he looked at his solicitor and said, "I don't see much use in messing about. My life is over anyway, so I might as well confess." The solicitor interrupted, saying, "may I have a word with my client in private, officer; I think he should be made aware of the seriousness of what he is proposing to do."

Berkowitz put up his hand and said, "I know what I'm doing. I can't live in a world where everyone knows who I am, and what I've done. In fact, you lot don't know the half of it. Those four women you say I've raped aren't the only ones. I've done some others, too, but I guess they decided not to do anything about it. Anyway, I want to get this whole business sorted out as soon as possible so that I can stop seeing coppers every time I look around."

Nathan Berkowitz was tried on four counts of rape and one of murder several months later. He was given a life sentence with a recommendation that he spend a minimum of fourteen years in prison. As it turned out, in his case, life meant life; he died of kidney failure less than a year after he began his prison sentence. When Liz saw the report of the death, she thought, "I can't think of anyone who deserved it more." Happy as she had been that Berkowitz had pleaded guilty, it meant that her rôle in the investigation of the murder of 'Miss X' had ended. Now she was spending all of her time chasing after illegal immigrants who were collecting for bogus charities.

Liz had been pleased for Lydia who had managed to expose and charge the two men who had organised the prostitution ring that used illegal immigrants. The men jointly owned all of the properties used by the ring, which assets, of course, had been seized by the immigration service. Lydia had thought briefly of going after the firms of solicitors who had acted on behalf of the two men. She was certain that some of the solicitors were fully cognisant of the true nature of their clients' business. Indeed, at least two of the solicitors had been caught 'on camera' during police surveillance of the West London brothels. However, in the end it was only the two principals who were charged and, ultimately, found guilty. Lydia counted it a small victory in the police effort to apprehend exploiters of illegal immigrants. However, she harboured no illusions that that victory would deter others from undertaking similar activities.

# Chapter Twelve

Upon returning from morning coffee in the canteen, Liz found a 'post-it' note stuck to her extension 'phone saying, "If you can, ring the number written below before eleven o'clock…Miss Parmeeta Khan wishes to speak to you." Liz looked at her watch, seeing that it was just after eleven. Fortunately, Miss Khan answered. After Liz identified herself, Miss Khan said, "there's good news, Sergeant Andresen. I've just had a note from the Home Office saying that Julia Gomes has been granted leave to stay in the United Kingdom. She can be released from the detention centre as soon as she has a place to go to. There still are some formal arrangements to be made, but even the man who wrote to me was sympathetic with the idea that Miss Gomes shouldn't have to stay in detention whilst they sort out papers for her. She will have to get herself a passport; presumably that will be Mozambican, and then they will provide her with a proper visa. However, all of that will take time, so she needs some place to stay in the meantime. Julia told me that she had stayed with you when she was helping the police; I wonder if it would be too much to ask if you would be willing to let her stay with you again. It would be just until she gets herself properly settled as a legal immigrant; then, of course, she will have to make her own arrangements."

Liz didn't hesitate. She told Miss Khan that she would be happy to have Julia staying with her. "The two of us got on famously when Julia stayed with me before. Also, there's the added bonus that she is a very good cook." Miss Kahn said, "well, that's all settled, then. As soon as I get a date for Julia's release, I'll let you know."

\* \* \*

Julia Gomes was almost unrecognisable when the young women entered the reception area of the detention centre where Liz was waiting for her. Quite patently, she had lost considerable weight; the clothes that she wore hung loosely on her body. When she saw Liz she rushed over to her kissing her on the cheek and hugging her. "Oh, Liz; I am so glad to see you. It is so very kind of you to let me stay with you for awhile. You are such a kind person; I don't know how I can ever thank you." It was quite noticeable from the way she spoke that Julia's English had improved considerably.

The detention centre in which Julia had been kept was located near the city of Cambridge. Liz had taken a taxi from the city. Once at the centre she had asked the driver to wait; despite his reluctance, he had done so. After the two women had got into the taxi, Liz had directed the driver to take them to the Arbury area of Cambridge. She told Julia, "we'll be staying overnight with my mother prior to going down to London.

\* \* \*

After she had spoken to Parmeeta Khan, Liz had done a lot of thinking about Julia, and what the young woman would do once she had been released from detention. Liz had hoped that she might be able to persuade her mum to have Julia stay with her in Cambridge. She knew that some weeks earlier Audrey had ruled out any thought of having a person other than her daughter or herself living in her house. However, 'living with Audrey' seemed such a perfect solution to the problems of both her mum and Julia. Liz would have someone to keep an eye on her mum, and the young woman would be able to attend school. Liz was hoping that she could get her mother to reconsider her position.

When Julia had stayed with Liz, the two of them had discussed Julia's ambition to finish her education in the UK. The young woman had completed secondary school in Mozambique and her primary aim once she got to Britain was to attend some form of higher education. She wasn't sure what subject she wanted to study, but she was interested in one that would be useful in her native country, perhaps nursing or teaching. Liz had no idea how much credit Julia would be allowed for the education she had had in her native country. She knew that one of the sixth-form colleges in Cambridge offered courses that led to examinations that would prepare her for university, the so-called A-level examinations.

Even though she was reasonably certain that Julia would agree to live with her mum, Liz knew that she would have quite a job persuading Audrey to allow Julia to live with her. In addition to the objection that her mum had voiced earlier: she did not want another woman living in her house, there was the problem that Julia was black. All of her life, Liz had heard her mum make derogatory references to black people. Also, Audrey had no love for people whom she described as "foreigners." Consequently, Liz was certain that her mum's initial reaction would be the rejection of any idea of living with a black foreigner.

In her mind Liz had planned carefully the way in which she would attempt to get her mother to accept Julia.

She and Julia would stay with Audrey after Liz had fetched the young woman from the detention centre. At first, she would not tell either Audrey or Julia of her plan. Liz hoped that after several hours together, her mum and Julia would get to know each other, and it would be possible to judge whether or not the two of them could live together.

After their first hour together, Liz was certain that her mum never would accept having Julia living in her home. Although the young woman was being her usual friendly self, Audrey had very little to say to her guest. When she did wish to say something to Julia, she would address her remark to Liz, saying something like, "does your friend like living in this country?" or "I don't suppose your friend knows much about our queen and what a wonderful person she is." Although Liz was bored with her mother's patronising attitude, Julia appeared not to notice, always speaking to Audrey in a voice filled with enthusiasm.

In order to keep the conversation going and to divert her mum's attention from Julia, Liz asked Audrey about her new hobby: weaving. As an alternative to going to the pub every evening, Audrey, at Liz's insistence, had begun going to night classes at the local secondary school. The woman had become intrigued with weaving and had taken to the craft with uncharacteristic enthusiasm. In order to encourage her mother, Liz had bought her a small loom which stood in one corner of the sitting room.

Audrey said that she wanted to show Liz some weaving that she had just completed, which she thought was really good. As she went to the closet under the stairs to get her work, the telephone rang. Liz picked it up to hear Pat's cheery greeting. Prior to going to Cambridge, Liz had telephoned Pat to tell her of her plans and to suggest that they should get together sometime during the visit. Liz wanted Pat to meet Julia.

Pat had rung to invite Liz, her mum and "your African friend" to come to her flat for lunch the following day. Liz accepted the invitation, and then the two women spent some time exchanging news about their latest activities. There was a method to Liz's retention of Pat on the telephone because she could see that Julia and her mum were holding what looked like a friendly conversation.

After Liz rang off, she joined her mum and Julia again; the two women were getting along together very well. Julia was explaining something about weaving to Audrey who appeared to be listening intently. After that exchange, Audrey and Julia appeared to get on much better with each other than they had when the two of them had first met. That gave Liz hope that her mum would agree to have the young woman living with her. However, she would wait for a few days before discussing the idea with her mum.

* * *

Back in London, Liz was enjoying having Julia living with her once more. The young woman had insisted that she would play the rôle of Liz's 'wife'. Liz had blushed when Julia had said that, even though she was sure that her friend had said it in all innocence. However, Julia had taken over the housekeeping and always had a lovely meal waiting even when Liz got home late from her work. Liz had decided that very soon she could get used to such spoiling and would wish it to continue. However, she knew that Julia's days with her were limited.

To her surprise and pleasure, Audrey's response had been to agree when Liz had broached the subject of Julia living with her and going to school. In fact, her mum had been uncharacteristically enthusiastic, saying that it would be wonderful to have a young person living in the house again. She even volunteered to get Mr Paltry next door to have a look at Liz's old bicycle to get it ready for Julia's use. For her part, Julia was very pleased at Liz's idea that the young woman might like to live in Cambridge, but she did say that she would be sad at leaving her good friend in London.

Liz had made enquiries at one of the sixth form colleges in Cambridge to find that Julia would be able to enrol in any of a number of courses. They said that the validity of foreign qualifications varied considerably, especially with so-called third world countries. Therefore, they would have to have an assessment made of Julia's qualifications by the government Department of Education.

Liz knew that the first priority in preparing the way for Julia to stay in Britain would have to be the commencement of the process of getting the young woman issued with a valid passport. It was obvious, from speaking to officials at the Mozambican Consul in London, that the process could be quite involved. In one conversation that Julia held with a consular official, the man insisted that she would have to return to Mozambique in order to make an application for a passport. Fortunately, that assertion was denied by another, more senior, official. Liz suggested that Julia should stay with her in London until the whole process was complete. The young woman took up that offer, with pleasure.

* * *

Julia had been living with Liz for over a month when an incident occurred that Liz hoped that she would not live to regret. A small packet arrived in the post one morning causing Julia to shriek with delight, hugging Liz and jumping up and down. It was her passport. All that would be necessary for her to do now would be to send it in to the Home Office to get the visa stamp indicating that she was legally present in the United Kingdom. Liz said that that evening they would have a special meal to celebrate, and that she would come home early to cook it. Also, she would stop at the off licence on the way home and buy a bottle of wine. "Then you and I will have a slap-up meal and get pissed." Julia's expression when Liz said that was at first one of puzzlement; then her face broke into a broad smile as she reviewed quickly the idioms that she and Liz had been practising. She recognised 'pissed', but she'd not heard 'slap up' before. However, from the context she assumed that it was good. Julia said that she would cook the meal, but Liz said, "no; this is your day, Julia. I shall do the honours!"

Liz was quite pleased with herself and the meal that she had cooked. It had been a long time since she had had the stimulus to cook such a meal. As she stirred the sauce that was to be poured over the pasta boiling away in a saucepan, she thought back to the days, not that long ago, when she had done this sort of thing regularly. However, since arriving at New Scotland Yard, her ambition had got in the way of regular meals at home. Since then, if she had eaten at all, it was some instant meal popped into a microwave for a short time.

As Liz was musing, Julia came to stand beside her, saying that the odours being produced were making her mouth water. She wanted Liz to teach her how to make the dish that was now being prepared. Liz asked Julia to seat herself at the table because the meal would be served shortly. She poured wine into two glasses and set them upon the table;

then she served the pasta dish that she had prepared. Julia kept offering to help, but Liz insisted that for the present evening her friend was to sit and be waited upon. The meal passed off uneventfully, except for Julia's periodic exclamations of delight at the tastiness of the food.

After Liz had loaded the dishwasher and had started it off, she suggested that she and Julia go into the sitting room and finish off the bottle of wine. She had been shocked at the price she had been asked to pay for the Sancerre, but she had to admit that it was quite nice. Liz was feeling very mellow and wanted to find out more about her young friend. She had no idea whatsoever what it would be like to grow up in a country like Mozambique; the idea of learning about it first hand intrigued her.

Julia seemed reluctant to say much about her childhood. She said that her father had come to Mozambique from Portugal when he was a young man. "He married my mother and settled down to become a farmer. Then they were living near Lichinga in the north of Mozambique. However, because of the civil war, it became very dangerous, so my parents fled to the south, settling in Maputo, the capital. That was when I was a little girl. In Maputo, my father was able to find employment as a carpenter, and we had quite a nice life."

When Julia had finished telling Liz of her memories growing up in Maputo, she asked Liz to talk about her childhood. As Liz was speaking, Julia lay her head on the back of the settee and listened, smiling at Liz in such a way that it made Liz nervous. Liz related how she was born and grew up in Cambridge and had only left there when she went to university. She said that she had gone straight into the police from university, and ever since then, she had worked and lived in London.

When Liz had finished speaking, Julia reached over and took one of Liz's hands in both of hers, saying, "you are such a wonderful person, Liz; I am so lucky to have you as a friend." Liz attempted to tell Julia that it was not difficult to be friendly with such a lively and resilient young woman, but she couldn't find the words. Also, she was aware of different feelings that were caused by the warmth of Julia's two hands as they held her hand in a tight grip.

It became obvious to Liz that Julia was being affected by the same feelings as she when the young woman said, "it is OK for women to love each other in England, isn't it, Liz?" Liz didn't know how to answer the question because she was frightened of learning about the reasoning that underlay it. She said, "why do you ask, Julia?" "I have been thinking about it ever since I was in the detention centre. In Mozambique, love between women is against the law. I have heard that in areas where the Muslim religion is strong, such women can be put to death."

"However, when I was put into the detention centre my body was examined by a nurse. As she looked between my legs, she began to manipulate me. I was frightened because I thought that it was against the law everywhere. I didn't know what she would do. I thought that she would get angry if I asked her to stop." Liz was sure that when Julia said, "manipulate," she actually meant "masturbate." She interrupted Julia, asking, "when you say 'manipulate', Julia; do you mean masturbate?" Julia said, "ah, yes; that's the word I wanted to use; I know it in Portuguese, but I couldn't remember the English word. When she finished examining me, the nurse told me that she thought I was a very nice young woman; she would try to arrange it so that I could assist her. I was frightened of saying anything, but I remember thinking that

I didn't want to get in trouble for doing something that was illegal. Later, when I asked her about it being illegal, she said that I didn't have to worry because in Britain it was OK. I didn't really want to do the things with her that she wanted, but I was frightened that if I refused her, she would make things difficult for me. For the next few weeks, she came to get me every time new female detainees came to the centre. I helped her with the examinations, and then we would stay together in her room and kiss and masturbate each other."

"Then a woman, a fellow detainee, told me that she knew what I was doing with the nurse, and that I should stop it because it was illegal. She said that the nurse had done it to her too, until she had found out that the woman had lied to her about it being legal in Britain. The woman said that if we got caught, I would be deported at once. Fortunately, a day after that, I was able to leave the detention centre. However, I don't know what to believe." Liz said that the official position in Britain, as well as the rest of Europe, was that love between women was not illegal. However, in Britain, and probably everywhere else where it was legal, there still were many people who opposed it.

Julia said that her experiences with the nurse in the detention centre had made her confused about herself. "I can't remember ever doing such things, even by myself. My parents raised me in the Catholic faith, and I can remember when I was a little girl being told that it was a sin to abuse my body by doing such things. Until I became a teenager in secondary school, I believed everything that the nuns and priests told me. Then I began to hear stories from my friends of what some of the priests did, sometimes with young girls, sometimes with young boys. From then on, I began to lose my faith, and now I'm afraid I haven't much faith at all."

The two women sat together talking of experiences that they felt had shaped their lives until Liz looked at her watch and exclaimed that they had best get to bed. As Julia delivered the two wine glasses to the kitchen, Liz made preparations to make up Julia's bed on the settee. Suddenly, Liz had an impulse she knew that she should resist, but she knew also that she would not resist. She said, "Julia, this settee can't be very comfortable for you, and I have a lovely, large, king-sized bed. I know that you will be more comfortable there, and there's plenty of room for the two of us. It will be for only a little longer, and then you will be going to Cambridge and will have a room of your own."

Liz tried to convince herself that her invitation to Julia to sleep in her bed had not been motivated by lust. However, their actions that night and for the nights following, belied that explanation.

Shortly after the two women got into bed, Julia was in Liz's arms and was enthusiastically kissing her all over her face, finally settling on her lips. Liz knew that it was the wine, but she was fully aroused, climbing on top of Julia and pushing her lower abdomen against that of her young friend. Julia continued to kiss Liz, but rather inexpertly, until Liz's tongue began to explore Julia's mouth. Then she felt Julia's hands go between their chests as the young woman unbuttoned her pyjama top and attempted to pull Liz's night-dress further up than it was already. At that point, both women giggled and paused long enough to undress themselves completely.

In the morning, Liz awoke early, as she did usually. However, now she saw the body of a beautiful young woman lying next to her. She lay on her front looking at Julia, who was lying on her back, the top sheet of the bed pulled down to the level of her navel. Liz wondered then if what she felt for Julia could be real love or just a physical attraction. She looked at the flattened breasts with their un-erect nipples and incredibly dark areolae. She resisted the urge to suckle Julia's breasts, realising that she should be preparing to go to work.

When she shifted her gaze from Julia's breasts to her face she saw that her friend was awake and looking at her, smiling. Julia turned her body, reaching over to take Liz's hand and pulling it toward her. Liz didn't resist the move-ment; consequently she was two hours late for work that morning, and she had not had any breakfast.

* * *

Finally, Julia's passport arrived back from the Home Office and the young woman shrieked when she read the official note that accompanied it: it meant that now she would be able to begin a new life. Julia expressed mock dis-appointment at the rather modest visa stamp that had been placed in the passport. She thought that the stamp should have been outlined in gold with illuminated letters. Never-theless, the young woman was sure that that stamp would change her life forever.

Early during Julia's stay with her, Liz had taken the young woman into the West End of London to shop for clothing. Julia never had had more than a meagre wardrobe since arriving in Britain. At one of the shops they visited, Julia had been very enthusiastic about a very brief 'shorty' night-dress. She called Liz's attention to it and said, "oh; isn't this beautiful Liz? It's just the sort of thing a wife should wear. Can I have it?"

Both Liz and Julia understood why Liz blushed deeply. During their time together, when alone, Julia had always referred to herself as Liz's wife. Several times, Liz had been on the point of discussing with Julia their relationship, explaining to the young woman that its sexual nature could not go on indefinitely. However, every time an opportunity would arise, Liz would be overcome by lustful feelings as she contemplated Julia's wonderful figure. Liz concluded, finally, that when Julia moved to Cambridge, her friend would be involved in a new life; consequently, the relationship that the two of them had had no longer would be possible.

\* \* \*

After her return from Cambridge, to where she had gone to accompany Julia and to make certain that her mum had got everything prepared for the arrival of the young woman, Liz was aware of the loneliness to which she once again was subjected. She knew that Julia had to lead her own life, but she regretted the loss of a friend with whom she had enjoyed a loving relationship; a relationship that she had not enjoyed with many people. She knew that she was being selfish, but she had wanted Julia to stay in London with her and to be the 'wife' that Julia had joked about. However, life was not like that, Liz knew. Julia had a new life that the young woman was determined to follow.

Audrey had quite outdone herself on Julia's behalf, having cleared all of the mess from the second bedroom in the house. It had been used as a dumping ground since Liz had left home. Also, one of the neighbours had given Audrey a sofa bed to replace the settee in the front room of the house. Unfortunately, Audrey's loom became a casualty to the sofa bed, having to be moved to her bedroom where, Liz feared, it would be 'out of sight, out of mind'. Because of the sofa bed, Audrey made it clear to Liz that now there would be no excuse for her daughter not to visit because even with Julia living in the house there would be beds for all three of them.

Liz opened the bottle of wine that she found in the fridge of her flat and used part of the contents to dull the 'pain' of Julia's loss.

# Chapter Thirteen

Liz had only just seated herself at her desk in the detectives' room when her extension 'phone sounded. It was Detective Chief Superintendent Rignell, who asked her to come to see him when she could spare a moment. Liz knew that when the super said, "when you can spare a moment," he really meant "drop whatever you are doing and see me at once."

A few minutes later the DCS greeted her warmly when she entered his office after knocking. "Liz, DI Mussett tells me that you are right in the thick of some mess with illegal immigrants, is that right? Tell me how you're getting on." Liz was puzzled by the super's direct approach to her when her progress on the case had been the subject of reports that she had compiled during the weeks that she had pursued the latest investigations. She had assumed that he had read those reports. Nevertheless, if he wanted to hear direct from her, she was not the one to argue. "Well, sir, I have been involved in a couple of areas since the prostitution ring was broken up. Some of us have been looking into the activities of illegal immigrants who are part of a ring that is going around posing as collectors seeking donations for various charities, all of which are bogus. We've managed to round up some of the collectors, but the people who organise the whole thing still are at large. Also, we had a look at some so-called sweat shops in the East End that have been employing illegal immigrant women making various items of clothing. All we've managed to do so far is close down two of them, but we've not been able to bring any charges against the owners and managers."

Liz was well aware of a lack of attention on the super's face as she spoke, so she discontinued her narrative quickly, saying that she had only just got a new lead from immigration that concerned a business employing illegal immigrants, this time from Eastern Europe.

Shortly after pausing, DCS Rignell made clear what had been the real reason for asking her to come to see him. "It sounds to me, Liz, that your investigation of illegal immigrants is not really a high-priority item. However, just yesterday I got a request from the Mile End police that I think should take a higher priority. I've had a word with DI Mussett, asking if it would be convenient to let you go back to your old 'haunts' for a short time. She has no objection, as long as it wouldn't be for too long. She reckons that young DC Blackthorne could take over on your team easily enough. Lydia thinks very highly of him." Liz said that she would be pleased to see DC Blackthorne take over from her; he was very competent.

The superintendent continued, "I'm sure that you'll remember Simon Lawrence from your time at Mile End? He certainly remembers you, and the fact that you are an expert in mathematics. I hadn't realised that you had spent a time undercover as a teacher of maths in one of the East End secondary schools. He told me that he had worried then that the police service might lose you; you did such a good job, the headmaster of the school in which you taught tried to convince you to stay on. Anyway, it seems that they need someone who is knowledgeable about mathematics. Their plan is to have you go undercover again, only this time as a university student. They are investigating two deaths by drowning of university students. When the first young woman died, it was thought that she had taken her own life. However, now a second has been found under almost identical circumstances, and they have concluded that both deaths may be suspicious. Both young women were reading maths at a place called Queen Mary and Westfield College in the East End and there is some suspicion that one of the college employees may be responsible for the deaths. The Mile End police want someone who can pose as an undergraduate in maths. DCI Lawrence said that he thought of you straight away. Neither DI Mussett nor I have any objections, but, how does it strike you? Do you fancy becoming a student again?" Liz was fairly certain that the question was not really a question. However, she thought that she should enter at least two disclaimers: "sir; I think it's possible that Chief Inspector Lawrence may have forgotten that whilst I was at the Mile End station, I acted undercover at Queen Mary College and Westfield College. At that time, I pretended to be a visiting undergraduate in the physics department. There may be people in the College, still, who will recognise me. Also, don't you think that I may be a bit long in the tooth to be convincing as a university undergraduate?" The DCS brushed Liz's doubts aside by saying, "well, let's wait until you've had a talk with DCI Lawrence before we come to any final conclusions."

When Liz thought about it, she decided that she would not be altogether displeased to be going back to the East End for a time. She had quite liked the atmosphere at that small station where she had begun her police career. However, at the time, she had not been overly fond of DCI Lawrence.

\* \* \*

On her way to the Mile End, Liz had got out of the tube at the Stepney Green underground station, which was an easy journey from her flat in Plaistow. At the police station, she was pleasantly surprised to see that very little had changed. She was to report directly to Detective Chief Inspector Lawrence under whose direct supervision she would be working.

During their initial conversation, the DCI said that he had not forgotten that Liz had posed as an undergraduate in physics at Queen Mary College when she was serving at Mile End. He said that he thought it unlikely that anyone would remember her. "You'll be in a different department with different students and different members of staff. Besides, most of the students who might have known you then will have left. Also, apparently now-a-days, there are increasing numbers of mature students going to university, so you won't be out of place if you appear to be a little older than the average undergraduate."

It was obvious to Liz that DCI Lawrence had thought through the task that she would be asked to undertake. She remembered his personality well enough to know that if she continued to express doubts, he would become irritated, bringing out his worst personality traits. She said nothing.

After pausing briefly to discover if Liz had anything to say, the DCI said that he would introduce her to the men who would be her colleagues. He took her to an office and rapped on the door. On the door was a sign that named the occupant of the office as Detective Inspector David Morgan. She had worked with him before, except then he had been a detective sergeant. After a brief, but friendly chat with 'Dai' Morgan, Liz was taken to the detectives' room where she was introduced first to Detective Constable Christopher

Houghton, another detective whom she had known previously. The only other detective in the room at that time was introduced to her as DC Clive Robinson; He was a "new boy," as DCI Lawrence described him, having graduated from the police college in Hendon only a short time earlier.

After the officers had become acquainted, the DCI took Liz to his office to explain in detail his thinking on the rôle that she would play whilst she was with his team.

In his office, the DCI took a file folder off his desk and handed it to Liz. The label on the folder read: "QMW Deaths." DCI Lawrence said, "all of the relevant details are in there, but let me fill you in on the background to the case we want you to help us with."

"About six weeks ago, the body of a young woman, Veronica Blanchard, was pulled out of the Grand Union Canal over near the college. You know the place, I think. As usual, the body was taken to the morgue at the London Hospital and autopsied. There was nothing overtly suspicious in the forensic reports, except, perhaps, the young woman must have died shortly after having sexual intercourse. Nonetheless, it looked like a straight-forward suicide by drowning. However, at the inquest the mother disputed the testimony of the girl's college tutor, that the young woman could have committed suicide. The mother was convinced that her daughter had been raped and murdered. She said that was the only conclusion that could offer an explanation of why the girl had sperm in various parts of her body, as the autopsy report had shown."

"To accommodate both versions of the means by which the girl met her death, the coroner insisted that the inquest jury return an open verdict. Dai Morgan was put in charge of the investigation, and he and Chris Houghton did a lot of asking around at Queen Mary where the girl was an undergraduate. Neither of them came up with anything that would rule out suicide. However, the girl's mother thought otherwise and threatened to raise a stink, saying that we were ignoring evidence that she says would prove that her daughter was murdered. More in an effort to calm down the mother than to learn anything new, I sent a woman police constable, WPC Hansen, to interview her and find out just what was her evidence. The transcript of the WPC's interview of the mother makes interesting reading, so I would look that over very carefully because it might help you in your enquiries at Queen Mary College."

"Then, about a fortnight ago, the body of a second young woman was pulled from the Grand Union Canal at almost the same place as the first. She, too, had drowned and she, too, had remnants of sperm in her body. However, when the DNA profile of the sperm was analysed it was found that it was from the same man whose sperm cells had been found in the body of Veronica Blanchard. In other words, it looks as though the dead girl's mother may have been right; her daughter, as well as the second young woman, may have been victims of a rapist."

"Now, the reason why you're here is because both young women were undergraduates in the mathematics department at Queen Mary College. For that reason we would like you to pose as an undergraduate to investigate the possibility that someone there was involved in their deaths." The DCI handed the file folder before him to Liz, saying, "everything we know about the two deaths is in here; I suggest that you go off now and have a good read of the file. After that, come back, and we'll have a talk about what I would like you to do."

At the desk that she had been assigned in the detectives' room, Liz opened the file folder that DCI Lawrence gave her. The transcript of WPC Hansen's interview of Veronica Blanchard's mother was the first item to be seen. Liz read that Veronica Blanchard's mother was a Mrs Susan Blanchard, and that she lived in South Hackney, a place that Liz knew was a quite pleasant part of East London. In her report, WPC Hansen had said that she had begun the interview of Mrs Blanchard by reviewing the information held by the police; telling the woman that she wished only to ascertain which aspects of her daughter's death Mrs Blanchard did not dispute. The WPC had told Mrs Blanchard, "I don't wish to drag up painful memories, but let me review the police files on the death of your daughter, Veronica Anne. Please interrupt me if I say something that differs from your view of events surrounding your daughter's death."

"Veronica Anne's body was found floating in the Grand Union Canal where it runs adjacent to Queen Mary and Westfield College, just off the Mile End Road. The body had been in the water for a time estimated to have been between one and two days. The body was autopsied by Dr Ramdan Marana, a pathologist at the London Hospital near where it was found. It was confirmed that drowning was the cause of death. The only other finding of the autopsy that had relevance during the inquest into the incident was the fact that remnants of sperm were found within the upper part of the vagina and the uterus. Because of that, the coroner assumed that Veronica had engaged in sexual intercourse, probably shortly before her death."

The WPC had written, "at that point I paused, expecting Mrs Blanchard to interrupt because the subject of intercourse was her point of disagreement with the coroner's findings. So I said, 'shall I proceed?' Missus Blanchard nodded in agreement, so I continued. I understand that Veronica Anne had not lived at home since she was eighteen. Initially, she worked as a shop girl, which she did for three years. Then she enrolled in an undergraduate course in mathematics at QMW. Her tutor there said that she had done quite well in her first year, but was not doing so well in the second year of the course. He blamed it both on personal problems and the fact that she was having financial difficulties. The tutor told both a police interviewer and the inquest jury that in his opinion, it would have been altogether possible that Veronica had taken her own life because of worries about her future."

"Missus Blanchard said that she could not and did not dispute any of the facts that I had recited except the fact that she thought it very unlikely that her daughter had committed suicide, saying, 'let me tell you something about Veronica, officer. She was a very determined young woman. When she started something, she would not give up easily. It is quite true that she left home after her eighteenth birthday and went to work. However, that had more to do with the attitude of her father than anything else'."

"'When Veronica was twelve or so, she told me that she thought that she was gay. She told me never to tell her father because she was sure that he would not understand. I am afraid that I had to agree with her. I knew that he would not understand; he hated the very idea of homosexuality and did not hesitate to let his opinion be known. Anyway, I told Veronica then that she should give it time to see how her feelings would develop. As time went on, my daughter made it fairly obvious, at least to me, the way her feelings had developed. She had friends who were boys, but for the most part she kept the company of girls, and her best friend throughout her teenage was a girl'."

"'Veronica was very studious, as well as ambitious. She didn't spend much time socialising. However, just before her eighteenth birthday, she completed the exams she had to take in order to go to university. To celebrate her success, we held a party for her. She had very few friends, but those she had, of both sexes, came to the party. She asked her father and me to attend and act as sort of chaperones. Veronica insisted that she should provide wine and beer for her friends, and she thought that our presence might be required to quieten things down, should that be necessary. Veronica's best friend, a girl whom her father and I knew well and liked very much, was to stay over with us after the party; she had stayed overnight with us often before. I was aware that Veronica and the girl were more than best friends, and I had appreciated that my daughter had been careful to hide her feelings for her friend from her father. However, I don't know what went wrong that night, but my husband found them in bed together, performing an act that he said was disgusting. He ordered the girl out of the house. He was so angry that he refused even to drive her home. I couldn't allow her to be on the streets at that hour of the night, so I drove her'."

"'The next day my husband made an impossible demand on Veronica. He told her that she had to change her ways and get herself a boyfriend, or he no longer would have her living in his house. I tried to get my husband to change his mind, but he never would. I hardly ever saw my daughter after that; it was so difficult because of my husband. Anyway, officer, perhaps now you see why I don't think that my daughter would have had sexual intercourse with a man.

That's why I believe that she must have been raped, and, very likely, murdered'."

The WPC's report went on to say that the constable had questioned Mrs Blanchard about friends of her daughter, who might be able to corroborate the contention that Veronica Blanchard was gay. However, the girl's mother had no information that was current, suggesting only that the police contact the QMW authorities.

A thorough search of the Blanchard file provided Liz with two puzzles: first, there was no indication that WPC Hansen's interview of Mrs Blanchard had been followed up by interviews of persons at QMW who might have known her. Both Dai Morgan and Chris Houghton, the detectives who would have investigated, were not available for Liz to ask.

The second puzzling feature of the Blanchard case was indicated by the transcript of a telephone call that had been made to the police by a female caller a day or so after an article on Veronica Blanchard's death had appeared in a London tabloid. The woman had said that Veronica Blanchard had not killed herself, and that she could prove it. However, when the police operator had asked the woman for her name and the telephone number from which she was calling, she had said, "oh, forget it; it won't bring her back!" Then she had rung off.

The call raised Liz's hopes that there might be at least one person, whom the police had not interviewed, who very likely would be able to shed light on the movements of Veronica Blanchard just prior to her death. It was obvious to her why DCI Lawrence thought that it was most likely that Veronica Blanchard's death was connected in some way with her status as an undergraduate at Queen Mary and

Westfield College. However, the nature of that connection seemed to be more than usually obscure.

Dai Morgan came into the detectives' room just after lunch, asking Liz how she was getting on. When Liz asked him about the follow up of the statement made by Mrs Blanchard, he said that, in fact, he had followed it up and that a statement by the dead girl's adviser at QMW should have been in the file. Liz suggested that perhaps the DCI had removed it and forgot to put it back. Dai said, "it wouldn't surprise me in the least, Liz. He's always going on at us for being sloppy about keeping our investigative files up to date, but he makes most of us look like amateurs when it comes to sloppiness. He's got it down to a fine art. It wouldn't surprise me to learn that he's lost the transcript that I made of my interview with the girl's undergraduate advisor. Hang on, let's go into my office and have a look; I did it on my computer, so I'm sure that I kept it in a file; all I've got to do is find the damn thing."

With that, Liz and Dai Morgan went into his office where he seated himself before a computer screen and began to manipulate the keyboard in front of him. "You know, this word processor is really great, Liz; when I think how much time I used to spend with my old typewriter... ah, there it is; hang on, I'll print off a copy for you. They've got us all connected up to a printer that's in the detectives' room; all we've got to do is remember to turn the damn thing on in the morning!"

A short time later Liz was reading over the statement made by Veronica Blanchard's undergraduate advisor at Queen Mary and Westfield College: Professor Robert Furner. Dai Morgan's narrative of his visit to QMW was remarkably detailed; either he had a very good memory, or he was well-schooled in taking notes in short hand. He said that he had consulted a Mrs Marks in the 'student-affairs' office of the administration to discover the name of Veronica Blanchard's tutor. "Mrs Marks informed me in no uncertain terms that the members of staff who looked after undergraduates were more than just tutors; for that reason they were called 'undergraduate advisers'. She told me that the advisers were there to get to know the students assigned to them and to follow them through their undergraduate careers, lending help where it was necessary. Finally, the woman gave me the information that I asked for: Miss Blanchard's undergraduate adviser was Professor Robert Furner, who is one of the senior members of staff in the department of mathematics. Then, she expanded on that information, telling me that formerly, Professor Furner had been a member of staff of Westfield College, and had transferred a few years earlier when the two colleges merged to form Queen Mary and Westfield College." Dai had added a note saying that he had thanked the woman for the history lesson; he had wondered why the institution was called Queen Mary and Westfield College.

Dai's report went on to say, "Professor Furner seemed a pleasant enough man, but after speaking to him for a few minutes I gained the impression that he was treating our conversation as a sparring match. It seemed as if he would intentionally misunderstand my questions. At one time, I had tried to get him to tell me his opinion of Veronica Blanchard's sexuality. He pretended that he did not understand the question. Finally, I came right out and asked him if he could or would venture an opinion about her sexual proclivities. He mistook that to mean, did she sleep around? He said that he couldn't possibly answer such a question; he didn't pry into the private lives of his advisees. I told him that it was my understanding that at least some knowledge of his advisees' private lives was a necessary requirement for him to do his job properly. He countered that by asking, belligerently, 'are you suggesting that I don't do my job properly?'"

"I was just on the point of concluding that he was an un-co-operative witness who I'd have to treat accordingly, when he asked me what I was accusing him of. That surprised me, so I said the first thing that came into my mind. I told him that I was not accusing him of anything, that I was speaking to him in the hope that he could clarify for me the reasoning underlying his statement to a coroner's jury that he thought that Veronica Blanchard may have committed suicide."

"Much to my surprise, the man's whole attitude changed. He said that he had known Veronica Blanchard well enough to know that she seemed to be a very lonely person. He said, 'she never seemed to be in the company of her fellow undergraduates. In their reports to me, her course tutors stated that she was punctual handing in assigned work, but that she rarely took part in the tutorial discussions. I knew that she was short of money, but then that's true of most of our students. Her financial problems forced her to get a part-time job, but I've no idea what she was doing; she never talked to me about it. I simply put together her 'loner' personality and the fact that she had money problems and ventured the opinion that she might have committed suicide. It was for that reason that I refused to answer your question about whether or not she was promiscuous'."

Dai Morgan's report continued, "I told him that I was sorry if I'd not made myself clear, but my question had not been about promiscuity. I said, according to Veronica

Blanchard's mother, the girl was gay. I think as you know, when her body was autopsied, sperm was been found in it. Veronica's mother says that her daughter would not have consented to sex with a man; she concluded that her daughter must have been raped and murdered. My question to you was designed merely to discover if you had any information that would confirm or deny what Veronica Blanchard's mother believed."

"Professor Furner responded by saying, 'no, officer, this is the first I knew about the sperm; I don't recall hearing about that on the morning I was called to testify at the coroner's inquest. I don't imagine that if I had known it would have changed my opinion as to Veronica's suicide, but then I didn't know that she was gay. However, now that you mention it, I don't think that I can ever recall seeing her in the company of a male undergraduate. Occasionally, especially during her first year, I would see her in the bar of the junior common room; however, if my recollection is correct, then she was either by herself or with a young female'."

Dai had added to his notes that he had come away from QMW thinking that the professor was a bit of an "elusive" character, although his latest testimony would be much more helpful than had been his opinion that Veronica Blanchard had committed suicide.

\* \* \*

As Liz read the contents of the file on the QMW deaths it became clear to her that very little in the way of police investigation had been made in the case of the second death: that of a young woman named Mary Roberts. Like Veronica Blanchard, Mary Roberts had just completed the second year of her three-year course in mathematics.

Also, like Veronica Blanchard, Professor Furner had been her undergraduate adviser. In the file, was a statement made by the professor, which indicated that he had no idea why the young woman had died: she had seemed to have been a normal, happy person. She had had some financial difficulties, but she seemed to have coped with them. He believed that she had had some kind of job in London during the summer vac, but he had no idea what it was.

The parents of Mary Roberts lived in North Shields, on the northeast coast of England. They stated that they had not wanted their daughter to go to university in London, but that she had been determined to do so. They had urged her to come home during the summer vac, but she had been determined to stay in London. If their daughter had had a boyfriend she had not made them aware of the fact. They had no idea what could have happened to her. They said that ever since Mary had gone off to London they had had little contact with her; they had little idea about what she had been doing during the summer that she had stayed in London.

The deaths of Veronica Blanchard and Mary Roberts had at least two features in common: firstly, both had had sexual intercourse with the same man. Probably the two young women had been murdered by him also. However, it was thought that a second feature common to the two deaths would be the one most likely to provide a successful conclusion to the investigation: the two young women studied mathematics at Queen Mary and Westfield College. Consequently, Liz had to agree with DCI Lawrence; the answer to the question of why and how Veronica Blanchard and Mary Roberts had died most likely would be found by an investigation centred on QMW.

# Chapter Fourteen

**H**aving familiarised herself with the case in which she would be involved during her stay with the Mile End police, Liz went to see Chief Inspector Lawrence to discuss the 'mechanics' of her task. She assumed that she would become a mature student in the mathematics department; at 26 it was unlikely that she could be mistaken for a typical undergraduate. Nonetheless, Liz was aware that whatever was to happen would have to happen quickly; the autumn term at Queen Mary was about to commence.

When she went to speak to DCI Lawrence, Liz discovered that he was not in his office. A little later she was informed that he had been called away from the station, unexpectedly. She was told to wait; the chief inspector intended to be back at the station by mid-afternoon. She returned to the detectives' room to review once again the written reports on the deaths of the two QMW undergraduates.

As late afternoon approached, and still there was no sign of the man, Liz decided to make her way home early. First she would walk over to QMW and 'scout out' the territory. Although she was fairly familiar with the QMW campus, she wished to renew her acquaintance with the place. Then, because she would be getting home early for a change, she thought that she would stop at a little market not far from her flat and do some shopping. Since Julia had gone to Cambridge to live, Liz had not had a decently-cooked meal.

Tonight she would take the time to prepare something, and, even better, she would have a glass or two of wine.

\* \* \*

That evening, feeling only slightly tipsy after consuming two glasses of red wine  with the pepper steak that she had prepared for herself, Liz seated herself in the front room of her flat, thinking that she would watch the six-o'clock news on the 'telly'.  Usually, she was home much too late to do that, and by the time the later news came on, she was in bed.  She had resisted the temptation to have a third glass of wine, knowing that that would make her feel terrible when she awoke the following morning.  Besides, she was looking forward to a nice hot bath and a long session reading a paperback: a detective story that she had bought that day in the shop at QMW.

The presence of fictional works in the QMW bookshop had surprised her; she thought that the shop would devote itself to academic books.  Obviously, QMW students occasionally lifted their eyes above their studies long enough to relax with a bit of fiction.

Liz wasn't fond of most detective stories, finding herself being irritated by the ease with which the central figures, almost all of them ever-so-heroic-males, solved really complex mysteries.  She couldn't help but contrast the reality depicted by fiction with the reality that she encountered daily.  However, the book that she had bought was one of a series which was different, if, perhaps, equally far fetched. The main human character of the story seemed to her to be a bit thick, and not particularly heroic.  On his own, very likely he never would solve any crimes.  However, he owned a pair of Siamese cats who, by their various actions, solved the crimes for their master. Liz had thought that the stories were well written and looked forward to the publication of each new episode, especially when it came out in paperback.

She had not got far into the first chapter of her purchase when the wine that she had drunk that evening exerted the effect it usually had on her: she had fallen asleep.

\* \* \*

Liz had no idea how long she had been sleeping when the telephone beside her bed awakened her with its ringing. It was her mum wanting to give Liz an account of how well Julia was doing. Liz was pleased to hear that her mum still was enthusiastic about the young woman living with her.

Audrey said that Julia was a wonderful girl, saying, "the sweet thing went straight out and got herself a part-time job so she would be less of a financial burden. You'll never guess what's she's doing, Elisabeth? She's delivering papers in the morning for the local newsagent. He said that he was as pleased as punch when Julia had asked him about it after seeing the card he had put in the shop window. He had been unable to find anyone for the morning and was doing that round himself."

"Also, Julia might not have to go to the sixth-form college. I didn't understand completely what she told me, but it involved the Mozambique High Commission. The college said that she should visit there and try to get them to confirm that she finished secondary school in that country. If she could do that she might be eligible to enter university straight away. Anyway, Elisabeth, what I'm ringing about is to ask you if Julia could come and stay with you for a few days whilst she sorts herself out with the Mozambique High Commission which is in London someplace. Mister Nardun, the newsagent, says that he will do her newspaper round whilst she's away."

After Liz had rung off she realised that she really had missed having Julia living with her. Unfortunately, the 'phone call from her mum had got Liz to thinking about the loneliness of her life; those thoughts had got her thinking about Pat. She thought that perhaps she should get in touch with her friend to see if they could get together some time in the not-too-distant future. Liz had rung Pat twice during the visit to Cambridge when she had taken Julia up there, but the only response she had got was from an answering machine.

She looked again at the clock, seeing that it was well past midnight. However, she knew that she might forget if she left it until the following day to contact her friend. After several rings, an answering machine began to recite a familiar message. After the tone, Liz identified herself and was starting to recite the message she intended to deliver when a sleep-laden voice came on the line: "Hi, Lizzie, it's about time you remembered that your best friend would like to hear from you every now and again!" Liz recognised her friend's tone of mock hurt, so she did as she usually did and ignored it. Almost half an hour later, Liz rang off, lying back on her pillow with a smile on her face and thinking, "there's nothing like a chat with Pat to give me a lift."

At first, Liz had worried slightly about the rather intimate nature of some of Pat's statements, thinking that Pat's husband, Roger would be able to hear. However, when Liz asked how Roger was, her friend had said that he wasn't there; he had gone to Peterborough on business.

Pat had been insistent that Liz and she should "get together" soon. Liz promised faithfully that it would not be long before she would come to Cambridge. She would ring Pat and leave a message on her answer 'phone when she knew when that would be.

After speaking with Pat, Liz found it difficult to get back to sleep. She kept thinking about her friend, and what they had meant to each other over the years. One of the things that Pat had said during their telephone conversation had brought tears to Liz's eyes: "it's taken me a long time to learn it, but I know now that there was only one person in the whole world who I know I can always depend on; that's you, Lizzie. I know that I'm not a very good friend to you. I married Roger when I knew that I didn't love him. I don't know why I started screwing him; I didn't even like it very much. However, as the two of us were going at it, I usually tried to pretend that it was you. I know that I shouldn't have married him, but I thought that it would be better for our baby to have a father. Now, however, I know that he and I aren't really compatible. I don't hate him; in fact I still like him. However, I don't love him, and I'm pretty sure that he feels pretty much the same about me. He's very good with Andrew, though. I don't know what to do, Liz; except I don't ever want you to give up on me, but stay my friend. Some day I will grow up; I promise." Liz had been sincere when, with tears in her eyes, she had promised Pat that they would remain close, always.

Thoughts of Pat reminded Liz once more that she was a very lonely person. The number of people in the world with whom she had been able to form a close friendship was just three: Pat, of course, Pat; always Pat. Then there was Reg. She knew that she loved Reg. In fact, the last few times she had been with him she had found herself wondering what it would be like to make love to him. She knew that he would be shocked at the very idea of such a thing; he was such a decent man. Nevertheless, that had not stopped her from thinking about it.

Finally, there was Lydia Mussett. Her friendship with Lydia had resulted in brief sexual encounters from time to time. Liz had wanted to continue them, but she knew that she had to agree with her friend: as serving police officers, they could not afford to have a prolonged love affair, either with each other or with other women.

Liz was well aware that there was a notable absence from her list; that was Julia. Ever since the young woman had left to go to Cambridge, Liz had agonised over her feelings for her. She had concluded that they were not love. She had become aroused by the sight of Julia's particularly lovely body and, because the young woman was willing, she had made love with her. However, she was pretty sure that her feelings for Julia were not love. Whether or not they could mature into that kind of feeling, she had no idea.

Liz knew that she was indulging in self pity, but she felt that her life lacked wholeness because she had no one to whom she could turn when she felt sad. She hated herself for doing it, but she began to cry. Her rational self tried to think of something to deflect the self pity, finally settling on thoughts of her childhood. In those days, when she was sad, she would talk to whatever animal she had at the time as a pet. Perhaps now it would be wise of her to acquire a pet. Would she be happy lavishing her love on some poor, dumb creature? Those thoughts then turned to the complications to her life that a pet would bring. Whenever she was away from home, she would have to be certain that it would be properly looked after. She knew of no way that she could do that. Finally she recognised the thought that she knew that she had been attempting to avoid. She was far too selfish to share her life with another being, either human or animal. She was sure that the only human for whom she would willingly alter her life style would have to be one of the three persons who now formed the total of her close friends: Pat, Reg or Lydia.

* * *

Julia arrived at the Mile End police station after her visit to the Mozambique High Commission, having followed Liz's instructions on how to get there. She told Liz that her business in London had not been completed; she asked if she could stay with Liz until it was completed. She said that she had to return to the High Commission the following day and, possibly, the day after also. She whispered to Liz, "I'm happy about having to go back into London because that means that I can stay with you until I go back to Cambridge." Liz smiled, but she made no reply. This time, she was determined to keep her relationship with Julia on a strictly platonic level.

Once the two women arrived at Liz's flat they had a 'quickie' meal that included a bottle of white wine. When it was time for bed, the two women went to Liz's bedroom where Julia, without hesitation, removed all of her clothing, revealing her lovely figure. Liz's resolve disappeared. She took Julia into her arms, and the first actions of the two women was a period of passionate kissing. Inevitably that led to other actions in which Liz had vowed that she would not participate with Julia.

Afterwards, as Liz was lying awake, staring into the night, she wondered if she ever would be able to resist her lustful feelings. She tried to blame Julia, who had initiated their contact that evening. Once they had got into bed, Julia had put herself in Liz's arms at once, telling Liz that she had missed her so. Then Julia had kissed Liz with a passion that was driven by lust also, thrusting her hand between Liz's legs and rather roughly manipulating her clitoris. However, it was when Julia placed her mouth where her hand had been, that all of Liz's self-imposed restraint had vanished. Their love making had got so vigorous that Liz was sure that she must be bleeding from a place where Julia had bitten her.

Fortunately for Liz's resolution, Julia's business at the Mozambique High Commission was completed the following day. Liz ignored hints made by Julia that she might stay in London with Liz for a few more nights.

Although Liz felt disappointment when Julia went back to Cambridge, upon reflection, she knew that the departure of her friend was a good thing.

# Chapter Fifteen

The Principal of Queen Mary and Westfield College turned out to be the same man that Liz had met when she first posed undercover at the institution four years earlier. He was different from most university officials whom Liz had encountered in the past. He was actually quite jovial. He welcomed Liz into his rather elegant office on the first floor of a building that overlooked the Mile End Road, saying how delighted he was to see her again. She was doubtful that he actually had remembered her from before, but she said nothing.

It was obvious that the principal was used to putting people at their ease, welcoming Liz with a little story about himself. He said that when the letter from the Metropolitan Police had been handed to him by his secretary, and he saw that it had been marked, "confidential," it had given him quite a start. He had thought that his past had caught up with him. "When I was a youngster I nicked a ball-point pen from Woolworth's. It was at a time when the pens had just come out and they were relatively expensive. I thought that my life wouldn't be complete unless I was the first person amongst me and my chums to possess one."

"However, once I read over the letter from Detective Chief Inspector Lawrence, I realised that I could rest easy, if perhaps a bit guiltily, for awhile longer! Although I must not rest too easily, remembering that the attractive young lady before me is a police officer to whom I've just revealed my criminal past!" Liz just smiled at the principal; not really knowing what to say.

The principal quickly got serious, saying that the reason for Liz's presence at the college was a matter of deep sadness for him; the college had lost two fine, young women. He said that when the body of Veronica Blanchard had been found, and it had appeared that she had killed herself, he had been profoundly depressed. "I have never been able to understand why young persons would wish to end their own lives. However, now that we know that the Veronica and, more recently, Mary Roberts, were victims of some kind of madman, it doesn't make it any easier to understand, but at least it is explicable."

He went on to say that he understood what the intention of the Metropolitan Police was in placing Liz at the college, and he would co-operate in every way that he could. He said that the main problem would be to insert Liz into the undergraduate programme in mathematics without questions being asked. "The primary difficulty is that I have been asked to keep all of this strictly confidential. In fact, even my secretary doesn't know about it, yet. That means that we shall have to come up with an excuse for you being here that will sound plausible to everyone you will encounter, but especially the lecturers in the mathematics department, including the head of the department. That will be the difficult thing."

"According to Detective Chief Inspector Lawrence, you have a first-class degree in mathematics from King's College, so that, at least, will make things easier. You shouldn't have any problems convincing the experts that you know a thing or two about mathematics. Anyway, Sergeant Andresen, as usual, I am doing all of the talking. Let me know what approach you think that you might wish to make during your time here."

Liz said that both of the dead women would have been starting their third and final year at QMW. Therefore, she thought that if it would be possible she should be placed in the third year programme. "I know that it isn't usual for students to transfer from one university to another in the UK, but I assume that it can be done." The principal said that she was right in saying that transfers weren't common, but it was not unknown. "Probably the greatest difficulty will be to find a university or college where the mathematics degree programmes are comparable to ours with respect to courses offered and B.Sc. requirements; that sort of thing."

"That isn't the only problem, of course. You may not know it, but the university world is a relatively small one. Mathematicians from Queen Mary can be expected to have friends and acquaintances in many other mathematics departments, not only in the UK, but abroad. Therefore, if you become a student here, having transferred from university X, your are as likely as not to be asked, 'ah, you're from university X, how did you get on there with my friend, Professor Smithers'? We shall have to be careful to give you a background that not only is plausible, but which can't be exposed easily. I think we can make some use of your age. We could have you returning to complete a degree that you interrupted some time ago."

"Forgive me for asking, but how old are you Sergeant Andresen?" When Liz told him he said, "well, let us say that you completed the first two years of your course at the age of twenty and then you got yourself a job working in London. Now you wish to return to university and complete your degree. How does that sound?" Liz said that she thought that it sounded most plausible to her.

"OK, we've got about a fortnight until the start of the autumn semester. I shall have a word with the academic registrar about you, and ask her to make up a letter to be sent to the mathematics department. They, of course, will have the final say on whether or not you're accepted here to read mathematics. However, that department has a chronic shortage of undergraduate students, so I think that they will be happy to see you come." "Unfortunately, I shall have to inform the registrar about your real identity because it will be her department that will approve the courses you will have taken during your two years at university. She is a rather proper lady, but I am sure there will be no problem getting her to go along with us in providing cover for you. So far, there has been no reason to inform the head of the mathematics of your true identity. However, if someone on his staff becomes suspicious of you, we shall have to think again. Nonetheless, we shall cope with that situation should it arise."

\* \* \*

Several days after Liz's visit to QMW she began her duties undercover officially. Until her assignment ended, she was to have only as much physical contact with the police as was necessary. However, she was to make a verbal report regularly. For the most part, that was to be done by telephone, but if that was not possible she was to use her radio transceiver. She was never knowingly to put herself in a dangerous position unless she had called for and received backup. In short, she was to play the rôle of a typical university student. Of course, very few university students lived in a flat on their own which was only a few tube stops away from the institution that they were attending.

Liz had got herself a prospectus for Queen Mary and Westfield College during her visit there to see the principal. She looked over the courses on offer for third-year undergraduates, most of which she recognised from her own studies as an undergraduate.

She rang her mum, and was relieved to find that Audrey had kept all of the reference books and notes that Liz had accumulated during the three years she had spent at King's College, London, studying for a B. Sc. in mathematics. Audrey said that all of Liz's "stuff" was stored in two large boxes in the loft space of her house. Liz made plans to visit Cambridge and sort through the notes, bringing back to London all of those that would be relevant to the studies she was soon to commence.

Also, Liz had got a letter from the principal of QMW telling her that the registrar of the college had had a letter from the mathematics department accepting her into the third year of the undergraduate programme in mathematics. The principle had included a photocopy of the letter that had been sent by the registrar to the director of admissions of the mathematics department, so that Liz would know the bases upon which she was accepted by that department.

The letter described a young woman, Miss Elisabeth Andresen, who had completed two years of the undergraduate mathematics course at Anglia Polytechnic University in Cambridge before she interrupted her studies for personal reasons. The letter went on: "subsequently, she moved to London and has been working here ever since. Now, she wishes to return to university to complete the requirements for a B.Sc. in mathematics. She has applied to Queen Mary and Westfield College for admission. Her qualifications have been checked and confirmed by this office. You will be pleased to know that Miss Andresen is a high achiever, having obtained no mark less than 95% on the examinations of her first two years of undergraduate work. It is hoped that the department of mathematics will be able to find a place in their undergraduate programme for such an able student."

In his brief reply to the registrar's letter, the director of admissions for mathematics said that his department would be pleased to welcome Miss Andresen as a third-year student.

In his letter to Liz, the principal explained that both he and the registrar thought it best not to stray further from the truth than necessary in setting up a false identity for Liz. He said that both he and the registrar had been pleased to have been able to tell the truth about Liz's academic performance when she was an undergraduate. He closed the letter by wishing her luck in her investigation, and he expressed his hopes that the results would not implicate anyone from the college. Liz thought over the closing sentences of the principal's letter. It seemed to her illogical that the deaths of the two young women had not been, in some way, connected with their status as undergraduates at Queen Mary and Westfield College.

\* \* \*

As Liz sat on the train taking her to Cambridge, she remembered something that had worried her slightly the previous evening when she had spoken to her mum on the telephone. Audrey had very little to say about Julia. To Liz's query as to how the young woman was getting on, her mum had been less than enthusiastic, saying that Julia was not often at home. Liz knew that her mother was prone to get 'downs' on people who did something to displease her; she hoped that that was not the case with Julia so soon after the young woman had begun to live with Audrey.

When the taxi drew up to her mum's house, Julia and Audrey were at the front door to welcome her. As far as she could determine from the way they treated each other during the first few minutes after Liz's arrival, the two women seemed to be getting on well together. Audrey said that she had decided that they would have a treat on the evening of Liz's arrival: she would take all of them to the pub where they would have some food and spend the evening chatting. Liz noticed that a slight grimace come over Julia's face when Audrey made her offer, and she wondered if perhaps her mum hadn't begun to frequent the pub once more. Liz didn't really want to go out that evening, but she could see that her mum had very little food in the house, so it would be impossible for either she or Julia to cook a meal.

It had been Liz's understanding that one of the reasons for Julia to live with Audrey would be to help in looking after the older woman's requirements. However, that appeared not to be the case. The Julia that Liz thought that she knew had not seemed like a person who would be remiss in her duties. She resolved that during the evening, in the pub, if the opportunity arose, she would get Julia aside, and question her about whether or not there was something wrong.

That evening, it became obvious to Liz that Audrey had once again begun to drink to excess. Whilst Liz and Julia each nursed a glass of wine, Audrey had made her way through two pints of bitter and had gone back to the bar to get a third.

Once Audrey had gone, Liz asked Julia whether or not her mother behaved all of the time in the way that she was behaving that evening. Julia said that she did not know what to do. "Your mother doesn't go to the pub, but she has been bringing home drink from a local shop, and she has quite a lot each night. When I first came to live with her she would give me money with which to buy food, but now when I ask her, she tells me that she doesn't have any money. I am spending the money that I earn from my paper round. Mister Nardun has been very kind and has let me take part of the afternoon delivery of papers, but I won't be able to do that once term begins and I have to attend classes."

Liz looked up to see her mum approaching them, so she told Julia that they would talk about it later.

After Audrey had seated herself at the table and had proceeded straight away to occupy herself with her drink, Liz, asked Julia, "what have you decided about your schooling? I've not heard anything about that since mum told me that you might be able to go to university." Julia said, "oh, Liz, it's wonderful! The Department of Education sent me a letter telling me that my qualifications had been recognised by them as equivalent to United Kingdom qualifications!

"Then I took the letter to one of the local universities, Anglia Polytechnic, and showed it to them, asking if I could do a course to become a teacher. A very nice lady there said that they did not do teacher training, especially of the type that I wanted which was to teach little children. They said that I could read one of the subjects that they taught and then go someplace else to earn what she called a PGCE or postgraduate certificate of education. I didn't think I wanted to do that, so they told me that I should go see someone at another place: Homerton College. The lady said that Homerton was primarily a teacher's training college."

"However, when I went there they didn't seem to be very happy to see me. Finally, I went back to Anglia Poly where I am going to start next week. I didn't know what I wanted to do, but finally I opted for something called sociology and anthropology. It sounded interesting, but I don't know anything about it."

It took all of Liz's efforts to persuade her mum not to have another beer and to go home with Julia and her. Audrey was sufficiently upset at being deprived of another drink that she wouldn't speak to either of her two companions as the three women walked to her house. Once Audrey got home she went straight to bed after bidding Liz and Julia goodnight in a rather grumpy voice.

Once Audrey was gone, Julia broke down saying that she was frightened about what was going to happen. She said that Audrey would not listen to her and "she gets angry with me all of the time. I don't know what I can do." Liz told Julia that she would have a word with Audrey in the morning; she was sure that her mum was just going through a bad patch. It was obvious to Liz that Julia, also, was upset; the two women talked for a short time, and then Julia excused herself and went to bed. The only gesture the young woman made that would remind them of their former close relationship was a brief kiss on the lips delivered by Julia to Liz.

Julia awakened very early in the morning in order to get up and do her paper round, awakening Liz, who was sleeping on the sofa bed in the sitting room. Liz made breakfast for herself and Julia, inviting Audrey to join them. Audrey refused, but she came down to the kitchen a few minutes after Julia had left. It was then that Liz began her campaign to make her mother see sense with respect to her young house guest.

Audrey went on the attack immediately, saying that Julia had been a disappointment to her. "She only ever wants to do what she wants; she never wants to do what I want." Liz asked about the drinking, knowing that Audrey could not deny it because the evidence was overloading the waste bin in the kitchen and the dustbin on the back porch. Audrey said that she only drank a small amount, and that Julia was a liar if she said otherwise.

Liz said that she was going to change the way that she sent money every month to help Audrey with the extra expense of supporting Julia. "From now on, mum, I will send the money directly to Julia. I will take her into town today and help her open a bank account. I can trust Julia to make certain that you are fed properly, but I can't seem to trust you to make certain that both you and she are fed properly. She is just starting a university course, mum; she really has no need to worry about you all of the time."

Audrey's face took on the 'poor little me' look that Liz knew well, telling Liz that she would regret her harsh words. Then she surprised Liz by saying, "you don't have to go to the trouble of opening another bank account. I will take care of Julia, you don't have to worry. I'll stop drinking so much; I know it's bad for me." Liz went to her mum and, for the first time for as long as she could remember, she gave Audrey a warm hug. Audrey said that she was sorry that she had 'slipped off the wagon', but the responsibility of looking after Julia just seemed to have got to her. She knew that she would do better in the future. "I will take up my weaving again; I haven't done that in a long time."

# Chapter Sixteen

Liz felt considerably older than her years as she stood in the large hall on the Queen Mary and Westfield College campus on the day that she registered for classes. All of the students who were milling around in the hall appeared to be so much younger than she. The students were endeavouring to get the necessary paperwork to complete the registration process. Liz had been assigned an undergraduate advisor, a Dr Boalt, whom she was supposed to meet sometime during the morning of registration.

Liz was quite impressed with the identity with which she had been supplied. The fact that she was born and grew up in Cambridge helped. Even if she was unfamiliar with Anglia Polytechnic University, at the very least she could answer most questions about the city itself.

Liz was pleased that a part of the registration materials that she had been given was a map of the QMW campus. Despite her previous experience at the school, she had only a vague idea where the mathematics department was located. The map made the journey from the registration hall to mathematics quite straightforward. Although her appointment with her adviser was for quarter past eleven, she found a queue seated outside of his office. She seated herself in a vacant chair next to a young man who was talking to another young man seated next to him. When a pause came in the men's conversation, one of them turned and extended his hand, saying, "hi, I'm Jeff Banks. You're new, aren't you?"

Liz introduced herself and explained that she was returning to university after a hiatus of a few years.

Liz asked Jeff why it was that it was necessary to see Dr Boalt. He explained about the adviser system in operation in the department, telling her that Dr Boalt was "a good bloke;" one of the better advisers in the department. Liz thought that she would mention Professor Furner's name to see what his reputation in the department was: she said, the only person in the department whose name was familiar to her was a Professor Furner. Jeff looked askance saying, "oh, he's OK, I suppose. As far as I've heard he has one of the better international reputations because of his work on numbers theory, but personally, he seems to be a bit arrogant. Also, you being female, it may be just as well that Boalt is your adviser; ol' Furner has a bit of a reputation, if you know what I mean."

Liz didn't wish to explore the subject of the professor any further, but she was interested to hear Jeff Banks' remarks. She remembered the comment that her colleague, Dai Morgan, had written in his notes of an interview of Professor Furner. Dai had said that the professor was a bit of an "elusive" character. Liz thought that he certainly would be one of the people on whom she would keep a watch.

Finally, the queue had diminished to the point where only she and Jeff Banks remained, and then Jeff's turn came. He was in Dr Boalt's office for only a few minutes, and then he came out again, motioning to Liz to enter.

Jeff Banks had been right. Doctor Boalt, who insisted that she call him Ron, short for Myron, proved to be a very personable young man, who, Liz guessed, was not too much older than she. He opened the conversation by telling her that he had been pleased when he had looked over her qualifications: he was sure that she would do well at QMW. He asked her about her personal background, saying that he was unfamiliar with Anglia Polytechnic University, but that he had visited Cambridge many times.

Liz was happy that she had reviewed written work done and several of the texts read during her undergraduate course in maths at King's College. Doctor Boalt outlined the course that she would follow during her year at QMW. During the interview he had used several mathematical terms that she had forgotten since taking her degree. However, her recent review had recalled them to mind. Finally, he explained that his job was to act as an adviser to her; that included helping her with any personal problems as far as he was able.

He ended the interview by saying that Jeff Banks had told him that several of the third-year students were meeting in the JCR bar; if she planned to go, undoubtedly he would see her there.

\* \* \*

The junior common room bar was packed with people, but almost the first person she encountered when she entered was Dr Boalt, who said that he had just got there himself. He told Liz that he would be pleased to buy her a drink, and asked what she would like. When Liz told him that she would like a glass of dry, white, wine if they had it, he said that he was sure that they did, and that he would bring it to her. He pointed to a crowd of undergraduates at one side of the large room, saying that most of that group were mathematicians. He said as far as he could see, most of the third years were there. Then Dr Boalt went off telling her that it would take a little while for him to 'battle his way' through the crowd to get to the bar.

As Liz walked toward the crowd of students, she recognised Jeff Banks who motioned to her to come over to
where he was. He introduced her to members of the group
of which he was one; each of them said, "hi," shook her hand
and recited their first name. Liz knew that she never would
remember all of the names, but she hoped that she would
learn them in due course as she encountered the young
men and women in her classes. Jeff asked if she was OK for
something to drink and Liz told him that Dr Boalt was taking care of it. Jeff winked at her and said, "Ron is one bloke
you won't have to worry about. However, this department
seems to have its fair share of randy old geezers." Then he
looked up and whispered, "speaking of randy old geezers..."
Liz looked where Jeff was looking and saw a middle-aged
man approaching the group of mathematicians, smiling and
saying "hello" to some of them. Liz asked, "who's that?"
Jeff whispered, "that's Professor Furner. I'm a bit surprised
to see him here. I should have thought that he would be
down at registration looking over the new crop of first-year
women. He's incorrigible!"

At that point Dr Boalt returned, giving Liz a glass of wine
and saying, "ah, Rob's here; come over and meet Professor
Furner. He teaches algebraic topology, which you will be
taking this year." Contrary to the impression gained by her
colleague, Dai Morgan, Professor Furner seemed to Liz to
be quite charming. He said that he had been to Cambridge
many times and had good friends in the Faculty of Mathematics at the university. However, he was not even aware that
there was another university in the city. Liz was relieved to
hear that; he wouldn't be asking her any embarrassing questions. As their conversation was slowing, she noticed that
she had lost the professor's attention after he had winked

and smiled at someone who was standing behind her. A short time later, he ended their conversation telling her that he looked forward to seeing her in his classes. Then he went off to speak to a young woman, obviously an undergraduate, with whom he held an animated conversation.

At home that evening, Liz reviewed her first day as a 'mature student' at QMW. She thought that it had been fairly productive with respect to the police investigation. She had had a chance to speak to one of the possible candidates for the killer of the young women who had been found in the Grand Union Canal. The candidate, Professor Furner, seemed to be more than usually interested in young females. Liz didn't think that either his appearance or personality was particularly attractive, but for some reason he seemed to be popular with his female students. She would try to discover what sort of relationships he might have had with the two dead undergraduates. Obtaining that information very likely would be difficult because it wouldn't be possible to simply ask questions about the dead women without making herself obvious. She could not have known either of them.

As well as observing the activities of Professor Furner, Liz was hoping to be able to identify the young woman with whom one of the dead women, Veronica Blanchard, had been friendly. Liz couldn't be sure that the woman she was seeking was a student in the mathematics department, or, for that matter, that she was a student at all. Liz concluded that there was only one way to proceed with her investigation. She would have to become friendly with as many as possible of her classmates and see what information they were able to divulge unwittingly in the course of conversation.

* * *

Liz's first break came a few days after the start of the autumn semester. One of her lecturer's had set the students a problem on wave theory, giving them a list of several references that had been placed on reserve in the college library. One of the references was in almost constant use, so that Liz had asked to borrow it overnight so that she could take it home with her. That meant that she had to pick it up after five in the afternoon.

She was just leaving the library, having signed out the reference book, when she heard her name called. Liz turned to see one of her classmates, a girl named Kay Trask, who asked her to wait up. Liz stopped until Kay caught up to her, asking if she was going her way. Liz said that she was going to the Mile End tube station to go home.

Kay asked where Liz lived. When Liz told her, she said, "wouldn't you rather get the tube at Stepney Green station? I have to go to Barking, but I won't walk from the college to Mile End anymore, not after what happened to two of my friends. Hasn't anyone told you about that?" Liz asked, "told me what? What happened?" Kay said that the bodies of the two girls had been found in the Grand Union Canal next to the college. She continued, "the police don't seem to doing anything about it, even though it looks like the deaths weren't by suicide as they thought at first. However, just in case there's a madman out there, I'm playing it safe and am not going anywhere near the canal. Why don't you come with me, and then we can walk together. We have to use the same tube line to get home." As she and Kay walked toward the tube station, Liz had no difficulty in getting her classmate to talk about the two students who had died.

Kay Trask said that she hadn't known Veronica Blanchard too well because Veronica was not terribly friendly. "Some of the girls said that they thought that she was gay. She always seemed to be in the company of Michelle Hufton, one of the research students in the department. I read in the papers that they thought that Veronica had killed herself. I remember thinking at the time that that seemed odd because they also said that she had had sexual intercourse just prior to killing herself. I didn't think that anyone would kill themselves immediately after making love. Also, as I said, there were some of us who thought that she was gay. I spoke to Michelle Hufton the other day, and she is still pretty broken up about Veronica. Anyway, now it looks likely that Veronica was murdered."

Kay continued, "a little while before the start of the autumn semester, another girl from QMW, Mary Roberts, was found in the canal. The newspapers said that Mary's death was being treated by the police as suspicious. Well, if Mary's death was suspicious, Veronica's should have been also. Mary and me lived in the same hall of residence then, and I knew her fairly well. She was a friendly, outgoing girl and not the sort to kill herself."

Fortunately, Liz stopped herself before saying that there seemed little doubt that both deaths were 'suspicious' because of the finding of sperm from the same man in both bodies She remembered that that detail: that the same man was involved; had not been released to the public.

Liz had enjoyed her talk with Kay, and was doubly delighted to have the name of the young woman who had been friendly with Veronica Blanchard. She tried to get Kay talking about Professor Furner, but by that time their tube train was entering the Plaistow station, where she would be leaving her classmate. Liz walked quickly to her flat from the tube station, wishing to write up notes of her interview with Kay Trask.

* * *

After her first fortnight as a student at Queen Mary and Westfield College, Liz was more than ever convinced that someone at the college had been responsible for the deaths of Veronica Blanchard and Mary Roberts. Her favourite candidate was Professor Robert Furner. He seemed to be an attraction to young women, of that there was no doubt. However, from Liz's observations of him, there was nothing to indicate that he was using his position to intimidate them into allowing him to seduce them. In fact, Liz had encountered no evidence at all that he was seducing the young women with whom he was so obviously friendly.

She had remarked upon the professor's behaviour when speaking to Kay Trask, but her friend had said only that she thought that he was merely a 'wanker'. "I think that he gets his kicks by 'chatting up' female students, and fondling their bosoms when they will let him, but I don't think that he would try anything beyond that. I remember dancing with him at the party the department had last Christmas. Obviously, he had had a fair amount to drink, which seemed to turn him into an octopus; his hands were everywhere. Just when I'd block one of them, the other would make a grab for my other tit. That happened to every girl that danced with him."

Some days after speaking with Kay Trask, Liz managed to make contact with Michelle Hufton, who, she had seen, sometimes came in to the college library whilst Liz was there. In order to speak to the young woman, Liz would feign ignorance about some aspect of one of the lectures she had attended, asking for Michelle's help. After the young woman would explain whatever it was that Liz had asked about, Liz would engage her in conversation. Those sessions of general conversation always were short-lived; Michelle Hufton was a very introverted young woman, obviously finding it difficult to hold a conversation with a person whom she didn't know well. As yet, Liz had had no opportunity to bring up the subject of Veronica Blanchard's death, when speaking to Miss Hufton. Nevertheless, as she reported to DCI Lawrence after her first month as a student at QMW, she believed that all of the elements were in place for her to discover if there was involvement of a member of the college in the murder of Veronica Blanchard and Mary Roberts.

The idea had entered Liz's head, although she had not acted upon it, that the elaborate plan put in place by the police: that of placing someone undercover in the college, possibly could be short-circuited by a ruse. She had noticed that Professor Furner travelled between his home and the college by car. Also, often during the early evening, she had seen him in the JCR bar talking with students: usually young women. At the same time, it could be seen that he usually had a half-finished pint of lager before him. It would be quite easy for him to be intercepted by the police when leaving the college parking lot after Liz had seen him in the JCR bar. Liz never had observed him long enough to see how much beer he consumed during the time spent in the bar. However, if he thought that he was over the legal limit undoubtedly he would refuse to take a breathalyser test. Consequently, it would be necessary for him to provide a blood sample at a police station. That blood sample then could be analysed to reveal his DNA profile, which then could be compared with the DNA profile of sperm found in the bodies of Veronica Blanchard and Mary Roberts. If they matched, the professor could be arrested on charges of rape and murder and analysis of a legally-obtained blood sample could be substituted for that obtained by the ruse.

Liz realised that her scheme had several drawbacks. The first drawback, and the most obvious, was the assumption that the professor was guilty of the murders. A minor drawback, which would lead only to a waste of police time, was the fact that if the professor drank only a pint or so during his periods in the JCR bar, it would be unlikely that he would refuse to be breathalysed. Consequently, there would be no reason to ask him to provide a blood sample. Finally, she wasn't too sure what would be DCI Lawrence's view of the police taking such a shortcut. She had seen such ruses utilised in fictional detective dramas on television, but she didn't believe that they were common practice. She concluded that she would wait a while longer to see how well legal methods served the police enquiries before resorting to more dubious procedures.

# Chapter Seventeen

For as long as Liz could remember her mother had been a gloomy person. At one time, Liz had assumed that her mum suffered from depression. She had discussed that assumption with Audrey's GP. He had said that he recognised that Audrey seemed to have a rather depressive personality. However, he didn't believe that she exhibited the usual signs of clinical depression: sleeplessness and agitation when things weren't going her way. He thought that her apparent inability to derive pleasure from her life was just a normal attribute of Audrey's personality. He had told Liz that he would prescribe an anti-depressant drug if her mother wished, but he thought it wouldn't have much benefit.

Liz knew that her mum would get angry were she to discover that her personal problems were discussed with a person whom she regarded as a stranger. It said something for Audrey's personality that she would categorise her GP as a stranger.

\* \* \*

Late one evening Liz received a telephone call from a very distressed Julia Gomes; she said that she was ringing from a public call box and hadn't much money on her. Liz took the number from which Julia was calling and rang her back. She was surprised that Julia had so little money because each month Liz had had transferred an amount into her mum's bank account which was supposed to be adequate to cover the added expense to her mum of having Julia living with her. Furthermore, she knew that Julia had continued her morning paper round which provided the young woman with a small income of her own.

Julia told Liz that Audrey was drinking again, and she didn't know what to do about it. "I have used up all of my own money buying food for the two of us; she simply refuses to make a contribution, accusing me of spending it on myself."

The news that Julia related quite upset Liz; it was obvious that Audrey was prepared to lie rather than have her daughter find out that she had begun drinking again. Liz had spoken on the 'phone to Audrey at least twice since her mum's promise to cease drinking. Each time, her mum had assured Liz that she and Julia were getting along fine, and that she was happy to have the young woman in the house. She had told Liz that having Julia there was like having a daughter again.

During the telephone call, Julia got quite emotional, saying that she didn't really know how to approach Audrey; "if I say the wrong thing to her she gets very angry. Two times she locked me out of the house, and I had to ask my friend from the university to let me stay with her for the night. I wonder, Liz, if I shouldn't give up my idea of going to university and get myself a job, instead. I am sure that I have not done well in my studies, so far." Liz said, "try not to be discouraged, Julia; I'll try to sort something out with mum. I'm afraid that I can't get away from here until tomorrow, but I'll come up on the train late tomorrow afternoon, so I'll see you then. I'm sorry that my mum is being such a bloody nuisance, but don't you even think about giving up your university course. We'll sort something out; don't worry."

After Liz rang off, her first impulse was to ring her mum and give her an earful. However, she knew what her mum's response would be: Julia would become the recipient of the full effects of Audrey's anger.

* * *

It was late evening, and a very drunk Audrey fumbled with the lock on the front door of her house as her daughter stood outside on the doorstep having arrived by taxi a few minutes earlier. Liz had had to ring the doorbell of her mum's house because, in her rush to get away from London, she had left her key in her flat. She had meant to arrive in Cambridge much earlier, but she had been delayed in London.

Through the door, Liz could hear her mother whining that she couldn't seem to cope "with this damn thing." Then Liz heard her mother shout, "Julia, get off your lazy arse and get down here to see who's at the door!" A few minutes later the door was opened. When she saw who it was, Julia gave Liz a hug and a kiss, telling her how glad she was to see her.

Liz went into the house, seeing that her mum had gone into the front room and had seated herself before the television; she didn't even look up until Liz was well into the room. Then her look was one of shock, and she blurted out, "what are you doing here; why didn't you tell me that you were coming?" Liz walked over to her mum, bending to give her a kiss on the cheek, saying, "I thought that I would give you a surprise. I've come to spend a day or so with you and Julia. How have you been keeping, mum?" Julia, who had been standing in the hallway, asked Liz if she would like a cup of coffee. Liz said that she would love one. When Julia asked Audrey the same question, there was no reply. Julia went into the kitchen, and Liz sat down next to her mum. She noticed that on the low table in front of the settee were three beer bottles, two of which appeared to be empty.

Julia served the coffee along with a sweet that Liz couldn't identify; when she asked what it was, Julia called it by its Mozambican name. Before Liz could comment further, Audrey said, slurring her words, "she's always serving that foreign rubbish!" Liz said, "mum; you don't really mean that. The cake is delicious, you should try it."

Audrey said nothing more whilst Liz and Julia talked, the young woman telling Liz all about the course that she was taking at university. As they spoke, Audrey sat slouched over on the settee occasionally taking a swallow of beer. When the third bottle was emptied, Audrey went to the kitchen, returning with another. Liz resisted the impulse to say something, deciding that it could wait until morning.

Not much later, Audrey rose and said that she was off to bed because it appeared that no one wanted to talk to her. Saying nothing more, she picked up the empty bottles on the table and took them into the kitchen. Then she went slowly up the stairs to her bed with both Liz and Julia watching her.

Once she was certain that Audrey was in her bedroom with the door closed, Liz told Julia that since the telephone conversation that they had had she had been doing some thinking about Julia's position. She had decided that she would have Julia open a bank account into which she would transfer the same amount of money each month as she had transferred into her mother's account. "I'm sure that that procedure won't solve all of the problems, but at least it should prevent my mother from drinking up the housekeeping money. I know that mum has been abusive toward you, but..." Julia interrupted to say that that happened only when Audrey had had too much to drink. Liz continued, "well maybe if she isn't able to spend the money I give you on booze, she won't get drunk so often. I really don't know what more I can do, Julia. I don't want you to have to quit your course at university. Also, I think that you shouldn't have to put up with my mum's drunken behaviour. Let's try it with you taking control of the housekeeping money and see how it goes. If that doesn't work, we'll have to try something else. In the morning, we'll go into town; I have a friend who works in one of the banks. I'm sure that she will help us set up a current account for you."

After they had finished speaking about Audrey, and Julia's problems with her, Liz suggested that the two of them should be getting to bed; they had quite a lot to do in the morning, because Liz had to return to London in the afternoon. She had to prepare for her classes at QMW the following day. It was obvious from the way that Julia looked at Liz that the young woman wished to continue the intimacy that they had enjoyed on previous occasions. Liz would have liked to have done so also; she found it hard to resist the allure of Julia's beauty and the loveliness of her body. However, Liz was determined to maintain her resolution that no more would she engage in casual sex. She liked Julia very much and wished her well, but she did not love the young woman. Consequently, she pretended that she had not detected the signals that her friend was sending.

The following morning, Liz was the first to awaken. She had not had a comfortable night on the sofa bed, whose mattress was lumpy and sagged in the middle. Also, she had lain awake for a long time wondering what she could do about her mum. She knew Audrey well enough to know that she would resent the move that Liz was about to make: putting Julia in charge of the housekeeping. However, there seemed to be no other way. Also, Liz had wished to get up early so to ring Pat before her friend went off to work at her bank. Liz would depend upon Pat to smooth the way for Julia to have her own bank account.

Liz wondered what she was doing wrong in her relationships with her friends. When she rang Pat, her friend spent the first ten minutes of the telephone conversation telling Liz off, saying, "why didn't you tell me you were coming up to Cambridge; I'd have arranged to have you over for a meal!" Liz wanted to explain the reasons for her visit and why it was so brief, but by the time an opportunity came: a pause in Pat's complaint; Audrey had entered the room. She stood by Liz, waiting to say something. Liz told Pat that she would explain everything when they met during the morning.

After Liz had put the 'phone down, she had to listen to her mum's apology for her behaviour the previous evening. Liz told her mum that the person to whom she really should apologise was Julia. Audrey patently was prepared to be very contrite because she admitted that, of late, she had treated Julia badly. She said that she would do better in the future. She said, also, that she knew that she shouldn't drink so much, but it seemed to help her to forget her loneliness when she came home in the evening from work. "Ever since your grandmother died, Elisabeth, I've had no one, and I have been very lonely. I know that you enjoy your work in London, but it would be so much better for me if you could work in Cambridge."

Liz purposefully left Julia out of the discussion that she was having with her mother. She hoped that when the young woman assumed her rôle in taking over part of the financial responsibility for the household, that Audrey's drinking problem would be lessened. The amount that Audrey earned in her full-time job was insufficient to support more than modest expenditure for alcoholic drinks, even assuming that Liz's mum made no contribution toward the housekeeping.

\* \* \*

Liz was pleased to get back to her flat in Plaistow and away from the stress of dealing with her mum's drinking problems and the smoothing of Pat's 'ruffled feathers'. With Pat's help, Julia had opened a current account at the bank, and Liz had deposited a cheque in that account which covered the first month's housekeeping money for Julia and Audrey. Liz would have to go into her bank in London in a few days time to alter an existing arrangement so that money would be transferred automatically to Julia's account instead of that of her mother. After they concluded their business, Pat offered to take everyone to a local pub for lunch. Liz wanted to say that she really had to be getting back to London, but she knew what Pat's reaction would be to that.

It was patently obvious during the meal that Pat was quite attracted to Julia. Most of her conversation was directed toward the young woman. At one point, Julia went to the loo. After she had left the table and was out of earshot Pat exclaimed, "she's gorgeous, Liz; where did you meet her? Ooh, it's all I can do to keep my hands to myself." Liz knew that Pat was attracted to women, but never before had her friend expressed herself quite so openly. Liz explained some of the background of the young woman, but she left out details that were only Julia's business.

As the three women parted after the pub meal, Pat issued an invitation to Julia to visit her whenever she liked, giving the young woman her business card and scribbling her home address on the back. As Liz and Julia walked toward their respective destinations, Julia going toward Anglia Polytechnic University and Liz going toward the train station, they could accompany each other for a time. Liz had told Julia that she was sure that the new arrangement with the housekeeping money would make a big difference to Audrey's behaviour. Although Julia had stated that she was sure that Liz was right, it was obvious that her words didn't carry much conviction in her own mind.

# Chapter Eighteen

It was late afternoon. Liz was seated by herself in the bar of the Junior Common Room at QMW, sipping a glass of wine that she had bought almost an hour previously. Although the wine was drinkable, just, the primary purpose of her visit was the surveillance of Professor Furner. He was across the room from her, talking quietly with one of the third-year students in mathematics. Liz had seen the professor with this particular student every time she had come into the bar within the past two weeks. She was convinced that there was something 'going on' between them. Then, Michelle Hufton entered the room and went to where the professor and the undergraduate were seated. She spoke to them briefly and then disappeared in the direction of the bar which was out of Liz's line of sight.

Liz was just at the point of leaving; she had seen that the professor had had only one pint of lager, and he still had not finished that. She thought it unlikely that he would be vulnerable to arrest because of an excessive level of alcohol in his blood. As she prepared to rise from her seat, a voice behind her said, "may I?" Liz turned to see that Michelle Hufton had come up behind her and was pointing at the seat that was opposite the one in which she sat. Liz replied, "yes, of course, surprised that the shy young woman had approached her." Michelle said that when they had spoken in the library a few times, she hadn't been too sure who Liz was so perhaps she had been a bit 'stand-offish'. "However, I've since learned that you're one of our third years who has taken up your undergraduate studies again after being away for a time. How are you coping?" Liz replied, truthfully, that it was a bit of a struggle. She said that the main problem was to force herself to 'think mathematically' again.

It was obvious that after the opening encounter that Michelle was not a conversationalist; she said only that she hoped that Liz would do well, then turned her attention to her drink; a glass of orange juice. Liz was not going to miss the opportunity of questioning Michelle about Veronica Blanchard, so she asked the young woman questions about herself. She'd learned long since that the best way of approaching people, whether they were shy or not, was to get them talking about themselves.

Michelle said that she was doing a Ph.D. in applied maths, and that she hoped to go into university research when she finished the degree. "However," she said, "job prospects in British universities, at the moment, are not very bright. There seem to be many jobs in financial services in the City of London, and places like that." The fact that the young woman did not continue made it clear to Liz that a job in the City held no attraction for her. As Michelle was speaking, Liz was trying desperately to think of a way of introducing Veronica Blanchard's death into the conversation.

When Michelle stopped speaking, Liz finished off her drink and rose from her seat as if to leave, saying, "when I first began my studies at QMW I came to the college and left by the Mile End tube station. However, I have been warned not to venture near the Grand Union Canal in the evening when it is dark, because two undergraduates from the college have died there. No one seems to know for sure what happened to them, but I'm not taking any chances, until they find out." Michelle said in a subdued voice, "yes,

I knew both of the girls; they were doing mathematics here. One of them was my best friend."

Liz, seating herself once more, said, "oh, I'm sorry. I didn't know." Then she said, truthfully, "that must have been terrible, to lose a very good friend like that. It happened to me once and it took me quite a time to get over it." Michelle gave no indication that she had heard what Liz had said, saying that she hoped some day her friend's killer would be found, "but I'll be surprised if the police ever get around to it. In my opinion they're just a bunch of incompetents!"

Liz said, "I thought that they didn't know how the two girls died. Didn't they suspect suicide in the case of one of them?" Michelle said, "they thought at first that Veronica; that was my friend, had killed herself. I know that Veronica would never do that." Liz asked why the police had thought that Veronica's death was a suicide. "Oh, I guess there were no signs of violence. Also, that wanker, Professor Furner, said that Veronica was a loner, and that she had financial difficulties. However, Veronica wasn't a loner. She didn't have many friends, that's true, but she wasn't a loner. Also, I know that she had had financial difficulties at one time but not at the time she was killed. She had found herself a summer job which paid her enough so that she could stay up in London."

Liz asked Michelle why it was that she thought that her friend had been killed. Michelle said that she didn't think; she knew that her friend had been raped and murdered: "the police found evidence in her body indicating that she had had sex just before her death. I happen to know that she wouldn't have done that. She would never willingly have sex with a man. She didn't like men." Liz asked Michelle if she had told the police about her idea that Veronica had been murdered. Michelle replied, "oh, I rang them and tried to tell them, but all they seemed to want to know was who I was. I finally got fed up. Even if they did catch the bastard, it wouldn't bring Veronica back."

Liz said that she understood that the second young woman to die also had had sex just before her death; did Michelle think that she had been raped and murdered also? Michelle said that she had no idea. "I knew of the girl, Mary Roberts, because she was also a student in mathematics, but I didn't know her personally. After her death I heard that she had had some kind of relationship with the lecher who was just sitting over there" Michelle indicated where Professor Furner had been seated until a few minutes earlier. "That man is incorrigible. How he keeps his job, I'll never know. He's supposed to be one of the world experts on numbers theory, so I suppose the college keeps him on because of that. However, no young female is safe around him. The department will be having a Christmas party at the end of the semester, so if you come, you'll see him in action then. I'd wear an iron bra, if I were you."

Liz decided that she had got all of the information from Michelle Hufton that she was going to get. She offered to buy Michelle another drink, but the young woman put her hand over her glass. Liz made her excuses and left the JCR bar.

As she sat on the tube train on her way home, she summarised in her thoughts what she had learned from Michelle Hufton. It was very likely that Michelle had been the person to telephone the police, anonymously, claiming that Veronica Blanchard had been raped and murdered. Also, Liz could tell by the way that Michelle spoke about Professor Furner that she did not think that he could have raped and murdered her friend. However, Liz wasn't so sure. The fact that there were no signs that either woman had struggled suggested that they knew their killer. Professor Furner had known both young women and, apparently, had been especially friendly with Mary Roberts. Whether or not he was a killer or just a 'wanker', as he had been described, remained to be examined. However, the easiest way to find out would be to discover if his DNA profile matched that of the sperm fragments found in the bodies of both young women. Liz decided that she would discuss with DCI Lawrence her idea that perhaps a ruse could be utilised to obtain a blood sample from the professor. However, contacting the DCI would have to wait until morning. Meanwhile, she would have a nice, properly-prepared, meal with a glass of wine or, perhaps, two, a hot bath and an early night.

Before going off to class the following morning, Liz rang DCI Lawrence. She told him of her conversation with Michelle Hufton and, also, asked about the possibility of using subterfuge to get a blood sample from Professor Furner. The DCI seemed cautious about the deception, but he said he would do some checking and ring her back. That evening, the DCI told Liz that he had had the name, Robert I. Furner, run through the police national database to discover if he had been arrested or had convictions for any offence, including driving whilst under the influence. He said that there was an old record of an arrest for sexual assault, but the charges had been dropped and there had been no proceedings. It was obvious that the man did not make a habit of driving under the influence, or if he did, he had been getting away with it.

Chief Inspector Lawrence was rather cautious about using a trick to get a sample of blood from the professor.

He told Liz that he had nothing against such tactics, *per se*, but that they would have to be successful. "When we stop him we would have to be certain that the professor had drunk enough alcohol to be over the legal limit. Otherwise, he could simply blow into the breathalyser and drive away. Maybe what you had better do, Liz, is keep an eye on him from time to time, and when you think that you have seen him drink enough to be at or near the legal limit, contact us on your radio. Meanwhile, perhaps you had best find out where he habitually parks his car and, also, get me the car's registration number and a description of it."

\* \* \*

Liz was growing restless with her rôle as a university undergraduate. On the rare occasions that she went into the Mile End police station, she had ignored the joking comments of her colleagues; they said that they envied the 'soft' life that she was leading. She tried to convince them that sitting in lectures, attending tutorials and spending long hours in the library did not constitute a soft life as far as she was concerned. "Then, when I get home in the evening, I have to review my lecture notes." This latter statement evoked mock cries of pity from some of her police colleagues.

Liz was looking forward to the end of the first semester when, she had been told, it was likely that her time undercover would be ended. Chief Inspector Lawrence was of the opinion that the police had got as much benefit from her activities at the college as it was likely that they would do.

Despite the fact that the two dead women were students in the same department of QMW, that fact seemed to have little to do with their deaths, unless, of course it could be shown that Professor Furner was involved. With the exception of an observation made by Liz's friend, Kay Trask, everything she had heard about the professor suggested that he never went so far as to attempt the seduction of those young women that he fancied. It was that exception that had aroused Liz's interest and had made her look forward to the Christmas party.

Kay had said that at the Christmas party the previous year, her friend, Mary Roberts, like several of the under-graduates there, had had too much to drink. "I left the party before it was over because I didn't want to get back too late to the hall of residence where we both lived; I had to catch an early train home the following morning. Mary told me that Professor Furner had offered to give her a lift after the party, so that she would be coming with him. Later, she told me that if she had been sober she'd never have gone with him, because he was a bit the worse for drink, also. Mary wouldn't tell me what happened, but I saw her when she came into the hall of residence. She was a mess. Her clothes were all mussed up; it looked like she had been wrestling in them, which, I expect, she had been. I'm pretty sure that ol' Furner had given her a pretty thorough going over. I did notice that she and the professor weren't friendly after that."

\* \* \*

The mathematics department Christmas party was held in the junior common room of Queen Mary and Westfield College about a week before Christmas and just after the semester had ended. It was quite well attended, with most of the faculty members of the department being present; in most cases with their wives. Of course, her fellow students were unaware that this was to be Liz's final appearance at

QMW in her guise as a student. She was there primarily to observe Professor Furner, so her movements between the JCR and its bar would be dictated by his behaviour.

Professor Furner was there already when she arrived, probably having remained at the college at the end of the day. Liz had gone home to change to an evening gown, which, she was pleased to say, had been purchased using police funds. Several people remarked on how well the gown suited her. Although Liz had never before worn such an elegant costume, she was pleased that this time she'd made the effort.

During the evening, she had been asked to dance by several of her male classmates. For the most part she was at least five years older than they; she was sure that they were asking her out of politeness. However, the lad that she had met during registration for classes on her first day at QMW, Jeff Barnes, stayed quite close to her during much of the evening. She had got to know him reasonably well as the semester progressed, and she quite liked him as a friend.

At times during the evening, it had proved to be difficult to socialise with Jeff and others and to keep an eye on Professor Furner. However, she was determined to keep track of the man's alcohol consumption. He seemed to alternate between a few dances in the common room and having a drink at the bar with his dance companion. Liz was sure that at the rate the professor was drinking, he couldn't possibly escape the consequences: a higher than legal blood-alcohol level.

As midnight approached, almost all of the faculty members and most of the undergraduates had left the party, and Liz was feeling conspicuous; only a few people remained in the bar, and she was the only person who did not have a companion. Jeff Barnes, the young man who had acted in that capacity during much of the evening, had left the JCR somewhat earlier and hadn't returned. Liz wondered if, perhaps, he hadn't had too much to drink. He was looking rather distressed.

Liz could see that Professor Furner was one of the guests remaining still. Hanging on his arm and much the worse for drink was a female undergraduate who Liz had seen around the mathematics department but did not know. Liz tried to assess the professor's sobriety by his behaviour as he prepared to go, but it was impossible to judge. She knew that DCI Lawrence had arranged for a marked police car to be parked on the road opposite the exit from the QMW car park. Upon receiving a signal from Liz by radio, the two uniformed officers within the car were to intercept the professor's car when it exited from the car park.

Liz left the JCR bar, following the professor, who was too preoccupied with his young companion to notice that Liz was not far behind him. When she was certain that his destination was the QMW car park, she stopped, waiting until the two people she was following were out of earshot. Then she removed the radio transceiver from her handbag and alerted the officers in the waiting police car that "the suspect" was on his way to his car with a female companion.

Liz had just stopped speaking when a voice startled her asking, "whatever are you doing, Liz?" It was Jeff Barnes. She hoped that Jeff had not heard any part of her conversation on the radio. Flustered, she said that she was trying to get a lift home on her walkie-talkie, but she couldn't raise anyone to come fetch her. "I'm not certain of the time of the last tube train from Mile End." Jeff said, "oh, your walkie-talkie looks like those radios that policeman use," then he laughed, saying, "I hope you're not a copper! It's OK, though, Liz; my dad lent me his car to go to the Christmas party, so I'll give you a lift if you like. I was feeling a bit off a little while ago, so I got out and walked around. I think I'm OK to drive now, though."

Jeff had been a good friend to her during her twelve weeks at QMW, and his behaviour was very gentlemanly when they arrived at her flat. She gave him a hug and a kiss on the cheek, and thanked him for the lift. Bidding him good night, and wishing him a happy Christmas, she entered her flat. He wasn't to know that very likely it would be the last time that he would see her.

\* \* \*

Once she was home, Liz telephoned the Mile End station to get a report on the results of the interception of Professor Furner. She was passed over to a PC Rider, who was the driver of the police car that had stopped the professor.

The police constable said that at first he and his companion had felt like they were taking part in something that "you would see on television. We saw the professor's car come out of the Queen Mary car park and swerve way across the Mile End Road, only narrowly missing a collision with another car. Then it started going at speed down the Mile End Road, so we turned on our lights and siren and started to chase him. Then the bugger came to an abrupt halt, and I had all I could do to avoid hitting him. Everything went fine after that, except I had to put up with a lot of verbal abuse from the man. He claimed that he had not been drinking, and that he had not been driving dangerously, but I finally managed to get him calmed down."

"Because of the dangerous driving incident, we were able to take him right into the station where, as arranged, there was a police surgeon waiting to get a sample of blood. The professor tried to argue that he didn't have to give his blood, but that urine would do. Fortunately, the surgeon was able to convince him that it would be in his interests to give the blood sample. He told the professor something I didn't know. He said that a urine sample quite often gives a higher reading than a blood sample taken at the same time. A urine sample may reflect the level of alcohol that was in the blood an hour or more before the sample was taken. Anyway, the police surgeon got the blood sample without further argument."

"I felt sorry for the young lady who was with the professor. I don't know who she was, but she looked young enough to be his daughter. She quite clearly had had a lot to drink because she was staggering all over the place at the police station. We got a WPC to take her home. We took the professor home, too. He'll have to come back to the police station in the morning to pick up his car."

After Liz put down the 'phone, she decided that she would celebrate the successful operation with another glass of wine. She had had only one all evening and really had not been able to enjoy herself at the Christmas party. She hoped her spoilt evening would prove to be worthwhile.

# Chapter Nineteen

**H**er last 'port of call' for the morning was Tara's least favourite; it was a flat in a three-story apartment building just off the Mile End Road. The feline occupant of the flat, a pure-bred Burmese, was the least friendly animal with which she had worked, and that included some rather nasty little dogs. Normally, she didn't look after animals in this part of London. However, her boss, Mr Volpi, had been very kind to her, so she had agreed to take over for one of the carers who worked for him part-time. The carer who normally looked after the Burmese had gone home for the Christmas vacation. Tara had no family or close friends in Britain, so she did not mind working over the holiday period.

She let herself into the flat, taking care that the cat didn't escape between her legs to go out onto the balcony; which the "little beggar" always attempted to do.

On one of her previous visits, the animal had managed to escape, and he had proved very difficult to recapture. He had run to one end of the long balcony outside the row of flats, and then had disappeared up the stairs to the floor above. Fortunately, a man who lived in one of the flats on the next floor up had been able to retrieve the animal, receiving, as a reward for his efforts, a severe bite on the hand.

On the present visit, having prevented 'Soong' from leaving the flat, and receiving a scratch on the ankle in thanks, Tara went into the kitchen. Her tasks were few. She merely had to top up his supply of dried food and refresh the water in his bowl. He, meanwhile, was all over her ankles, constantly rubbing them with his jaw except during the times that he was alternately lifting his front paws and very loudly uttering the somewhat strangled cry peculiar to the breed. She checked his litter tray, seeing that he had deposited a few oblong objects in the past twenty-four hours. However, the odour still was manageable. She had been cautioned by her boss not to change litter unless it smelled badly, and then only during the last visit before the pet's owner returned. Some owners had complained that they thought that the carers were stealing the litter because it had disappeared so rapidly.

As she was preparing to leave, the cat abandoned its attentions to the food bowl and jumped onto the table in the middle of the kitchen floor; Tara knew that this was his invitation to her to stroke him for a brief spell. The spell had to be brief because if it was prolonged beyond a time span known only to Soong, Tara would receive a bite on her wrist to tell her that the time was up.

She had just begun to stroke the cat when she felt an arm encircling her chest and a noxious-smelling object clamped over her nose and mouth. She tried to struggle free, but she was fighting a losing battle against the loss of her consciousness.

Some time later, she became aware that she was lying flat on her back with her arms enclosed in some kind of garment that held them crossed over her chest and immovable. She tried to roll from side to side, but that movement was prevented also. Her mouth was filled with some kind of material that prevented her from drawing air into it. She tried to shout, but the only noise she heard was a muffled sound inside her head. The place in which she found herself was entirely darkened. It was obvious that she was nude and her body was covered by coarse material of some kind whose texture she could feel as she attempted to turn. As she became more alert, she realised that her genitalia were sore; when she concentrated on that feeling, she knew the likely source. She had had much the same feeling there for a time after her first experience of sexual intercourse. Her memory of that event was relatively fresh in her mind because it had occurred only a few months earlier. It was obvious to her that she had been raped. Because her feet and legs were not tethered, she tried to release herself by lifting her hips and kicking her legs. All that action accomplished was the dislodgement of the material that was covering her body. Now she became aware that the place where she was being held was cold. Since she could see nothing and, for that matter, she could hear nothing, she decided to close her eyes and await events. Eventually, she returned to a state of sleep.

When next she awakened, it was the result of the feel of something rasping at her genitalia. After a moment of puzzlement, she realised what was happening to her. When she was a youngster her parents had had a cat as a family pet. Whenever Tara or her brother had scraped themselves, drawing blood, the animal would lick at the wound as long as she or her brother would permit it. Tara remembered being surprised by the roughness of the tongue of the cat. Now she was feeling that same roughness on her genitalia. Obviously, Soong had discovered her and, very likely, now was licking at places where she had been injured during the rape. She tried to turn the lower half of her body so to discourage his attentions, which were hurting her. However, her efforts proved to be futile. She had thought that the discomfort that the cat was causing her could not get worse, when she felt it biting her. Her only thought was that she was going to be savagely attacked by the cat; his second bite was so painful that quite involuntarily, she heaved her hips into the air, patently dislodging the animal because its activities halted for a time. She heard the sound of the cat's cry several times, and then she knew that he was at her again. However, now she felt no sensation other than a tugging in the area of her bottom. She didn't know what he was doing and her attempts to dislodge him by turning her body seemed futile.

The next time she was awakened, it was because the room lights came on and she heard a male voice say, "sheiss! Aus, you shtupid animal!" She looked up to see a man who was doing something at one side of the surface on which she lay, which she now could see was a bed. He did not look at her but was intent upon pulling at tethers on one side of the bed that helped fasten her to it. He then walked to the other side of the bed and tested the integrity of the tethers on that side. Then she heard him say, "that should keep you still for a little while longer, meine Liebchen. Let me treat you to a little show." Saying that, he went to one side of the room where there was a table and a chair. He seated himself in the chair and removed his shoes and socks. After that he stood and continued to undress himself. Tara tried not to look but she knew exactly what the man had in mind.

When the man was undressed he held his fully-erect member in one hand whilst he walked to the side of the bed. "There you are Liebchen; what do you think of that. You didn't seem to appreciate it when I used it before, but maybe you'll like it better this time." With that, he got onto the bed and proceeded to rape Tara. She closed her eyes, wanting to cry out but the gag in her mouth prevented any but the smallest of sounds. Her rapist's only contribution to the sound of the room was a slight grunting noise, as though his thrusting was an exertion on his part. He stopped after a brief time and got off of Tara's body. He said, "Jesus, you're a tight Teufelchen, but I'm loosening you up." This time she could not feel her genitalia; they were numb. Then, her arms were tugged alternately. Her captor obviously once again was checking the fastness of the bindings that held her in place. Then the room was darkened. She heard a door open and close; then silence returned to her.

It was at that point that Tara gave in to thoughts that her consciousness had been fighting to avoid: she was going to die. Her captor had made no effort to hide himself from her. As she thought of her likely fate, tears began to flow from her eyes; they came in such a rush and volume that her nose became partially blocked. Unable to breath through her mouth, she felt a sense of panic as she gasped, attempting to bring in sufficient air through her nose to satisfy the increased needs of a body in panic. After regaining control over the state of panic, she breathed slowly and deeply until, finally, she experienced the return of calmness.

\* \* \*

It had never occurred to Tara that what was happening to her in the darkened room in which she lay could happen in her adopted country. One of the reasons for leaving her homeland was because she knew that such things as abduction and rape happened there quite regularly.

A year earlier at the age of seventeen, she had left her native Romania and had travelled first to Italy. There she found employment in a hotel in Rome that was operated by an order of nuns. Although she had come from an educated family, she was more than happy to accept employment as a menial. She was part of the domestic staff of the hotel. The ladies of the nunnery were very protective and quite kind, seeing in her a very inexperienced young woman. One of them even volunteered to teach the young woman rudimentary English when she discovered that Tara wanted, ultimately, to go to England to live.

During her stay in Rome, Tara met, and became friendly with, a young Englishman who was in Rome working as a language assistant at a secondary school that was associated with the nunnery. He was in his third year of a modern languages course at a British university. His stay abroad was a requirement of the course he was taking. He had been accommodated in the hotel that had employed Tara. Although the young girl had become friendly with the Brit, she successfully resisted his efforts to become more than close friends. The nun with whom she was particularly friendly had cautioned her: "you have a precious commodity that the young man wants very much; I can see it in his eyes. However, make certain that you get a good price for it." Tara had not had much experience of the Catholic religion, or, for that matter, any religion. However, she thought that the words of the woman, who, supposedly, was not supposed to be knowledgeable about the ways of the world, were very wise indeed.

When it was time for the young Englishman to return to Britain, Tara agreed to pay his price for helping her to return with him: she lost her virginity. The young Brit persuaded his sister, who was about Tara's age and bore a vague resemblance to the young Romanian girl, to send her passport to him. He had warned Tara that smuggling her into Britain was risky, not so much because of immigration controls in

Britain but because of checks that would be made at the Rome airport from which they would fly. He said that the passports would be scrutinised closely by the airline when they checked in for their flight. If the airline got it wrong, then it was their responsibility to put it right, and that was expensive. However, he said that when they checked in for their flight, he would do something to distract the check-in attendant.

Secretly, the young Englishman hoped that Tara would be stopped because he didn't fancy her hanging around once they got back to Britain. He had a story prepared in case they should be stopped. He would say that Tara had been staying with him and had stolen his sister's passport without his knowledge. However, the woman at the airline check-in counter at the airport only glanced at the pictures in the two passports that were presented to her. Obviously, Tara looked enough like his sister to be able to fool someone not looking closely at the picture and comparing it to the person standing before her. At Heathrow, Tara encountered no difficulty passing through the immigration-control barrier.

Once in Britain, Tara and the young Brit went to the home of his parents in Northwood, one of the more prosperous suburbs of London. She had been invited to stay there for a few days by the parents of the young Brit. To that point, their sexual liaison had occurred only once, and that was only a few days before their departure from Italy. Once they were at the home of the young Brit, and despite his efforts to continue, she proved to be quite adept at avoiding further sexual intercourse; furthermore, she managed to do that without creating noticeable resentment on his part.

Not long after their arrival in Britain, the young man returned to his university to commence the fourth year of his course. Tara stayed on in London, at first taking advantage of 'free' overnight accommodation afforded by London's railway stations. She had arrived in Britain with a reasonable amount of money, so it was not necessary for her to beg like many of the homeless who frequented the railway stations. However, there were at least two hazards to loitering around the passenger halls of the stations at night: being moved on by the police and being subjected to pestering by men wishing to use her body for sexual purposes. She coped successfully with both hazards by using her natural acting ability. Although the help given her by the nun in Rome had improved her use of English greatly, she was able, successfully, to feign a lack of understanding of both the admonitions of policemen and the importuning of her sexual harassers. Usually, they gave up trying to communicate with the "stupid foreigner" and would leave her where they had found her.

Before her financial resources were depleted, much to her relief, she found a man who would employ her almost her first time of trying to find a job. He ran an agency that looked after people's pets whilst they were on holiday. It was called by the rather unimaginative title, "Holiday Pets." The company owner was, himself, an immigrant from Romania, so Tara had a natural alliance with him. At first she assumed that he was in Britain illegally, also. However, he was at pains to make it clear to her that he did not hire people he knew to be illegal immigrants. She had taken the hint and never again mentioned her illegal status.

After working for a short time, Tara had discovered that she was not the only employee of Holiday Pets who was in the UK illegally. One of the others had explained to Tara that their boss preferred to hire illegal immigrants because they were unlikely to complain if their terms of employment didn't conform to those laid down by the Department of Employment. All of her fellow employees were temporary; their numbers being dictated by the amount of work there was for them to do. However, Mr Volpi had taken a fancy to Tara. His obvious admiration for her body was not discouraged by the young woman. She had no intention of stopping him looking, but should he venture to touch, she knew that she would have to object.

* * *

As Tara's thoughts dwelt upon her immediate past and how she had come to be in the present predicament, she heard a noise. She thought that the noise came from the opening of the door of the room in which she was lying, helpless. She waited for something to happen, suddenly aware of just how cold she had became and how precarious her position was. Moments later, a regime began that repeated one that had played out when? Hours ago? Days ago? The lights were turned on. The same man that she had seen previously had come into the room and was undressing himself. Tara could not look, so she closed her eyes and lay there, waiting for the inevitable. This time he did not speak, but the noise of his exertions still were to be heard. When he had finished, all became quiet, and she lay there, eyes closed, wondering how long it would be before the man did what she was sure that he was going to do. Tears filled her eyes, once again making breathing difficult, as they drained into her nose.

After she had lain for a time, her eyes tightly closed, she slowly opened them and looked about. No one was in the room with her. She wondered what had happened because the light was on still. She saw that the man's clothes still were laid over the chair upon which he had sat to remove his shoes. A short time later, he came into the room. It was then that she noticed a familiar sound; the running of water into a bathtub. Her thoughts were sufficiently confused that she placed no significance on that sound; she was expecting only that the man would once again be directing his attentions toward her body. She wondered what he was going to do now. Her genitalia were numb, so whatever he did would have little significance for her.

The man left the room, and a short time later Tara heard the running water stop. The man came back into the room, going to Tara and untying the bonds that held her to the bed. She tried to move her arms, but they had not been released. She then felt herself being lifted and carried. A short time later she felt herself being lowered into a place she immediately recognised as a bathtub. It was full of water which rose quickly over her face; so quickly, in fact, that she had not been able to fill her lungs with air. Instead, her actions only filled them with water. Despite contortions of her body brought on by suffocation-induced panic, it was all over very quickly. Once again, Tara was in darkness.

# Chapter Twenty

As Liz entered the police station on her first morning back at work after staying with Reg over the weekend, the station sergeant greeted her with, "you missed some excitement on Saturday, sarge. We pulled the body of another young woman out of the Grand Union. Looks like another suicide, but forensics are still working on it. I don't know what anyone sees in bumping themselves off that way, except that it's probably sure fire. If they don't drown, they'll sure as hell die of the pollution!"

Liz smiled at the sergeant's sentiments, even if, probably, they weren't entirely accurate. It seemed like every time she passed the canal during the day there was someone fishing from its banks. She reasoned that if fish could live in the canal, the water couldn't be that polluted. As she turned to go, the duty sergeant called after her, "oh, I almost forgot to tell you, sarge; Chief Inspector Lawrence told me to tell you that he would like a word as soon as you get in."

As Liz walked toward the DCI's office, she thought to herself that she would be surprised if the woman had killed herself. Very likely, it would prove that she had been murdered, and by the same man who murdered Veronica Blanchard and Mary Roberts. Liz found herself concluding in her own mind that the young woman would prove to be another mathematician from Queen Mary and Westfield College. Liz hoped that it wouldn't be someone whom she had got to know during her time there.

When Liz entered the DCI's office, he said, "I expect you've heard about the most recent drowning in the canal. We've not got much information yet; it's too soon. However, I did manage to get the morgue to photograph the dead girl so that we can start our enquiries."

The DCI handed a colour photograph to Liz, who looked at it carefully, and then said that she was fairly certain that she'd never before seen the young woman. "However, if, like the other dead women, she was a student at QMW I might be able to establish an identity for her very quickly. The college has identification photographs of all of their three-thousand-plus students. I'm sure the registrar will co-operate in allowing me to go over the student records to compare this photograph with theirs. I'll ring the registrar's office, and see what she has to say. If she throws up any obstacles, we'll probably have to get something official, but I don't think that there will be any problems."

Liz's telephone call to the Registrar's office at Queen Mary and Westfield College was transferred automatically to a male voice that identified itself as a security officer. He said that the college had closed for the Christmas period and would re-open a few days after the New Year. She was irritated by the delay in her investigation that Christmas could cause.

After ringing off, Liz thought about it for a time deciding finally to try another tact. She rang the QMW College operator again, and again was transferred to security. She asked the man who answered the phone if she could be put through to the principal's office. He asked who she was, and Liz identified herself adding that she was calling on official police business, and that it was urgent. The security man said that he had seen the principal only a short time earlier, so he knew that he was in college. Moments later a voice came on the 'phone saying, "principal." Liz identified herself and listened as the principal told her how nice it was to hear from her, and had her stay at Queen Mary been successful. Liz waited patiently for him to finish being his usual jovial self. Finally, she had a chance to explain to him the purpose of her call. The principal said, "I happen to know that the registrar has gone to Scotland for the holiday season; she has family up there. I could certainly let you into her office, but I would have no idea where to look for the files you are seeking, and I'd never be forgiven by the registrar if I was responsible for leaving a mess. Let me make a few 'phone calls, and I'll get back to you, Sergeant Andresen. I expect that I can chase up someone who knows their way around the registrar's office."

Liz had no idea how long it would take the principal to sort something out so that she could look at the registrar's files. However, whilst she was waiting she thought that it would be useful to search the missing persons' database. It was much too early for the dead woman's details to appear on the database unless she had gone missing well before the time of her death. Nonetheless, it would be worth a few hours of Liz's time.

Liz had only just got started on her search, when the principal rang her back, saying that he had got through to one of the young clerks who worked in the registrar's office. "She has very kindly agreed to come into the college tomorrow morning, if that would be convenient for you. Her name is Hyacinth Fogg, and she'll meet you at the front entrance to the college administration building tomorrow morning at ten o'clock. It was lucky that I was able to contact Hyacinth because she is the person who is responsible for student records, so she'll know where everything is that you will wish to see." Liz thanked the principal for his help, to which he responded, "oh, don't thank me, officer; Miss Fogg is the one doing all of the work."

By the end of the day, Liz had completed her search of the national database that listed all known missing persons, finding no match for the dead woman's photograph. On the following day, Liz spent most of the morning looking through the record files for all students at QMW. Some of the student photographs were rather poor quality, but Liz was certain that the dead woman had not been a student at the college. She finished her search just before lunchtime, so she offered to take Hyacinth to lunch.

After a most enjoyable lunch with Hyacinth Fogg, who turned out to be a very outgoing person, monopolising the conversation during the lunch, leaving it to Liz to do that at which she was best: sitting and listening.

Hyacinth had yearnings to go on the stage. She said that her father was rather old fashioned and had insisted that she go to secretarial college when she left school. That she had done, but the school was near Swiss Cottage which also had a theatre where amateur productions were staged. She had joined a group that used the theatre, and now she was hoping to make acting her career. Meanwhile, she had to eat, so she had got a job as a clerk at Queen Mary.

Liz had so little in common with Hyacinth that she found it difficult to do other than a rather dull recital of how she had got where she was in the police. The two women parted on friendly terms, but no mention was made of the possibility of getting together again, socially.

Liz went back to the Mile End Station, reporting the results of her searches to DCI Lawrence. She knew that it would be several days before the results of the forensic examination of the dead woman would be complete: the Christmas season was slowing everything down. Also, she was anxious to know the results of the DNA analysis of Professor Furner's blood sample, but that wouldn't be available until after Christmas either. Fortunately, the professor's blood had been shown to have an alcohol level almost fifty percent higher than the legal limit, so there would be no repercussions following his arrest, as he had threatened.

In short, the fact that Christmas was imminent was not very helpful to the investigation in which she was engaged. Liz decided that she might as well begin her preparations for that event. She was hoping that she would have time to socialise more than had been the case during her undercover work at Queen Mary and Westfield. She planned to spend some time in Cambridge. Based on telephone conversations that she had held recently with her mum, it sounded as if Audrey and Julia now were getting on well. Also, she felt bad about neglecting Pat and had promised her friend that she would have a meal with her and her husband one evening during the few days she would be in Cambridge over the Christmas period.

# Chapter Twenty One

Cambridge was an especially attractive place over Christmas. Liz was looking forward to being there and spending a few days doing nothing more than eating and drinking and relaxing with people whom she loved. She even found herself fantasising about Julia, and what the two of them had got up to. She was aware that she was not the only one fantasising about Julia. When she spoke to Pat over the 'phone her friend had expressed some disappointment because to that point she had been unable to find a time when Julia would be free in the evening to come to Pat's flat for a meal, and, Liz surmised, perhaps other activities.

Liz had learned from Pat that Julia had little free time during the evenings not because of her academic work, but because she was working. Julia had said nothing to Liz about working except, of course, her early-morning paper-delivery round. Liz hoped that Julia didn't feel that she had to work because of Audrey's awkwardness about money. Unfortunately, Liz had become aware that her mum quite often would lie if it suited her purpose. Consequently, Liz had no confidence that her mum was being truthful when she assured her daughter that Julia and she were getting along well together. Liz hoped that the Christmas break would not be marred by unpleasantness.

\* \* \*

There was no response when Liz called out to her mum and Julia after unlocking the front door to her mum's house, and entering. There were no lights on in the house, which was an immediate cause for concern. She knew that Audrey was expecting her, so she was sure that unless something had happened to her mum, she should have been at home.

She went next door to the house of the neighbours and friends, the Paltrys. Rose Paltry answered the door, telling Liz that Audrey had mentioned a Christmas party where she worked, saying, "however, I thought your mum decided not to go because you would be arriving. Maybe she changed her mind. You can stay here with Fred and me if you like, Elisabeth." Liz thanked Mrs Paltry. She was looking forward to having a chat with them, anyway. She hoped that they would be able to give her an honest accounting of her mum's activities over the past several weeks.

Fred Paltry offered Liz a beer which she accepted although it was a drink of which she was not overly fond. The Paltrys explained to Liz that they had not seen very much of Audrey over the previous several weeks. Fred said, "we used to have her over here most evenings complaining about that 'darky', as she called her, who was living with her. However, either they're getting along better or the young woman isn't staying there anymore." At that moment, the lights of a car could be seen through the front window of the Paltry's sitting room. Fred drew aside a curtain and announced that he thought it must be Audrey arriving home by taxi. Liz thanked the Paltry's for the beer, saying also that it had been nice to talk with them. Perhaps they could get together sometime over Christmas.

Liz stepped out of the Paltry's front door in time to see the driver of the taxi, that had brought Audrey home, just leaving her mum's house. When he saw Liz, he asked, "are you headed for that lady's house? I would look after her if I was you. She's so incapable she couldn't even get out of my cab. I've picked up some Christmas party goers in my time, but that lady takes the biscuit. All the way here, I was worried she was going to make a mess of my motor."

Liz apologised to the driver and went into the house where Audrey was lying back on the settee in the front room. Liz tried to talk to her mum, but it was obvious that Audrey was not in a mood for conversation; all she wished to do was go to bed. Liz helped her up the stairs to her bedroom and helped her to remove her clothing and prepare for bed.

Back in the kitchen she was surprised to find that there was plenty of food to be found, including an 'instant' meal consisting of a packet containing two quail which had been stuffed with dressing. Unfortunately, the only thing alcoholic to drink was beer, so she decided that she would have milk instead. Liz was pleased to see the food because it meant that Julia had been keeping up her end of the bargain to look after Audrey.

Looking at her watch, Liz saw that it had only just gone seven; she had only a few days in Cambridge and she didn't want to waste them by doing things that she could do easily at home in her flat, like reading. She knew that if she rang Pat her friend would insist that Liz should come to her flat, using the excuse that she couldn't leave her young son. Liz wasn't in the mood for much socialising, so she thought that she would just go along to the local pub and have a few glasses of wine.

Just as she was about to leave the house, the telephone rang. Almost automatically she lifted the receiver only then realising that she might be making a mistake. Upon leaving the Mile End station for her Christmas break, Liz had had to leave a number at which she could be reached in case she had to be contacted. However, even before she got the receiver to her ear she heard a female voice say, "Liz? Is that you? Hi, it's Julia." Liz replied, "Julia, hi. Where are you?" Julia said that she was working late, but that she planned to be home soon. She wanted to have a nice, long visit with Liz. Liz said that she was thinking of spending an evening in the pub, and asked Julia if she would like to go also. Julia said that she would love to go and she would be home just as soon as she could. Liz told her to take a taxi, and that she would pay for it.

Julia looked to be a new person. She had changed her hairstyle to reflect the modern 'frizzy' look and the clothes that she was wearing looked not only trendy, but expensive. However, the person wearing the clothing was still the same affectionate young woman that Liz knew. Julia gave Liz a firm hug, and kissed her on the lips, telling her that she had so looked forward to a time when Liz would be coming home. Julia's kiss was rather more prolonged than a kiss of greeting between two friends. Liz was aware of feelings that she had resolved that she and Julia never again would explore. However, of late, she had been feeling rather depressed. She hoped that an evening spent with her friend would cheer her up, and if the young woman was agreeable, they might spend the night together after returning from the pub.

At the pub, Liz asked Julia to be seated whilst she bought a round of drinks. Usually, Liz prepared for the worse when she took her first sip of wine served over the bar in a pub, but she was pleasantly surprised by the wine that was served that evening.

When she got back to where Julia was seated, her friend was full of news about the new life that she was living.

She told Liz that when she started at Anglia Polytechnic she had made friends with a girl, Leeanne Palmer, who was taking the same course as she. She said, "Leeanne was very friendly and the two of us just seemed to hit it off from the start. She was especially good to me during that time when your mum was being difficult, and I was running out of money. She offered to lend me some, but I told her that I couldn't do that because I had no way to pay her back. However, one day she told me that if I was free she would like me to go with her to a job that she did part time for her dad. I knew that Leeanne had a job of some kind because occasionally she missed classes, and she would ask to copy my lecture notes. She said that I shouldn't tell anyone, but the reason she missed classes was because of the job. It wasn't until later that I found out what she did, but I assumed that the job involved irregular hours because of the classes she missed."

"However, one day when I had a free afternoon, she asked me to go along with her and see where she worked. Only then did I discover that she modelled clothing. Her dad is a photographer. He has contracts with some shops that sell fashionable clothing to young people. His biggest contract is with Marks & Spencer; for them he photographs women wearing clothing that is to be marketed by that chain of shops. Leeanne is just one of several models he has used for that contract. I thought that the whole procedure was very interesting; I'd never seen a fashion photographer at work before. I noticed that he kept looking at me as he was working. Finally, when he was finished with Leeanne he asked me if I would like to pose for him. He said that he might be able to use me, if I would like some work. I suppose I was flattered that he wanted to photograph me, so I spent a few minutes putting myself into the poses that he wanted me to do. As Leeanne and I went back to the university, we discussed what working for her dad would involve. She said that the hours were fairly flexible, and when she mentioned what he paid per hour, I was certain that I would do it if he asked."

At that point, Julia insisted upon buying a round of drinks and went off to the bar. Liz thought to ask Julia about the work that she had ended up doing for Leeanne Palmer's father, but she didn't wish to pry; it was none of her business. Liz was aware that Julia had a figure that very likely would attract large sums of money were she to pose for erotic photographs. However, then she told herself to stop acting like a copper: suspecting everyone; the fact that Leeanne's father used his own daughter, indicated that his motives very likely were quite innocent.

Liz needn't have bothered herself, because when she re-turned with their drinks, Julia explained what she had been doing for Leeanne's father: "Mr Palmer told me that he was hoping to get a contract with a group of shops that sold clothing to women who were tall. However, he had been having difficulties finding models that were tall enough. He told me that the minute he laid eyes on me, he was sure that I would be perfect. So, he took some photographs of me. Then, about a week later, Leeanne told me that her dad wanted to see me because he had got the contract that he had been hoping to get. Since then, I have done quite well, financially. In fact, that's the good news I was going to spring on you this Christmas, Liz. I haven't been using the money that you have been transferring into my current account. I have been using my own money to buy food for your mum and me, and I hope that you will let me contribute something to pay for my room. I'll never be able to repay you for all that you have done for me, but there's no reason why I should continue to be a financial burden on you."

Liz was quite touched by Julia's thoughtfulness. She had intended to question her about her relationship with Audrey, but the two women got off onto other subjects, principally, Julia's impressions of her university course, and whether or not it was fulfilling her ideas of what it should be. Julia said that she now found herself to be confused about the future. She wasn't so sure any longer that she wished to teach, but she couldn't make up her mind what it was that she wished to do instead.

Julia changed the subject expertly by asking Liz to tell her what she could about what had happened to the prostitution ring that had been responsible for Julia coming to Britain. Liz had to tell her that she was out of touch with that investigation. However, the last time she had spoken with her boss, Lydia Mussett, about it, she had learned that a few people had been arrested as the ringleaders, but that the case against them was building only very slowly.

Liz and Julia had another glass of wine and then decided to leave the pub to walk home. On the way, Liz monopolised the conversation, attempting to keep the subject off events that might occur once they arrived at Audrey's house. However, once the front door of the house was closed behind them, Julia's mouth was pressed to Liz's mouth and two tongues met and intermingled. Some time later a naked form left the sofa bed in which a great deal of activity had taken place. Before departing, the form whispered, "I love you Liz; you're my favourite person in the whole world.

I know we can't be together very often, but when we can, let's do it."

After Julia had left the sofa bed, Liz once again was plagued by doubts that disturbed her. She was no longer certain that she didn't love Julia, but if she decided that she did, it would involve her rethinking her plans for her life.

# Chapter Twenty Two

Liz awakened in the morning when a fully-clothed Julia seated herself at the edge of the sofa bed and took her hand. Julia said, "I just got back from my paper round; do you want to have breakfast with me?" Liz expressed surprise that Julia still was doing the paper round; the young woman explained that although she no longer needed the money, Mr Nardun had been so good to her, she didn't want to let him down. Julia said that she had just looked in on Audrey who appeared to be sleeping soundly. "Do you think that we ought to wake her up, Liz? Sometimes she gets angry with me when I do it, especially after she has gone to bed drunk." Liz would have liked to have had a quiet breakfast with Julia, but she knew that her mother would take offence and would be in a foul mood for the rest of the day. Liz agreed to awaken her mum and give her any assistance she needed whilst Julia fixed the breakfast.

Audrey did not disappoint Liz and Julia. For most of that day she was proving to be very awkward. It was obvious that she was suffering very badly from drinking excessively at the Christmas party she had attended. Finally, toward late afternoon, Liz had had enough of her mother's disagreeable behaviour and told her so, rather bluntly. She knew of no way to gently tell her mother that her behaviour was unacceptable, and that she and Julia were not going to put up with it. As had happened quite often when Liz displayed her temper, Audrey came around immediately. She apologised for being such a 'misery'. Liz put her arms around her mum and said that she understood. She said that she and Julia would cook a nice meal that evening, so that Audrey would have to tell them which of her favourite dishes she wished to have included.

Despite Liz's attempts at cheering up her mum, Audrey was incapable of joining Liz and Julia in their efforts to maintain a pleasant mood. Both during the meal and after Audrey insisted on drinking, consuming several bottles of beer. Not that she needed an excuse, but she said that it was the holiday period, so she felt that she could celebrate.

By late evening, Liz was in despair. Audrey was much the worse for drink and was being antagonistic toward Julia, complaining to Liz that the young woman never was at home, so what good was she. It wasn't long before Julia was sufficiently upset that she had excused herself and had gone off to bed.

Liz tried to speak to her mum, saying that if she was trying to drive Julia away she was succeeding. "Julia is now working and making enough money so that she could afford to get a place on her own. The only reason that she stays here is to look after you." Audrey replied by saying "oh, Liz, what you say just isn't true; she isn't interested in me. I hardly ever see her. Even when she's here she hides herself in her room and doesn't talk to me." Liz thought that very likely what Audrey had just said was true. Probably Julia spent quite a lot of her time in her room, studying. However, that was the inevitable consequence for her mum of having a university student living with her. She said to her mum, "Julia tells me that she used to get home every evening and cook a meal for the two of you, but you never would eat what she cooked. Isn't that true?" Audrey said that Julia did cook sometimes but that she never could eat the food. "She won't cook what I like; all she wants to cook are things that she likes. I can't eat that African food." Liz said, "mum; you know that's not true. I know the dishes that Julia likes to cook. It's true that some of them are dishes she learned to cook when she was growing up, but also she loves to cook dishes that she has learned to cook since she came here to live."

After a period of trying to reason with her mum, Liz concluded that the effort was futile. Her mum's objections to Julia were not based on anything rational. The woman simply did not like Julia, probably because she was both black and foreign. She knew that she would have to have a talk with the young woman and relieve her of any further responsibility for looking after Audrey.

Liz excused herself to go to the loo. When she returned she found that Audrey had turned on the television, but instead of watching she was seated on the couch, sleeping, with her head resting against its back, snoring loudly through her gaping mouth. Liz used the opportunity to go to Julia's room, knocking gently on her door. Julia invited Liz to come into the bedroom. Liz told the young woman about the conversation that she had attempted to have with Audrey. Julia said that to some extent what Audrey had said was true, "I do tend to stay in my room when I am at home. When I first came to live with your mum, I tried to talk to her after I got home from the university, but it was difficult. I didn't know what to talk to her about except my courses, and she didn't seem very interested in them. I tried to ask her about her job, but then she would say that I wouldn't be interested in her boring job. I don't even know what her job is, Liz. I know she works in a shop, but what she does there

I don't know." Liz asked if Julia thought that she would rather find someplace else to live.

She knew she had stated the question badly because Julia got a worried look on her face and asked, "don't you want me to stay here?" Liz said it wasn't that at all; "it is obvious that my mum is treating you badly; nobody should have to put up with that. All I'm saying is please don't feel that you are obliged to stay." Julia assured Liz that she had agreed to stay with Audrey and that she would do that so long as Liz wanted her to do so. "Your mum is fine until she starts drinking, Liz. I just wish that there was some way that we could stop her doing that. When I go shopping, I don't buy beer, but she buys it herself, except when she runs out of money. I have learned not to give her any money because it just goes for booze."

\* \* \*

Pat had invited Liz, her mum and Julia for a meal with her husband and son at their flat on Christmas Eve. Although Pat wasn't aware, her invitation proved to be a very effective means of keeping Audrey sober during the day.

In her youth, Liz used to make pocket money by conducting tourists around Cambridge. As an activity to occupy their time prior to visiting Pat and her family, Liz suggested that she, Audrey and Julia might go on a tour of Cambridge. Julia was immediately enthusiastic, saying that despite living in Cambridge for almost three months she had never really seen anything except those places that were obvious like King's College Chapel. Audrey was less enthusiastic, but she agreed to be taken along. Liz knew that her mum wasn't really interested in the historical sights of the medieval city, so she appreciated her mum's agreement to go along with

Julia and her. She thought that as a reward to her mum, Liz would suggest that they stop in a pub in town for lunch.

Soon thereafter, Liz began her stint as tour guide. She began in the usual place for her: Magdalene Bridge on the north end of the town centre. Soon after, Liz came to realise that she could remember which buildings to include on the tour, but she found herself to be a bit hazy on some of the historical detail. However, as did some tour guides, she improvised shamelessly.

It was obvious that the only part of the tour enjoyed by Audrey was the brief stop for lunch at a pub in the centre of the city. Fortunately, the pub was very crowded, so it was difficult to obtain service, thus limiting Audrey to only one pint of beer. Liz had long suspected that it was her mum's preference for unhealthy food that had put her off the healthy meals that Julia had cooked for the two of them. That suspicion was again confirmed when the three women ordered their pub lunches. Given a wide choice in the pub's menus, Audrey found it difficult to choose between the pork pie and chips or sausages and chips. Liz earned her mum's gratitude by suggesting that Audrey should have a double helping of chips with whatever she chose.

The women finished their tour in time to get a taxi home and to begin their preparations for the visit to the Moffatts. When Pat had made the dinner invitation for Christmas Eve, she had insisted that Liz should bring nothing. However, Liz had violated her promise to her friend, buying some wine and beer and a gift for Andrew. Liz knew that neither Pat nor Roger Moffatt drank beer, so that she thought that she had better provide for her mum.

At the Moffatt's flat, the evening went very well. As Liz had hoped would happen, Pat's small son, Andrew, immediately took control of Audrey and insisted that he show her how well he was doing with his numbers and reading. Liz had not considered that her mum was that fond of children, but she seemed to 'have a way' with Andrew, and, equally, Andrew was able to charm her.

Whilst Audrey and Andrew were occupied, it was the turn of Pat and Roger to turn their attention to Julia. Liz had learned already of Pat's attraction for the very pretty young woman, but it became obvious very quickly that Roger was attracted similarly. At one stage, Liz excused herself to go to the toilet. As she left the sitting room of the flat she was followed closely behind by Pat who, before Liz entered the bathroom, whispered, "are you watching that 'letch' of a husband of mine? I'd keep an eye on Julia, Liz. Roger'll have her knickers off and into his bed before she knows what's happening!" Liz treated what Pat had to say as a joke, but she could see that Roger was quite smitten with the young lady. Julia was sufficiently pretty that Liz thought it likely that many, perhaps most men were attracted to her. Liz wondered how Julia felt about that, or if she even noticed.

During the taxi ride home, Audrey opened the conversation by saying that she had thought the night would never end. "Andrew's a cute little soul, but my god his parents don't get on, do they?" Before Liz could defend Pat and Roger, Julia said, "no, they seem to disagree with each other a lot; aren't they happy together?" Liz knew that Pat and Roger were not getting on, but she hoped that it was just because their marriage was going through a bit of a 'rough patch', and she said so.

When sober, Julia was not one to criticise people. However, she had had sufficient wine during the evening to remove that inhibition. She began by saying that she liked Pat better than Roger. "He was always looking down my front. I don't like men who do that. However, Pat is very kind. She has invited me to come visit her whenever I would like whilst I am attending university." Liz debated with herself whether or not to warn Julia off Pat, deciding finally that very likely the young woman could look after herself.

Later that night, at home, Liz managed to persuade her mum to have no more than two bottles of beer. In that way she hoped to ensure that Audrey wouldn't become incapable by bedtime. Also, because all of them would be going to bed very late, there would be little opportunity for Julia and her to get up to anything on the sofa bed. Liz knew that she was taking the coward's way out, but she couldn't trust herself when Julia crept into her bed. She would have just one more night to be brave, and then she would be back in London. She had agreed to spend Boxing Day with Reg.

# Chapter Twenty Three

Liz had had to get an early morning train to London on Boxing Day, making the excuse to her mother for leaving by saying that she had to be back at work early. She didn't like lying to her mum, but she had got used to the necessity of doing it. Train services on the holiday were restricted, so it took Liz longer than usual to get to London, allowing her only to have Boxing Day supper with Reg. He had quite outdone himself, roasting a very small turkey that he had bought from a poulterer who, Reg said, bothered to 'hang' his meat properly. He said that when he was a lad his family had got poultry that had been 'hung' in a cool place for a minimum of two weeks after it had been killed, allowing the meat to 'mature'.

At first, Liz was rather dubious about the whole procedure, especially when she saw that, prior to placing the bird in the oven, parts of its carcass were covered in green mould. However, once she tasted the result, she was in doubt no longer.

Reg had chilled a few bottles of a type of white wine which, he said, he had discovered during a holiday he had taken in south-eastern France. The wine was from the Savoie region and was called "Abymes." He said that he had been unable to find Savoie wines in London until a few days earlier when he had run into a small stock of them in a Kensington off-licence. He had bought all of the Savoie wine the shop owner had which consisted of two other types, Apremont and Chignin, as well as the Abymes. He had tasted all of them, finding that he preferred the Abymes.

Liz stayed at Reg's flat that night, going into the Mile End station in the morning. The journey had seemed longer than usual because she was somewhat the worse for having drunk too much wine the previous evening.

\* \* \*

The Christmas holiday being over, Liz arrived back at her desk in the detectives' room at Mile End and exchanged pleasantries with her colleagues, most of whom had the same complaint as she: too much indulgence over the Christmas period.

The next order of business for her was to obey the instructions in a note that she had received from Lydia just before the Christmas break: after the holiday, she was to ring Scotland Yard to discuss with her boss what the future would hold.

When she spoke to Lydia, Liz asked to stay on a bit longer in the East End because she was sure that there would be a break soon in the investigation into the rape/murders. Lydia said that things were rather quiet at the 'Yard' at that time, but they were likely to 'hot' up after the New Year and she might have to be recalled then.

Liz's next task was to shuffle through the contents of her IN basket. As she had hoped, there was a full report of the forensic examination of the unknown woman whose body had been found in the Grand Union Canal near QMW before Christmas. Marker points of the DNA of sperm found within the body were identical to those found in the body of Veronica Blanchard and Mary Roberts. Furthermore, there were insufficient similarities between the DNA markers of the rapist and of Professor Furner to be of significance. In other words, the professor was not the rapist/murderer. Liz had anticipated this result, more or less, once she learned that the third woman to die was not a student at Queen Mary and Westfield College.

An unusual feature of the body of the unknown woman was that it showed evidence of parts of the genitalia having been removed, probably before death. That finding puzzled Liz sufficiently that she telephoned the London Hospital where the autopsy had been performed and asked to be put through to the pathologist who had signed the autopsy report, a Dr Lemoine. She was hoping that he could explain a detail that had been stated in the report: the inner and outer labia on one side of the dead woman's genitalia were missing. She wondered if, in addition to being a rapist, the dead women's attacker was a sadist.

As she feared would be the case, Liz was informed that Dr Lemoine had not returned from his "Christmas hols," but that he would be coming in the following day because he had to perform an autopsy. The woman to whom Liz spoke said that she would leave a note in his pigeonhole for him to ring her.

As she did always, Liz listed the main conclusions that she had drawn up to certain points in investigation that she was pursuing. She did the same for the present investigation: that of the suspected rape/murder of three young women. She hoped that listing of the conclusions would provide a hint to her as to productive avenues of further investigation. Aside from the fact that all three dead women had had sexual intercourse, either voluntarily or otherwise, with the same man, there appeared to be no other factor that was the same for all three deaths. Liz was sure that there must be some connection between the women other than the fact that all very likely had been raped and then murdered. What had caused them to become victims of the rapist murderer? She was quite certain that the finding of that connection would go a long way toward answering the main question that she had posed: who was the rapist/murderer.

Liz decided that she would attempt to persuade DCI Lawrence to back her in making a public appeal. On national television there was a programme that highlighted a few serious crimes that had remained unsolved for some time. The programme was rather over-dramatised, but, in general, it produced results. During the programme, details of the crimes that the police wished to reveal would be given; often there were reconstructions of the crimes highlighted. Liz had no idea how crimes were chosen to be featured in the programme; she hoped that it would prove to be possible to have the rapes and murders that she was investigating included as part of one of the programmes. If that proved to be impossible, she would try other means to publicise the crimes. Through official police channels, of course, she would ask the London newspapers to help in the enquiry.

For either a television programme or the newspapers, Liz would supply photographs of the three dead women, describing where and how they had died. She would even reveal that it was known that the women had had sexual intercourse with the same man, although how that was known would not be stated.

The man who had been involved sexually with the three women would be asked to come forward so that he could be eliminated from the enquiries. That statement would cover the possibility, probably remote, that the man with whom the women had had sexual intercourse and the murderer were not the same person. Chief Inspector Lawrence agreed to relay the details of Liz's scheme to higher authority, telling her not to become too anxious should it take a little time.

It took almost a week, but finally, Liz got approval to release her account of the deaths of the three possible victims of rape/murder to the newspapers, along with colour photographs of the facial features of the young women. The same information was approved for use on television, also, but she was informed that the delay there might be too long to be useful. Liz was relieved that the 'higher authorities' had not altered the account.

A day later an article containing the pertinent details of Liz's scheme appeared in the London tabloid newspapers. One of them substituted the rather prosaic information supplied by the police with a lurid account about a mad fiend who was at large in the East End of London; the newspaper dubbed him "Jack-the-Raper."

The response of the public to the newspaper appeal was much more vociferous than it was helpful. All of Liz's detective colleagues were drafted in, as were several members of the uniform branch, to enable the police to handle the volume of calls. However, after a couple of days of hectic activity only thirteen calls had been received that had been considered worth following up, which was just as well. Dai Morgan and Chris Houghton had been assigned to the investigation of a murder that occurred two days after the newspapers had published Liz's account, so they were available no longer for the investigation of the rape/murders.

Liz and DC Robinson were left to follow up the thirteen useful leads that had resulted from the public appeal. Most of those involved the woman whose identity was unknown, and one sounded like it might result in the woman's identification. That call had come from a university student whose home was in London suburb of Northwood. He said that he had come home for the term break and, by chance, he had seen the article about the dead woman. He said that he was pretty sure that he had known the girl whose identity was unknown; her name was Tara Ionescu, and she was from Romania. He said that Tara had stayed with him and his parents for a time, so, very likely, they could back him up in his identification. Liz agreed to visit the young man, Kevin Price, and his parents late that evening to take a statement from them.

The entire Price family, including Kevin's sister, were able to identify, positively, the unknown dead woman as a girl all of them had known as Tara Ionescu. Kevin stated that Tara had accompanied him to Britain from Rome where she had lived for a time. He said that he hadn't paid much attention at the time that he and Tara had passed through the immigration barrier together, but as far as he could remember he thought that she had travelled on a Romanian passport. Liz was puzzled by that statement. She knew that Tara Ionescu and Kevin Price would have had to separate when going through immigration controls, she being a citizen of a country which, at the time, was not a member of the European Union.

Kevin Price said that after Tara had entered Britain, she had stayed with him and his family for a time. He said he had no idea where she went after he had gone back to Durham to commence the fourth year of a course in modern languages. Liz asked about Tara's family name, whether or not she had its correct spelling. Kevin had said that as far as he knew it was spelled the way that he had indicated. Liz told the Price family that she would have to make enquiries of the Home Office; in order that Tara Ionescu had entered the country legally, they would have to have a record of the circumstances. She informed Kevin that very likely the Home Office would wish to question him further, especially if there were any irregularities.

After Liz got back to the Mile End police station, she received a telephone call from Kevin Price who, it became clear quickly, wished to modify the statement that he had made, but he didn't wish to implicate himself. Liz had suspected that Tara Ionescu had come into the country illegally, and Kevin Price had helped her. Liz short-circuited the rather long-winded explanation of his action by the young man by getting straight to the point: "Mr Price, I believe that it will help solve the murder of Miss Ionescu if we know whether or not she was a legal immigrant. If she was in the country legally, a wide range of jobs would be open to her that otherwise would not be available. If she had been forced to make a living at a job that occupied the fringes of society, such as prostitution, then it would be useful to the police investigation to know that. Now, if you can tell us something that will be of help, we are not going to worry about it too much if you have done something foolish; especially in view of the fact that the unfortunate young woman is dead. Does that help?"

As Liz had hoped he would, Kevin Price confirmed that Tara Ionescu had entered Britain illegally, although he wouldn't say how she had managed it. However, he did say that he would be surprised if she had taken up prostitution.

"She struck me as a very proper young woman. She slept with me, but I'm pretty sure that I was the first."

\* \* \*

As the woman at the London Hospital had promised, the day after Boxing Day Liz received a telephone call from the pathologist there, Dr Lemoine, who had autopsied Tara Ionescu. When he discovered what Liz wished to know, he said that he remembered the autopsy because the damage to the genitalia was unusual. However, to be sure of his facts, he would review notes and photographs made at the time of autopsy, and then get back to her.

When the pathologist rang back, he reiterated the statement in his report that the body had been mutilated by partial removal of the genitalia. He went on to say, "personally, I think that the body may have been attacked by some kind of carnivore; perhaps a cat or a small dog; maybe even a small fox, if it had lain somewhere out of doors. Liz asked how he could be certain the young woman had been alive when her body had been mutilated. He said, "there's irrefutable proof that drowning was the cause of death. It is possible, I suppose, that the animal attack could have occurred after death; the body had been in the water long enough that it was not possible to be certain whether the wounds to the genitalia were pre or post mortem. However, if they were post mortem, the body would have had to have been removed from the water for a time after death and then replaced there. That doesn't make sense to me; perhaps you can make some sense out of it, sergeant." Liz said that she would not argue with Dr Lemoine's logic.

Liz then asked, "how can you be so certain that the wounds to the genitalia were caused by one of the animals you mentioned, rather than some madman with a knife or, perhaps, a carrion-eating bird, like a crow?" Doctor Lemoine replied, "no, sergeant; part of the woman's genitalia were chewed away. I don't know if you've ever noticed, but when dogs and cats eat 'largish' pieces of meat, they tend to turn their heads at an angle to their food. This is to bring into use the so-called meat-eating or carnassial teeth that they have on either side of their mouths. Those teeth are composed of a combination of upper premolar and lower molar teeth, to form a set of 'shears' for cutting. Only mammals that belong to the group called 'Carnivora' possess those teeth, and, as far as animals you're likely to meet every day, that means dogs, cats and foxes. The wounds were caused by flesh being cut away, not by pecks, so that eliminates birds. The flesh was sheared away raggedly, rather than cut cleanly, indicating that it had been done by biting, rather than cutting. Finally, from the size of the bites, I would guess that the animal's jaws were rather small, more like a cat or a quite small dog, rather than a fox. Of course, sergeant, I could be completely wrong; I am merely giving you my opinion, in case it would be helpful."

All the time that Dr Lemoine had been speaking, Liz had in her mind a colour photograph of the damage done to the genitalia of the woman about whom he was speaking. The damage had been quite extensive. As Dr Lemoine was about to ring off, Liz fairly shouted, "oh, doctor; just a moment! As I look at the photographs of the poor woman, I can't help thinking that she must have been in terrible pain if she was alive still when an animal was attacking her." The doctor said that Liz need not worry, "very likely she would have felt the first bite or two, but then tissue shock would have seen to it that she lost sensation in the area. Of course, had she stayed alive long enough, sensation would have returned to the area, and very likely she would have felt pain then."

# Chapter Twenty Four

The identification of the unknown woman whose body was found in the Grand Union Canal should have helped Liz with her investigation, and it did. However, that investigation was then complicated further by the revelation by Kevin Price that Tara Ionescu was an illegal immigrant. That status on her part bore no relevance to the deaths of either Veronica Blanchard or Mary Roberts. Therefore, Liz reasoned, if there was a connection between the three women other than the fact that they had had sexual intercourse with the same man, it had to be some other aspect of their lives. Either that or perhaps all three of the young women had engaged in prostitution, which seemed most unlikely in the case of Veronica Blanchard.

The Christmas break at Queen Mary and Westfield College was not yet over, but Liz hoped that Veronica Blanchard's friend, Michelle Hufton, might have returned to college from her holidays. Liz telephoned the mathematics department and was put through to Michelle on the extension 'phone in the room the young woman shared with three other graduate students. Michelle didn't seem very welcoming, but she agreed to see Liz that day.

From the subject matter of the conversation that passed between them it was obvious that Michelle thought that Liz wished to talk about the mathematics course. Liz didn't disabuse her of that surmise. However, it was likely that it would be necessary for Liz to inform Michelle of her real identity if for no other reason than to get the young woman to co-operate.

Liz decided she would combine a trip to QMW with a little exercise; she walked briskly from the police station down to the Mile End Road. During the walk to the college, Liz thought about what she would say to Michelle Hufton; she concluded that it would be best for her to start the interview with Michelle by telling her the truth: she was a police officer who had been acting undercover at QMW.

There were two other graduate students present in the room where Michelle had her desk, so Liz suggested that perhaps they might go to the Junior Common Room and have a cup of coffee or tea while they talked.

When Liz revealed to Michelle who she was, the young woman said, "but you seem so intelligent!" Then a look of fright came over her face and she said, "what I mean is you seemed to know so much about mathematics!" Liz smiled at the young woman's initial outburst. She had learned long ago that the perception held often by the more educated levels of society was that police officers were the dull 'plods' sometimes depicted in the media. Liz no longer attempted to dispel the myth, saying merely, "well, it helped during the time I was at QMW that a few years earlier I had taken a B.Sc. in Maths at King's College, London."

Michelle surprised Liz by saying, "so it **was** you, then. I went to a meeting at Kings over the Christmas vac, and I got to talking with one of the applied mathematicians who's on the staff there. Your name came up because of that brilliant project you did last semester in applied maths where you compared the results of investing £10,000 with five financial advisers with the result of investing the same amount of money in an index-linked fund. You may not have realised it, but I've heard that at least one member of staff changed his investment strategy when he read your report! Anyway, not to get too far off the subject, the woman that I spoke to said that she had had an undergraduate named Elisabeth Andresen in one of her tutorial groups when she had been a research student at Kings. She said that the Elizabeth Andresen she had known had got a first-class degree in maths and then had joined the police."

"It was funny; I told her that despite the same name you had only completed two years of a maths course and that had been at some polytechnic. To think all along you were sitting there acting as if you didn't know things that you did know!" Liz said that in point of fact quite a lot of the material of the third-year course she had taken at QMW had been new to her, and she'd had to work pretty hard at it just to keep up.

Liz hoped that the opening friendly exchange between herself and Michelle would lay a proper groundwork for talking about Veronica Blanchard. She told Michelle that she had posed as a student in the mathematics department at QMW because the police had been of the opinion that that department, in some way, was connected with the deaths of Veronica Blanchard and Mary Roberts. "However, as I'm sure you will have heard, just before Christmas the body of a third young woman was found near where the bodies of Veronica and Mary had been found. She had died in a manner that was almost identical to that of what Veronica and Mary. However, the third woman had no connection with Queen Mary and Westfield College or the mathematics department. In fact, we are fairly certain that she was an illegal immigrant."

"The death of the third young woman has caused us to revise our thinking about the deaths of all three women.

We think still that their deaths may be connected with some aspect of their lives that they held in common, but, patently, that was not student status. For the time being, probably, there is little that we can learn about the life of the third dead woman prior to her illegal entry into Britain. However, I hope that you and Veronica Blanchard's parents may be able to tell me something about Veronica's life. Details that might have been identical to aspects of the lives of the other two dead women. Similarly, I shall be speaking to those who knew Mary Roberts well, hoping that they can supply me with similar details."

Obviously, Michelle was thinking, but she sat silently munching on one of the biscuits of a small packet that Liz had bought for her. Liz decided that she would ask a question that had been bothering her for some time: she wondered if the common thread that held the murders together was prostitution. Kevin Price had denied that Tara Ionescu could have been involved in prostitution, but Liz was not convinced that the young man really had known Tara that well. Liz asked Michelle if there was any possibility whatsoever that Veronica had sold her body to a man who had then had murdered her.

Michelle's mouth came open and she said, simply, "impossible. Veronica would rather have died than sleep with a man, let alone do so for money." Liz told Michelle that she didn't want to bring up distressful memories, but was she absolutely certain of her opinion. "I have heard of gay women who have become prostitutes, so it is not unknown."

Michelle said that Veronica never would have sold her body either to a man or anyone. "You didn't know her like I did, Sergeant Andresen. She wouldn't even live with me until I had promised her that I would never be unfaithful to her. In fact, we broke up just before summer because of a misunderstanding about a female cousin who came to stay with me. Veronica was killed before we could sort that out; she could be very stubborn at times. She had a 'thing' about loyalty in friends and relatives. She said that her father had turned her out of the house for being what she could not help being. No, Sergeant Andresen, there must be something else where Veronica was concerned." Liz could see that tears had filled Michelle's eyes; she thought it better not to continue on the subject of Veronica Blanchard's sexuality.

Liz found herself agreeing with Michelle Hufton; it seemed most unlikely that engagement in prostitution was the commonality between the three dead women.

She asked Michelle if she knew what the summer job that Veronica had taken up was. The young woman said that Veronica had stopped speaking to her by then, but she thought that before they parted her friend had said something about working with animals. Liz asked, "do you mean working at the zoo or some place like that?" Michelle said that she really didn't know, but she was pretty sure that it had not involved working with zoo animals. "It was some place local, I'm pretty sure, because she told me that she wouldn't have to spend a lot of time travelling. She was 'dotty' about cats. She wanted us to have one, but, unfortunately, I'm allergic to them. As I recall she may have said that another advantage of the summer job would be that she could be around cats again. Maybe it was with a veterinary clinic or an animal shelter."

Liz asked Michelle several more questions about Veronica's activities that might have led her to meet people. None of the activities that Michelle mentioned appeared to be those in which Tara Ionescu would have engaged except, possibly, jogging. Apparently, Veronica had jogged occasion- ally, and when she did, usually, she would go along the foot- path that bordered the Grand Union Canal.

Liz concluded that she had learned as much as she was going to learn by speaking to Michelle Hufton. Therefore, af- ter requesting that the young woman notify her if she could think of anything else, she gave Michelle her business card and left.

As she walked back to the police station, Liz wondered if interviewing Veronica Blanchard's parents would pro- duce any further results. At the station, she telephoned Mrs Blanchard to ask her the same questions that she had asked Michelle Hufton. However, the woman could say only that she had no idea what her daughter had done in order to finance her course at university. "It has been a very long time, officer, since Veronica has asked me or her father for anything."

The registrar's office of Queen Mary and Westfield Col- lege supplied Liz with home addresses for the family of Mary Roberts and the address at which Kay Trask might be con- tacted. She thought that she would contact Kay first, rather than risk dredging up sad memories for the Roberts family. She learned that the young woman had gone abroad for a short skiing holiday and was not due to return until just be- fore the start of the new semester at QMW.

The mother of Mary Roberts told Liz over the telephone that as far as she was aware, her daughter had planned to stay in London during the summer to catch up on her stud- ies and prepare for her final year at university. It was only after her daughter had died, that she had discovered that that had not been the case. Her daughter had been working at a job and living with a boy. Missus Roberts said that she did not know who the boy was, or what job her daughter had done. She said that she thought it likely that Mary's friend, Kay; she didn't know her last name, would be able to answer Liz's questions.

After she put down the 'phone, Liz couldn't help but feel frustrated at her inability to get definitive information that would allow her to make a connection between the three dead women. She was worried that a perceived lack of progress in the investigation would mean that her boss would insist that she should return to Scotland Yard. She didn't want to turn the investigation over to someone else; she was sure that as soon as she could interview Kay Trask, she would be able to find a feature that was common to the lives of the three dead women.

# Chapter Twenty Five

Liz was pleased that she would be getting home before late evening for the first time in several days. She was looking forward to a properly-prepared meal preceded by a glass or two of a white Bordeaux that she had bought over a week earlier, and which had remained in the fridge, unopened, ever since. Then she would spend a quiet evening reading, followed by a hot bath and an early night.

As she approached her flat, she could hear a telephone ringing so she rushed through the front door, grabbing the 'phone and shouting, "hello" into the receiver. It was her mum. Liz was irritated to hear by the hesitation in the speech and the slurring of words that her mother had been drinking. Audrey said that she was not feeling well, and would it be asking too much of "my only daughter to come home for a few days." Liz asked what had happened to Julia and was told, "oh, her! She ran out on me. I knew I never should've trusted her. She was never here when I needed her." Liz did wonder what could have happened that would drive Julia away, but she knew that it was useless to expect her mother to make much sense in her present state. She thought quickly to consider if there was a likelihood that she could get away, even if it were only for a day or so. She would have to make the attempt, yet again, to smooth out difficulties Liz knew would have been created by her mother's drinking.

Liz told Audrey that she would enquire of her superiors to see if she could get some time off. "If I can manage it, I will come up on the train this evening, mum. Meanwhile, you get your rest."

After she had rung off, Liz thought quickly about the approach she would have to make to DCI Lawrence; she would have to make her mum sound much more ill than she was actually. The DCI had given her his home telephone number, in case she had to contact him in an emergency, so she rang him at home immediately after speaking with her mum. He was most sympathetic and told her to take as much time as she needed. "If you find you've got to stay up in Cambridge longer than you anticipate now, all you've got to do is give me a tinkle at the station and I'll arrange some cover."

Liz debated with herself whether or not to prepare a meal at home or to try to grab something at Liverpool Street Station whilst waiting for the train to Cambridge. She opted to fix something at home, since there were several packaged meals in the freezing compartment of her fridge.

After finishing her meal, she packed an overnight case and was just on the way out the door, when her telephone began ringing again. She raced back into her flat. It was Julia. She said, "I've been trying to get you for quite some time. I tried to ring you at Scotland Yard, but they said that you weren't there and gave me another number to ring. When I telephoned that number, they said that you'd gone home, so I tried your flat, and, finally, I got you. Liz, I really must talk with you. Your mother and I have had another disagreement, and she ordered me to leave the house. I know that she doesn't mean it; it was the drink talking to me, but I don't know what to do now. I don't want to leave your mother all alone, but sometimes, when she is drinking, she can be very cruel. Would it be possible for me to come to

London and talk to you?" Liz asked where Julia was staying. "My friend, Leeanne, is letting me stay with her." Liz told Julia about Audrey's 'phone call, telling her that she was coming to Cambridge that evening. She and Julia made arrangements to meet in the town centre the following day.

Liz did not allow the fact that the downstairs of her mum's house was unlighted to detain her long at the front door. She thought it likely that the woman had collapsed in a drunken stupor either on the settee in the front room or on her bed. As it turned out, it was not the front room. Then she went directly to her mum's bedroom, seeing that Audrey was lying on her back on the bed, fully dressed, with the lights still on. Liz found a blanket in the wardrobe of her mum's room and used that to cover the form, which remained unconscious all during the covering operation. A search of the kitchen relieved one of Liz's worries: it was obvious that Julia had been there sufficiently recently so that there was food in the house.

Audrey was permitted to sleep the following day until it was necessary for Liz to make preparations to go into town to meet Julia. A badly 'hung over' Audrey came down the stairs in response to Liz's call to breakfast. As Liz had anticipated, her mum wished for nothing more than tea. Also, she would not explain why it was that she had ordered Julia to leave, beyond saying that she was fed up having the girl in the house. Her attitude made Liz realise that it would be futile to try to argue her mother into continuing to let Julia live with her. Besides, she thought that Julia deserved to be treated much more kindly than Audrey seemed prepared to do when she had been drinking.

* * *

As was always the case, Liz's spirits were lifted when she saw her friend. Julia was seated at a table in the Starbuck's coffee shop where they'd agreed to meet. Julia rose when she saw Liz, coming to meet her and giving her an affectionate hug. After the preliminaries, Julia opened the conversation about Audrey by asking how Liz's mum was getting on. Liz said that she was very worried about her mum, but she felt helpless to do anything about it. "One of the things I wished to discuss with you, Julia, was where we go from here. You shouldn't have to put up with my mum's nonsense. She wouldn't tell me what she said to you the other evening, but I can imagine. You mentioned when last we met that the modelling that you're doing paid you reasonably well; do you think that it would be possible for you to rely on your earnings to support yourself? I can help out a little, if that would make it possible."

Julia hugged Liz again, saying, "you are so kind to me, Liz, but it won't be necessary for you to do that. I am earning quite a lot of money modelling. In fact, I don't spend it all, so I keep it in my bank account. I can easily support myself. I would have suggested it before, but I didn't want to let you down by not looking after your mother. Also, I don't want to lose you. I know that if I am living in your mother's house, I will see you when you come to visit her." Liz told Julia that they must always try to stay in touch, inviting her to stay with her whenever the young woman visited London. Also, Liz assured Julia that the two of them would get together in Cambridge whenever Liz came to visit her mum.

However, despite their mutual assurances, Liz could see already that the young woman was growing away from her.

She had taken on an image that befitted her youth, using the word, "cool," as an exclamation and prefacing most every description with the word, "like." Also, it was obvious to Liz that the clothing that Julia wore was the latest in fashion; consequently it was expensive.

# Chapter Twenty Six

Liz and DC Clive Robinson were making their way, slowly, through the remainder of the list of people who had called the police to give information about the woman now known to be Tara Ionescu. It was necessary for each of the callers to be interviewed, and that involved finding a time mutually convenient for both the caller and either Liz or Clive. Most of the callers had sighted a young woman looking like Tara in various parts of London, including three of the main train stations, where she had been seen, usually late at night, acting like she was homeless. She had been remembered both because of her youth and a rather striking appearance; she didn't look like the sort of person who should be homeless.

Neither Liz nor DC Robinson asked the interviewees the question that had entered their minds: what should a homeless person look like? However, Clive's interview with one person immediately caught Liz's attention when he mentioned it to her. A man who worked as a local-authority dustman said that he had had an "argy-bargy" with a young woman looking like the one in the photograph just before Christmas. He had encountered her in the dust-bin storage area behind a block of flats in Stepney. He said that he had caught her in the act of dumping "shitty, smelly" cat litter loose in her dustbin. "I told her that the stuff went all over the place when the dust cart picked up the bin to empty it. I told her to tie it up in a plastic bag, but she didn't seem to know enough English to be able to understand me."

Constable Robinson said that he had asked the dustman to show him the place where he had encountered the young woman; "I checked around the front of the building which is a collection of one and two bedroom council flats set in a three-storey apartment building. So far, I've talked to the residents in about half of the twenty-four flats, and none of them has the foggiest idea who the young woman is. I did find out, however, that one of the residents keeps a cat. My informant pointed out the flat where the cat lives, but the owner wasn't at home. My informant did say, however, that the cat's owner was an older woman; not the one whose picture I showed her."

Liz was very pleased by the constable's discovery. If, as seemed possible, Tara Ionescu was the woman to whom the dustman spoke, there was a chance that her movements could be known at a time that probably was only a few days before her death. Liz suggested to Clive that the information about the woman with the cat was of sufficient potential importance that it would be worthwhile making an approach to the local council to obtain name and contact details of the flat's occupant.

\* \* \*

Liz checked her diary, seeing that Mary Roberts' friend, Kay Trask, should have returned from her foreign holiday. She rang the telephone number that she had for the young woman, learning that, indeed, Kay had returned. She was spending the last few days before the start of the new semester at QMW studying in the college library.

Liz welcomed the opportunity to get out of the police station to get some exercise, so she again walked down to the Mile End Road and then to the QMW library. She had to search for a time, but ultimately she found Kay seated at a table in one of the alcoves off the large reading room. After whispered greetings and enquiries after the sort of Christmas vac that each of them had had, Liz requested that Kay accompany her to the part of the library were they could speak without disturbing anyone.

Liz had wondered how Kay would react when she learned that Liz was in the police and not a bona fide student. Kay was surprised at Liz's revelation. However, she caught herself before saying what she very obviously was thinking: that Liz seemed to be too intelligent to be a police officer. Liz covered over the potential gaff quickly by telling Kay that she had been chosen for the undercover work at QMW precisely because she had taken a degree in mathematics prior to entering the police. Finally, the two women got down to the subject of interest to Liz: the job at which Mary Roberts had been working at the time she had died. Kay said that Mary was taking care of the animals of people who were on holiday. She couldn't remember for whom Mary had been working; in fact, she wasn't sure whether or not her friend had told her. "She liked the job because the hours were fairly flexible. However, I don't think that it paid her very much. She seemed to be 'skint' all of the time."

As Liz walked back to the police station she concentrated her mind on a thought that had formed the moment Kay Trask had told her that when she died Mary Roberts was doing a job working with animals. Assuming that the young woman to whom the dustman had spoken was Tara Ionescu; that indicated that at least two of the dead women were involved in some way with animals. Furthermore, if what Michelle Hufton had said was true: that Veronica Blanchard had worked with animals also, perhaps the common factor in the deaths of the three dead women was that they were doing jobs where they looked after animals.

Where that conclusion would lead was not at once clear to Liz. Just offhand, she had had experience of three kinds of businesses that looked after animals: kennels, veterinary surgeries and animal shelters. Perhaps it would be necessary to contact all such enterprises in the East London area to learn if any of the dead women had worked as kennel girls for them. It was unlikely that there would be many such enterprises, so Liz decided that she would begin with that aspect of the investigation as soon as she got back to the station.

Having got the work of the immediate future sorted out, Liz thought about the place that she had left a few minutes earlier, Queen Mary and Westfield College. She had enjoyed her time being an undergraduate again. In particular she had found the relationship that she had had with Jeff Barnes, Kay Trask and the rest of her fellow third-years, to be very pleasant. She knew that she would miss them and some of the college staff, such as Dr Boalt, but she would not miss the academic life. She concluded that she had made the right decision, a few years earlier, when she had chosen to enter the police service rather than pursue a career in academic research.

Liz could find only one listing for a kennel for household pets, and that was a cattery. She rang the number to be told that the cattery was run by a man and his wife, and they did not take on part-time workers. In the same category was a business that called itself, Holiday Pets, but there was no reply when Liz rang the telephone number listed. There appeared to be only one animal shelter in the East End of London, and that one catered for stray and abandoned cats.

The person to whom Liz spoke at the cat shelter said that all of their present employees had been with them for at least two years, so it would not be necessary for her to examine their employee records.

There were not as many veterinary surgeries in the East End as Liz had feared there would be, but only one of those that she rang had had an employee leave them during the six months prior to Christmas. That had been one of the three veterinary surgeons on the staff; he had emigrated to South Africa.

In the meantime, DC Clive Robinson had not managed to get any details of the woman with the cat. He discovered from his enquiries with the local council that the flat in which the woman lived was no longer owned by the council but had been sold to a sitting tenant. Clive got the name and address of the owner and was able to contact him. The owner said that he didn't live in the flat any longer; it was too small now that his elderly mother had come to live with him and his family. He gave Clive the name of his tenant, a Ms Beddoes, but he had no idea where she worked; indeed, whether or not she worked. Therefore, Clive would have to catch her when she was at home. The DC told Liz that he would run 'round there that evening, hoping that she would be there.

The following morning, Clive greeted Liz with the news that still he had not been able to make contact with the woman with the cat. However, he had managed to find someone else who could place Tara Ionescu at the same block of flats. He said that he had got no response after knocking loudly at the door of the woman's flat. As he turned to go a man was coming along the balcony that ran along outside the flat doors. "He was just entering the door of the flat next to hers. Since he was one of the flat owners I'd not yet questioned, I thought that I would question him then so my journey wouldn't be completely wasted. He said that the young woman in the photograph taken of Tara Ionescu looked very much like one he had seen a couple of times because she had been looking after his neighbour's cat. He said that he probably wouldn't have noticed her except that she had knocked on his door to ask where she could take cat litter to dispose of it."

"He told me that he had a hell of a time understanding her at first because of her peculiar accent. He said that she pronounced litter as 'leeter' and so on; it was kind of funny because he said that it took him the longest time to discover that the girl wasn't talking about drinks or some sort of bottles, but the stuff that cats do their business in." Clive went on to say that he had tried to find out more about Tara Ionescu, but Ms Beddoes' neighbour couldn't help much. He said that the only reason he had even seen the girl was because of the cat litter. According to DC Robinson, the man didn't know whether the girl was a friend of his neighbour or if she was being paid by someone. The DC finished by saying, "I put my card through the mail flap of Ms Beddoes' door, asking her to telephone me. However, if I don't hear from her in a couple of days, I'll go back. I would telephone her but directory enquiries has no listing for her under the spelling of her surname that the flat owner gave me, and that's not because she has an unlisted number."

# Chapter Twenty Seven

Liz felt really rather weary as she let herself into her flat much later than the time at which she usually arrived home. During the day, DCI Lawrence had got a telephone call from Detective Inspector Lydia Mussett, Liz's boss at Scotland Yard. Lydia was making 'discrete' enquiries about "Detective Sergeant Andresen's work;" obviously it would not be long before Liz would be 'requested' to return to her duties in Southwest London. Liz hated to leave jobs undone; she knew that she would be particularly unhappy to have to turn over to a colleague her part in the rape/murder investigation just when it looked hopeful that a successful conclusion was in sight.

The main reason for her late arrival home was a long discussion about the progress of her investigation that she had had with DCI Lawrence after he had called her to his office to tell her about Lydia's telephone call. Liz had given the DCI regular written reports of the progress of her investigation, so she wondered why he wanted her to go over the same material. However, he had explained his reasoning, saying that he was rather old fashioned and liked to hear things "from the horse's mouth, so to speak." He offered her no advice, but he did agree with her that the possibility that all three dead women had worked with animals was a promising lead.

Liz had come away from the meeting feeling much the same about the DCI as she had felt about most of the superior police officers she had met. It appeared that a requirement for those that aspire to high office was a large element of arrogance in their personality. There had been some exceptions, however; Lydia Mussett being one.

Liz decided that she would have a meal, courtesy of her microwave, and then she would follow that by a long, hot bath. Finally, she would spend a period in bed reading a detective story. She had been reading the same story for almost two weeks, having to go back over material she'd read already because the long intervals between reading sessions caused her to forget important details of the plot. Just once, she thought, she would like to enjoy the luxury of reading a book straight through.

She had just lowered herself into the bath when her telephone rang. She cursed to herself; it was at times like this that she wished that she had given in to an earlier inclination and had had an extension 'phone installed in the bathroom. At least then she would stand a chance of answering it before the caller had rung off. She decided to let it ring; if the call was important, whoever it was would try again.

\* \* \*

A persistent ringing of the telephone awakened Liz. She had drifted off to sleep whilst reading. The caller was Julia who said that she was thinking of making a change in her life, and she wanted to discuss it with Liz first. When Liz asked what was the change, Julia said that she would tell her when she saw her; would it be OK for her to come down to London the next day? Liz replied that of course Julia was always welcome; did she wish to stay overnight? Julia said that she had hoped that Liz would invite her to do so. Liz said that she would either take Julia out for a meal, or that she would cook something special at home. Julia said that she had been eating in snack bars and pubs far too much, and that she would prefer "one of your delicious meals, Liz."

After the telephone conversation had ended, Liz thought over what Julia had said; it was worrying that her friend was contemplating a change in her life. She hoped that the difficulties that the young woman had encountered with Audrey had not disrupted her friend's routine so badly that she was fallen hopelessly behind with her coursework. In Liz's experience that was the commonest reason, aside from finances, for undergraduates to discontinue their studies. Of one thing Liz was sure: she and Julia would not sleep together. To be certain that she kept that resolve, she would not serve wine during the visit.

Prior to Julia's visit, Liz spent a day in further efforts to discover possible employers of young women to look after animals. She tried two further categories that had been suggested by DCI Lawrence: pet shops and garden centres. Her enquiries at those enterprises that were listed in the Yellow Pages met with disappointment. Representatives of the three garden centres that she contacted said that no employees were hired specifically to look after animals that they might have for sale. Usually, one of the general shop clerks would make certain that the animals were well cared for, but that wasn't their only job. Liz couldn't be certain of the terms of employment of the dead women, so she asked the representatives to search their employee records for the previous six months and to telephone her if they had hired any or all of the women whose names she gave them. One man, the manager of a garden centre, said that he could answer the question without looking at his records. None of his employees had left during the previous six months, although he had taken on extra staff over the Christmas period.

The manager of the one pet shop listed said that she looked after all of the animals except when she went on holiday; then her assistant took over.

Liz discussed her results for the day with Clive Robinson who said that he still had not heard from the lady with the cat. He guessed that he would have to call around there again that evening.

On her way home, Liz stopped at a small market near the Plaistow underground station to buy items for the special meal that she was going to prepare that evening for Julia and her. She had a favourite pasta dish that she had not prepared in quite some time, so she thought that she would try that if she could find some Parmesan cheese. She negotiated her way successfully through the market, finding the cheese and resisting the temptation to remove a bottle of white wine when she passed the chilled-drinks cabinet. She was determined that that evening she and Julia would confine their joint activities to talking about the change that her young friend wished to make in her life.

Julia was in buoyant spirits as she entered Liz's flat. Her first act was to give Liz a kiss whose intention was unmistakable. Liz felt her resolve weakening the longer the kiss endured, but finally, Julia stopped kissing and handed her hostess a bottle of chilled white wine. She said, "I bought that only a few minutes ago at a nice little market near the underground station. I know that you like Sancerre." Liz knew what the wine had cost because she had bought it at that same market. She hoped that Julia was not overextending herself.

Julia had arrived earlier than Liz had expected, so that she had not yet completed the preparations for the evening meal. Liz suggested that her friend come into the kitchen and talk whilst she completed the pasta sauce and made the salad. Julia volunteered to make the salad, so that left Liz free to concentrate on the sauce. Liz insisted that a glass of wine would make their tasks very much easier. Julia said that she had to agree.

Liz didn't discover what the change in her life was that Julia contemplated until much later in the evening. As usual, Julia was the perfect guest, enthusing over Liz's pasta dish, even occasionally using a word other than 'cool' as an adjective.

The bottle of wine was finished off during the meal with the consequence that what little remained of Liz's resolve not to let lust rule her relationship with the young women disappeared completely. Their encounter that evening was more passionate than anything they had managed previously. They had bathed together, giggling at their efforts to make both of them fit into Liz's tub. Once they emerged from the tub, Julia insisted upon drying Liz, kneeling before her as she did so and beginning to orally masturbate her. At first, Liz felt embarrassed, but then her arousal dispelled that feeling as she held Julia's head to her.

Before their session together that evening had ended, Liz no longer cared that she had given in to her lustful feelings. In fact, she had engaged in acts that she had not done before with anyone. The whole of the front of her body from her neck to her thighs bore abrasions; the result of Julia's passionate biting. Liz was aware also of damage that she had done to her friend's body. Julia had winced later in the evening when Liz had begun to massage the young woman's clitoris. Liz guessed that during one of their sessions when passion was peaking, she very likely had nibbled too vigorously. Finally, the two women had exhausted themselves and lay in each other's arms, ready to talk.

To start the conversation, Liz said, "now, tell me what is the change in your life that you contemplate. It sounded very serious over the 'phone." Julia said, "I don't want to let you down, Liz. I love you and respect you too much. However, I want to tell you what has happened, and I want you to tell me what you think that I should do."

"You know that I have been modelling for the father of my friend, Leeanne Palmer, in Cambridge. About a week ago, Leeanne's father introduced me to a man who spoke with an American accent. Leeanne's father said that the man would be watching the session, if I didn't mind. A few days later, Leeanne told me that her father wished to speak to me, would I please telephone him. Well, I did, and he told me that the man that he'd introduced me to was interested in me. He said that the man was a big American agent who handled several famous models. He mentioned some names, but I don't know anything about models, so the names didn't mean anything to me."

"Anyway, Mr Palmer said that this was my big opportunity if I wanted a career in modelling. He said that most young women, including, he suspected, his own daughter, would sell their souls for a chance like that I was being given. He said that this man, the American agent, wanted me to come to London for a photographic session; the agent had thought of a couple of modelling assignments where I might be just the person the client was looking for. Well, one thing led to another, and now I have been offered a contract by the agent. There is some legal reason why the contract has to go through a British agent; something to do with me not being of legal age in the place in America where the American agent has his business. Please tell me what you think, Liz; am I being stupid? Leeanne says that I am. She suspects that the

American is just trying to get me into bed. Of course, Lee-anne doesn't know about me and you. I wouldn't get into bed with him no matter what inducement he offered me."

As Julia had been speaking, Liz had been anticipating the question that it was very likely her young friend would be asking; a question that Liz would find it impossible to answer for anyone but herself. Put in its simplest form, should she, Julia, lead a life based on self interest or should she try to adhere to the principle of altruism that had been guiding her life for the previous several months. She was fairly certain that Julia genuinely was seeking an answer to her question; she was not merely using Liz as a sounding board for an idea about which she'd made up her mind. Finally, Julia stopped speaking and said, "tell me, Liz, what would you do if you were me?"

Liz could think of no other way of approaching the question than to pose several questions for Julia to answer. "How old are you, now, Julia, twenty?" Julia said that she had just become twenty years of age. "Do you enjoy modelling, or have you done it just because of the money it pays." Julia said that she did enjoy the work, but she didn't know if she would like doing it full time. She said that Leeanne had said that it could get terribly boring. However, Julia had to admit that the money was useful, especially when it came to buying nice clothes. Liz continued, "let me suggest something for you to think about: don't make up your mind right away, but think about it. Why don't you say 'yes' to the American agent? Try being a model for a year or so. I should think that you would learn by then if it is the career for you. If you find that it is what you want to do, continue doing it. If you discover that it is not the sort of life you wish to lead; quit. You'll be only a little older then than you are now. Nothing will prevent you from coming back to Britain and resuming your career in education."

It was obvious from Julia's enthusiastic response that Liz's idea was not foreign to the young woman; probably, she had been thinking along the same lines outlined by Liz. She hugged Liz, and her kiss conveyed the message that she would like them to continue with their lovemaking. However, Liz looked at her watch, saying that she would have to be at work early in the morning so perhaps they had best get some sleep. Liz didn't mind, however, when Julia cuddled closely with her whilst both women made their way to sleep.

Liz was kept awake for a time by a thought that she had neglected to voice some minutes earlier. She would have to get Julia to give her some details of the agent with whom she would be dealing. It would be a simple matter for Liz to check into his 'bona fides', making certain that his sole interest in Julia wasn't that that was suspected by Leeanne Palmer.

# Chapter Twenty Eight

Clive Robinson greeted Liz with a uncharacteristic boast: "I've cracked it, Liz!" Liz said, "oh, you've finally chased down that woman with the cat? Good going, Clive. What did she have to say for herself?" At that point Dai Morgan broke in, "no, Liz, I think that he's cracked the whole damn thing. Your three dead women and my murdered man. Tell her about it, Clive." Liz looked at Clive whose smile was very broad. "Well, I finally found the woman with the cat: Ms Beddoes. She's OK, but the cat is a little bugger. Whilst I was talking to the woman, the damn animal jumped up on the table in front of me. To be friendly, I stroked it a couple of times, and the little bastard bit me, drawing blood. The woman didn't apologise or anything; she just put the cat on the floor."

"Anyway, she said that she works for a publishing company, and has to travel away from home for brief periods fairly frequently. She doesn't have a car, so it's not convenient for her to take the cat to a cattery, the nearest of which is way out in Romford. Consequently, she uses a company called Holiday Pets, which sends in people on a daily basis to feed the animal and make sure that it has plenty of water, and that the litter tray is kept clean. She said that she had never laid eyes on any of the people who came to her flat. Whenever she was to go away, she would ring the Holiday Pets people and arrange to leave them a key to her flat door."

"Now get this, Liz. She told me that when she rang Holiday Pets she usually talked to a man whose name was

Mr Volpi!" Liz looked at Dai Morgan, asking, "isn't that the man whose death you and Chris have been investigating?" Before Dai could say anything the penny dropped: "oh, Tara Ionescu was working for Volpi and, probably, the other two were also. Was that why he was killed?" Dai said that he didn't know, but now it was possible to make some sense of the whole thing.

Dai Morgan continued, "Chris and me weren't aware of the Holiday Pets thing. We thought that Volpi was involved with his wife's business. She is an Indian or Bangladeshi lady, and she runs a business making Asian clothing. Whether or not there is a connection, the wife's business was attacked by an arsonist right around the time Volpi died. Missus Volpi has not been very helpful in our investigation so far, leading us to suspect that she had something to hide. Just looking around her premises it looks like she has six women working for her, all of 'em Asian. Probably at least some of the women are illegal immigrants, but we've no proof of that, as yet. I think what we had better do, Liz, is combine our efforts. I've already put Chris on the job of looking up employee records for Mrs Volpi's company with the department of health and social security. If her employees are legitimate, both they and she should be paying National Insurance contributions." Chris broke in to say, "I've not heard from the DHSS, as yet; they move like a bunch of snails!"

Dai Morgan continued, "if it turns out that Mrs Volpi is not making National Insurance contributions, we can haul her in for questioning. She doesn't have to know that it's not our job to investigate those sorts of irregularities. However, maybe we can frighten her enough that she will tell us what we want to know about Holiday Pets. Volpi must have kept some records for his company; maybe, at the very least, we can get his missus to show us those."

Liz thought for a moment, wondering how to suggest an alternative approach without offending Dai Morgan. She said, "that sounds like a good idea to me, Dai, but I suspect that we had better wait until Chris hears from the DHSS. We don't want to end up with egg all over our faces when Mrs Volpi pulls out her company records detailing the National Insurance contributions for both her employees and her company." Liz's warm opinion of her colleague was confirmed when he said, "you're right there, Liz. We'd never get anything out of her if her business is completely legitimate. She'd probably haul in a solicitor who would make all kinds of demands. Have you got a better idea?" Liz said, "I wonder if it wouldn't be better to use a more 'softly, softly' approach. We must assume that Mrs Volpi loved her husband and is still grieving over his death. Might it not be a good idea to try to enlist her co-operation in the solution of her husband's death? If we tell her of our suspicion that all three dead women worked for her husband's company, she may help us to confirm that. If that was the case, then she may have access to records that will give us details of all of the clients of Holiday Pets. It is very likely that one of those clients is the murderer both of Mr Volpi and the three young women."

Liz knew that she had got a bit carried away with the logic of her argument, causing her to worry that Dai Morgan would react negatively. Throughout her life Liz had been no stranger to the reactions of others to what was often described by them as her 'know-it-all' attitude. She always had found this puzzling. She valued informed opinion even if it displayed insight that was superior to her own. However, she needn't have worried in this instance. Dai Morgan made it clear that for the immediate future the four detectives should follow Liz's ideas. Later, when she and Dai were alone, he paid her a compliment that brought tears to her eyes and a hug and a kiss on the cheek for Dai: "I can see why they wanted you at the 'Yard', Liz. That was good thinking back there. I'm proud of you." Dai insisted that Liz should be in charge of the now combined investigation of the deaths of Volpi and the three women who had been raped and then, very likely, killed by drowning them. He voiced concern that the contacts that he and Chris Houghton had made had accomplished no more than getting Mrs Volpi's back up. He hoped that Liz's 'softly, softly' approach would have more success. The excuse that Liz could give to the woman for yet another visit by the police could be the new evidence that Clive Robinson had turned up when he interviewed the woman with the Burmese cat.

Liz telephoned Mrs Volpi to make an appointment to see her. She could tell by the reaction when Liz identified herself, that Mrs Volpi was not inclined to co-operate with the police. The woman was unfailingly polite as she spoke to Liz, but she said that things were very difficult for her at that time. "Part of the building that my company occupies was subjected to an arsonist attack a short time ago, and we are very crowded at the moment. Also, as you know, my husband has been attacked and murdered. It is not a good time for the police to call 'round." Liz exercised great tact in making it clear to Mrs Volpi that the police investigation into her husband's death could not be delayed. "I will try not to take up too much of your time."

Just as she and Clive were preparing to leave for the interview with Mrs Volpi, Chris Houghton came over to Liz's desk saying that he'd just heard from the DHSS about the company run by Mrs Volpi; it was called Asian Enterprises. "At present, the company has a clean bill of health; all of the employees for whom National Insurance contributions are made have legal documentation. That goes for the company as well; it makes regular contributions for its employees. However, apparently that has not always been the case. It has been suspected, but never proved, that the company has made use of illegal immigrants in the past. The DHSS would appreciate being informed if we discover any irregularities during our investigation."

Liz introduced herself and her colleague to Mrs Volpi, who shook their hands saying that she was Kamini Volpi. At once, she launched into excited exclamations that caused her voice to take on a 'sing-song' metre. She made it clear that she could not contribute any more information about her poor husband's death than she had already done. She said, "this part of London is full of bad people. I don't know why any of them would want to garrotte my Grigore; he was such a nice man; a kind man. He never carried any money on him, so they would not have got anything."

Liz waited for Mrs Volpi to stop speaking. When she did, Liz said, "as I mentioned over the 'phone, Mrs Volpi, we now have evidence that your husband's death was not due to a mugging attempt, but perhaps, it was connected with a business that he ran. We would like your co-operation in telling us about that. If you will help us there, it is possible that we will be able to clear up your husband's murder."

As Liz was speaking Mrs Volpi's eyes grew wide indicating that what she was hearing had relevance for her. She said, "yes, I wonder if that was what it was all about. One of the ladies who works for me told Grigore that she thought at least one of the girls whose picture was in the paper the previous day had worked for him; she thought that she had seen the girl in the office of the company. Grigore didn't pay much attention to newspapers; his English reading was not very good. However when the lady employee told him that the police wanted people to contact them if they knew any of the women, he asked to see the newspaper article. He was astonished. He said that all three of the dead young women had worked for him; he had thought that they had just quit and gone off without telling him. He said that he was going to telephone the police when he got a spare moment. That same night, an arsonist attacked my company. Fortunately, the fire was put out before it got to the main plant where all of our expensive machinery is located. However, we lost all of the company records that were kept in two filing cabinets in the office where the fire was started. I suppose the arson attack distracted my husband because he never got around to calling the police; the day following the fire, he was attacked and killed."

Liz asked Mrs Volpi to tell her as much as she knew about Holiday Pets, the business that her husband had run. "Oh, Grigore loved that. He made a good living from it, and he hardly had to lift a finger. Also, he had quite an eye for young ladies; nothing improper, mind, but he hired pretty girls to do the work of the company. To be honest, I was surprised that the company was as successful as it was." Missus Volpi's eyes became tear-laden as she said, "we still get many calls from people wanting him to look after their pets. I hoped to get my brother to take over the business, but he wasn't interested."

Liz tried to keep Mrs Volpi on the subject by asking details about the running of the business; did it have premises, was there some office staff, etc. Missus Volpi said that her husband had run the business from her office. "He thought that he was being very clever, the sly devil; he kept saying that he could get by without paying a secretary, but then my secretary handled most of the calls that came in for his business." Liz asked if the records of Mrs Volpi's husband were available; would it be possible for her to see them. Missus Volpi said that Holiday Pets had had one drawer in one of the filing cabinets in the office of her business, where her husband kept his written records. "However, like the records for my company, the written records for Holiday Pets were destroyed in the fire. Fortunately, Grigore was very good with computers and he had duplicated all of my company's records as well as those of Holiday Pets on a computer that we keep at home. I don't understand about computers, so now I have had to hire someone who is computer literate to handle the company accounts and records. I think that anything you wish to know about Holiday Pets would be on that computer, if you wish to look there. When we are finished here, I will introduce you to Miss Sanjeera, our computer expert, she should be able to help you."

\* \* \*

Grigore Volpi kept the records of his business in a spreadsheet programme in which each sheet in a workbook was devoted to a single client. Also, there were individual sheets for each of his employees. Miss Sanjeera said that she thought that that was an odd way of keeping records, but it was interesting because it made calculations of both client's bills and employee's hours easier. At the head of each client sheet Volpi had entered the full name of the client, the address, and other pertinent details such as contact telephone numbers, number and kinds of pets, their names and the sort of attention that they required. The rest of the sheet consisted of columns headed "Visit Date," "Visitor," "Approximate Duration," "Tasks Completed." Figures in the columns marked "Visit Date" and "Approximate Duration" transferred automatically to a sheet devoted to the record of an employee whose name was indicated by that recorded in the "Visitor" column.

The first step in the search for the killer was to print off copies of all of the spreadsheets that showed visits to clients by young women named Veronica, Mary and Tara. The second step was to see who the three young women had visited up to a week before the discoveries of their bodies. That time period was well outside the time it was estimated that the women had been dead when their bodies were found, but, of course, it was possible that the victims had been held captive for a time.

The analysis of the data very quickly turned up the name of just one client: Ms Beddoes, the woman interviewed earlier by DC Robinson. Her animal, a cat named Soong, had been attended by all three of the murdered women within a week of their deaths. However, DC Robinson was of the opinion that it was unlikely that the woman had any knowledge of the murders. "When I spoke to her, she told me that she never saw the girls who had looked after her cat whilst she was away, but that she thought that they were very conscientious. That was why she had continued to use Holiday Pets. She appeared to be quite shocked when I told her the reason for my visit." DC Robinson's doubts led Detective Inspector Morgan to voice the opinion: "she may not be aware of it, but very likely she knows the man we're looking for. It may be someone she allows to use her flat whilst she is away on her trips."

Liz was asked by Dai Morgan to make contact with Ms Beddoes and attempt to interview her. She was told, "if that fails, we may have to obtain a search warrant and examine her flat."

When Liz rang Ms Beddoes at her place of work, she was pleased to hear that the woman was there, not off on one of her trips. Liz identified herself and was on the point of attempting to set up a time when they could talk, when the woman said, "oh, sergeant; I have been thinking of ringing the police. I wonder if it would be better for me to drop in at Mile End on my way home during the evening. I live not very far from the station, so it won't be out of my way. I think there's something that I should tell you." Liz agreed to meet Ms Beddoes that evening around seven.

After Liz rang off she paused briefly to think over Ms Beddoe's side of the conversation. She hoped that she wasn't wrong, but she thought it likely that the woman had come to the realisation that she knew something that might help in the murder investigation of which Liz was part.

\* \* \*

The woman identified herself to Liz as Hermione Beddoes. Liz introduced herself and DC Robinson before taking Ms Beddoes to an interview room. The woman said, "I've been doing some thinking since talking to you, sergeant, about those horrible rapes and murders of the girls whose bodies were found in the Grand Union Canal. I wonder if

I don't know someone who may be involved. He is a man who stays at my flat from time to time, particularly when I'm not there. I turned over my second bedroom to him, so he can pretty much come and go as he pleases. I can't remember if he was here at the time those poor girls were killed, but I thought I had better tell someone. If he's not involved, presumably he will have nothing to worry about."

Liz asked who the man was, and how well did Ms Beddoes know him. She said, "his name was Karl Hübner; he is a German, but he visits the UK from time to time. He works for a German optical-instruments manufacturer. I used to know him when we were kids. My dad and his both worked for the same company, and during my summer hols we quite often would go to a small house the Hübner's had in the Bavarian Alps. They would invite us there, and Karl and I would play together. I didn't see him for a long time; in fact, I had forgot about him, when one day, six months or so ago, he rang me where I work, wanting to visit me. He said that he was now coming to the UK regularly, and he would like us to renew the friendship that we had when we were kids."

"I only saw him to be polite, but he turned out to be a rather 'pushy' individual. Before I knew it, he had more or less got me to agree to let him stay with me whilst he was in London. Since then, he's been here four or five times that I know about, mostly during times when I've been away. I prefer it that way. He's sort of...I don't know; not exactly 'creepy'; more kind of over familiar, if you know what I mean?"

"I suppose it is sort of funny, but when I first spoke to the police, Karl didn't even enter my mind when I was asked about men friends. He's not really a friend; in fact I have been trying to figure out a way of politely asking him not to ask to use my flat again. Until I got to thinking about the possibility that Karl could be involved in the murders, I had overlooked curious things about him. He seems to be a cleanliness 'freak'. The flat is always spotlessly clean when I get back from a trip, and he's been staying there. At least twice, I've come back to find that he'd bought a new set of sheets for the bed he sleeps in. In fact, one time the sheets he replaced were new ones he'd bought a previous time; neither he nor anyone else had slept on them as far as I knew. I just thought that he preferred stiff sheets or something like that, 'cause I never iron mine. I'm not sure what else I should say, but I just thought that I should speak to someone about Karl."

\* \* \*

Just over a fortnight after the interview of Ms Beddoes, Karl Hübner was arrested when police in Retzlar, Germany, called at the premises of a prominent manufacturer of optical instruments. In his statement to the German police he claimed that he had no knowledge of the deaths of any of the three young women, Veronica Blanchard, Mary Roberts or Tara Ionescu. However, forensic examination of the room occupied by him in the flat owned by Ms Beddoes, had provided more than enough evidence for the German police to agree to act.

Although the room of Ms Beddoes' flat occupied by Hübner contained no obvious evidence connecting him with the rapes and murders of three young women, several potential sources of DNA were found on the covering of the mattress of the bed. These were sent off for DNA analyses. It was positive matching of the DNA profiles of those samples with those of the rape/murder victims that provided evidence allowing the German police to act. A blood sample taken from Hübner at the time of his arrest ultimately provided the conclusive DNA evidence that he was the rapist/murderer.

Several days after his arrest on a holding charge, Karl Hübner was re-arrested and charged with the murders of Veronica Blanchard, Mary Roberts and Tara Ionescu. Marker characteristics of his DNA profile closely matched those of the sperm cells found within the bodies of the three women. However, there was no forensic evidence to connect him with either the death of Grigore Volpi or the arson attack on Mrs Volpi's company premises.

Once Hübner's DNA profile was known it was posted on police databases, both national and international. A short time later it was became clear that for almost ten years the man had waged a campaign of rape and, latterly, rape and murder, across much of Western Europe.

Shortly after the arrest of Karl Hübner, Liz was recalled to Scotland Yard so that she lost close contact with the investigation of Hübner's crimes. However, she was able to follow the progress of the investigation because of reports that appeared at intervals in the IN tray on her desk. It became clear that the man was a thoroughly evil person. He was known to have been responsible for the rape of thirty-three women throughout Western Europe. Of those, it appeared likely that he had murdered at least eight.

# Chapter Twenty Nine

Liz arrived in Cambridge just after lunchtime on Saturday and took a cab from the train station to her mum's house in north Cambridge. Audrey opened the door to the house as the taxi drew up. Liz had to alight from the cab into the road outside her mum's house because parked cars lined the kerb on either side. Liz kissed her mum, noting the smell of alcohol on her breath.

Drinking during the day had been started by her mum only after the death of Liz's grandmother. Liz knew that the loneliness her mum had felt most of her life had been exacerbated by her Nan's death, probably because Audrey assumed that she had been responsible. Liz's Nan, Deirdre, had been killed by running into the path of an automobile just outside a pub where she had spent the evening drinking with Audrey and some neighbours. It was an argument with Audrey, fuelled by alcohol, which had caused Deirdre to leave the pub; obviously she was sufficiently the worse for drink that she had not seen the automobile that had killed her. The driver said that Deirdre had simply stepped in front of his car; there was nothing that he could have done.

As Liz had feared, her mum was completely unprepared for her visit, explaining to Liz that she'd got nothing in because she had expected that the two of them would go out that evening for a pub meal. Liz didn't say anything that could be interpreted by Audrey as criticism of the plan for the evening. She hoped thereby to prevent the anguished tones that her mother had come of late to use almost every time she spoke to her daughter. According to Audrey, Liz was being very disloyal by making her life in London instead of returning to Cambridge to look after her mum. Audrey was forever reminding Liz that she, Audrey, had given up her life after her husband had died in order to look after not only her only daughter, but her own mother. In a voice that was always filled with self pity she would utter words to the effect: "I've asked for little enough from you throughout the years; I should have thought that you would have some consideration."

Before her mum could get started on drunken critical monologue, Liz said, excitedly, "mum; I've just had a brilliant idea. Remember, when I was a little girl, you used to take me to the botanical garden? You said that you loved going there because you couldn't have a proper garden here, and everything there looked so nicely done? Why don't you and I go there this afternoon for a visit? I'll pay for a taxi to get us there and back. What do you think, mum? It's a gorgeous day; we don't often get them like this."

Liz could see at once that Audrey had no interest in leaving the house until it was time to go to the pub that evening. However, Liz was determined to raise her mother from the mood of depression within which her mind dwelt. Audrey always lapsed into such a mood after having a few drinks. Liz went at once to the 'phone and ordered up a taxi to arrive within half an hour, giving Audrey no choice but to accompany her daughter to the botanical garden.

As Liz had hoped, once her mum began to see sights that not many years before had delighted her, the atmosphere brightened. Liz made no concessions to her mother's complaints that she no longer could walk as fast as when she was young; Liz reminded her mum that she was hardly old. Liz was never certain of her mother's age, because that had been something the two of them never had discussed. However, judging from her Nan's age, which she had learned at the time of her grandmother's death, Liz had estimated that Audrey couldn't be older than her mid forties.

As her mum sobered up, Liz picked up the pace of their walking. Before long she and her mum had covered the whole of the grounds of the relatively small botanical garden. Liz suggested that the two of them walk toward the centre of town which was not far away; perhaps they could visit the market square and pick up some fresh vegetables and fruits from one or more of the stalls to be found there. Liz was pleased to see that Audrey's mood had brightened sufficiently that she didn't even hesitate before agreeing to accompany her daughter.

The centre of Cambridge had not changed; it was as crowded with Saturday shoppers as it always had been during Liz's lifetime. She had to admit to herself that she did love Cambridge, and if the opportunity ever were to arise she was sure that she would return to the city to live.

The wait in the queue for a taxi to take them home was quite long, but Liz was enjoying the conversation she was having with her mum. Audrey was enthusing over the few hours the two of them had spent together: "oh, Elisabeth, it was just like old times when your Nan was with us. Wouldn't it be wonderful if we could do this all the time?" Liz said that they must plan on having an outing of some kind every time she came to Cambridge. She saw the change in her mother's expression that usually signalled a lapse into recriminations, so she spoke quickly to retain the initiative: "I know, mum; I don't get up to Cambridge as often as I should, but I promise that I'll do better in the future. When we do things like we've done today, it's an absolute pleasure to be here." After she said it, Liz could kick herself for making the last remark; she waited for her mother to say something that would confirm the destruction of the pleasant mood that Liz' careless statement very likely had begun.

Surprisingly, Audrey said nothing, changing the subject to ask if Liz knew that Eaden Lilley's, one of the familiar shops in the centre of Cambridge, no longer was there. Liz hadn't known, and didn't really much care, but to keep the conversation going on a neutral subject, she agreed with her mum that it was true; Cambridge was changing too rapidly. Finally, they got to the head of the queue, and the driver who helped them into the cab proved to be very jolly. When he lifted their bags of vegetables and fruits into the boot of the cab he remarked that he hoped they'd left a little for him. He was under orders from "the missus" to pick up some things from the market square. "If I go home without them, the missus will turn me out on the street." His mood was matched by Audrey who surprised Liz by saying, "don't worry; if she does that you can come and stay with me."

That evening, in the pub, Liz met the usual cast of characters. Audrey's close friends and neighbours, Rose and Fred Paltry, were there. Ever since she had been aware of such things, she had known Fred to be a keen gardener. In fact, he was almost obsessive about it. As a consequence of this, it never was necessary for Liz to think up subjects of conversation when she was in the company of her mother's neighbours. Fred saw to it that everyone within earshot learned all about his gardening exploits. He was especially proud of his collection of a plant that had magnificently-decorated leaves; plants of the genus Hosta. Any garden pest that so much as looked at his Hostas would be doomed to a swift and horrible death, as far as Fred was concerned.

Fred particularly hated woodlice and pill bugs, for which his term was "the insects from hell." The only time that Liz ever could remember that Fred had got angry with her was when she was a child of about nine. She loved animals of all kinds and always was eager to learn about them, and, perhaps foolishly, tell others of that knowledge. She knew that woodlice were not insects, but were actually crustaceans; more closely related to prawns and lobsters than to insects. She made the mistake of correcting Fred. Liz remembered the exact words of Fred's response because they had both surprised and frightened her: "listen, young lady; when you grow up a little and learn more about the world, then you can start correcting your elders. Until then keep your know-it-all attitude to yourself. I don't care what you think they are, when they chew holes through the leaves of my Hostas they're the insects from hell!"

Liz remembered that she had run from Mr Paltry, crying. Some time later, he had apologised to her, but she had remembered the incident as one of the most frightening during her childhood. Until then she had loved Mr Paltry, but after that until she became an adult, she'd given him a wide berth.

During the evening in the pub, Rose Paltry had got Liz aside to tell her that she was worried about Audrey's drinking. "She's being fairly abstemious tonight, but usually halfway through the evening, she is feeling no pain." Liz thanked Rose for the information, explaining that she thought that her mum drank to combat depression. "I'm hoping that the two of us can get together more frequently than we've done in the past; maybe that will help." Rose agreed, saying, "Audrey's always telling Fred and me how much she misses you."

Liz and her mum walked home from the pub, having left well before closing time. Audrey seemed quite cheerful and obviously was enjoying the intimacy of walking arm in arm with her daughter. As Audrey spoke of her happiness, Liz was thinking of the lie that she had planned to tell her mum about having to get back to London early the next day. In reality, she had planned to visit her friend, Pat. However, Audrey came away from the pub in such a buoyant mood that Liz decided that she could not tell her mum the lie. She thought that perhaps she could ring Pat in the morning and suggest that they all meet for lunch someplace. However, when she mentioned the possibility, her mum said that she really wasn't interested. She would prefer to stay home with her daughter; perhaps they could make a nice salad with all of the fruit that they had bought in the market square. Liz agreed that her mum's plan for the following day was probably the more practical thing to do. She wanted to keep her mother's good mood going, and the best way to do that was to refrain from disagreeing with her.

The disappointment in Pat's voice when Liz telephoned her the next day to tell her friend of the change of plans only added to her thought that she was finding it difficult to control her own emotional life. Somehow, she had to see Pat before she went back to London, if only long enough for them to kiss and give each other a hug and make plans for a future meeting. Then Pat made a suggestion that Liz thought might work. She asked Liz to put her mother on the 'phone. As Liz listened to her mum's end of the conversation she heard her mother say, "I'd love that, Pat; yes, he's a darling little boy. Yes, of course, we'd love that. No there's no need for that; we can take a taxi. Yes, I do insist. You've got enough on your plate if you're going to feed us lunch. We'll look forward to seeing you then, Pat. G'bye."

Audrey turned to Liz after putting down the 'phone, saying, "I hope you don't mind, Liz, but I've changed my mind about today; I've accepted Pat's invitation for the two of us to go to her place for lunch. I said that we'd take a taxi 'cause we can't have her driving over here to fetch us; her having to look after her little boy 'n all."

Liz felt like ringing Pat once more and telling her what a genius she was. Not only had she made it possible for them to see each other, but she had made Audrey pleased to be involved. She couldn't help thinking the thought, "why couldn't I have thought of a subtle way of getting 'round my mum. Pat, bless her, just seems to have the knack."

* * *

On the train back to London, Liz found herself musing about her visit with Pat. Day dreaming was a habit that she had had for as long as she could remember. Usually it occurred when there was little else to do. Although she had brought with her the detective story that she had been trying to finish for several days, she preferred to daydream during this journey from Cambridge to London. She wanted to think about the brief time that she had spent alone with Pat.

Little Andrew, unknowingly, provided his mother and Liz with the opportunity to be together. Just after the lunch had been completed, Andrew had approached Audrey with his favourite book, saying, "you read me, peez." Audrey had told him that of course she would read to him, taking him onto her lap.

Then Pat had said, "Liz; come with me into my bedroom, there's something there I want to show you." No sooner had the two of them got into the room when Pat closed the door and rushed to Liz, kissing her and pushing her tongue into her mouth. "Oh, Liz; it's been so long. I have imagined doing this with you so many times." Pat pulled Liz's blouse free from her skirt and, pushing her bra above her breasts began to suckle. Liz wanted to respond, but she was aware of her mother's presence just on the other side of the bedroom door. She wanted to relax, but she couldn't. However, she didn't resist when Pat pushed her hand into her underpants and between her legs. She had become so aroused that tears came to her eyes; she wanted to ignore her mother's presence and engage with Pat in a way her emotions told her that she should do, but her rational mind told her that that was impossible.

Finally, Liz pulled Pat's hand free, kissing the two fingers that had been giving her pleasure, and, gasping, told Pat that they had to be sensible. Pat said that she was tired of being sensible. She wanted the two of them to be lovers; she didn't want to wait. Then she stopped what she was doing and said, "oh, I know you're right, Liz. I get so frustrated not having you here in Cambridge any more." As Liz rearranged her clothing they had agreed to have a long chat on the telephone; maybe they could arrange to meet again soon either in Cambridge or in London.

The slowing of the train as it commenced the approach to Liverpool Street station and the end of her journey to London caused Liz to end her daydream. She felt the moistness between her legs which caused her to be impatient to get to her flat where, later that evening, she would allow her fantasies to control her actions completely.

Made in the USA